W9-BZC-117

≡ BENEATH ≡
the *Bellemont*
SKY

Eagle Public Library
100 N Stierman Way
Eagle, Idaho 83616
208-939-6814

OTHER BOOKS
BY RANEÉ S. CLARK:

Playing for Keeps

Double Play

Love, Jane

= BENEATH =
the Bellemont
SKY A NOVEL

RANEÉ S. CLARK

Covenant Communications, Inc.

Cover image: *Woman Embracing a Soldier* © Lee Avison / Trevillion Images

Cover designed by Christina Marcano
Cover design © 2018 by Covenant Communications, Inc.

Published by Covenant Communications, Inc.
American Fork, Utah

Copyright © 2018 by Raneé S. Clark
All rights reserved. No part of this book may be reproduced in any format or in any medium without the written permission of the publisher, Covenant Communications, Inc., P.O. Box 416, American Fork, UT 84003. The views expressed within this work are the sole responsibility of the author and do not necessarily reflect the position of Covenant Communications, Inc., or any other entity.

This is a work of fiction. The characters, names, incidents, places, and dialogue are either products of the author's imagination, and are not to be construed as real, or are used fictitiously.

Printed in the United States of America
First Printing: March 2018

23 22 21 20 19 18   10 9 8 7 6 5 4 3 2 1

ISBN 978-1-52440-278-5

To my siblings and their spouses; DJ, Ashleigh, Jordan, Jill, Nikki, Jeff, Sean, Jenn, Keesha, Savanna, and Mat; without whom I wouldn't know how to write about a family who loved each other through anything.

≡ ACKNOWLEDGMENTS ≡

FIRST, A BIG THANK-YOU TO my husband. I feel blessed beyond my ability to express (which is saying something!) to have his support and his belief that I can accomplish anything. Thank you to three extremely cool boys who write stories and make their mom's heart flutter with possibilities. I love your imaginations.

More thanks to my family, both the Clarks and the Savages, who always support me.

As always, to the writing community—I wouldn't be here without you all. To Kaylee Baldwin, who is not only an extraordinary critiquer but also an amazing friend. Thank you to Jenny Proctor, who always answers when I call or text to ask some silly question keeping me up at night. Thank you, thank you to all my CPs—Gina Denny, Kate Watson, Natalee Cooper, and the girls of Suite Sisters. Thank you to Kimberly VanderHorst, who helped me with the French terms—any mistakes are all mine.

Thank you to the friends who help me balance my real life with the pretend one, the ones who've been around nearly twenty years and the ones it feels like it's been that long—Brook, Jana, Brittany, and Suz.

And, of course, to Covenant and the lovely people who champion me there—thank you for letting me write about the things I love and making my ideas shine.

★

PART I

A MOST CIVIL WAR

= CHAPTER ONE =

Bellemont, Wyoming—September 1946

VERA DICED THE TOMATO IN front of her with far more force than necessary, each slice coming faster with every noise she heard from the bedroom down the hall—where her kids were supposed to be sleeping.

She closed her eyes, took yet another deep breath, and scooped the tomatoes into her hands to deposit into the waiting bowl for the latest batch of tomato soup her mother, Kathryn Larson, was working on. Then Vera counted to ten while she rinsed and dried her hands. This happened every night. And who could blame them—four of them stuck in one room, even though they'd crammed in another bed and hung a sheet to separate the older boys from four-year-old Tom and two-year-old Audrey, the usual troublemakers. It may have been two years since they moved from California back to Wyoming to live with Vera's family, but was losing a father and being uprooted something a child ever got over?

In any case, it'd been fifteen minutes since her last—unfortunately unsuccessful—lecture on going to sleep when told and it was time for another. But another interruption in the tomato canning meant it would take extra time for her and her mother to finish up preserving what they'd harvested that day from their large garden. Vera Larson Trumbell had grown up working hard—there'd never been an easy day on the Larson farm—but that workload had tripled when her brothers and father went off to war. *One more day*, she told herself, and they'd have a few more hands to help with the work.

But a few more hands couldn't make life normal again. Not for her children. Not for Vera. Not for anyone living in the Larson farmhouse.

As Vera passed by her mother at the stove, Kathryn ducked her head to hide a grandmotherly smile. It did lighten Vera's mood that her not-so-little family's continued presence in the old farmhouse didn't bother her mother too much.

Once Vera had crossed the worn but well-kept carpet in the living room, she pushed open the bedroom door, not going inside. One never really could get inside. The door couldn't open all the way with one of the two full beds on old iron frames in the way. Both were pushed up against the far corners of the room, and only a foot or so of space and a sheet separated them. Certainly no room for dressers. The kids' clothes were piled into some old, wooden milk crates in Vera's room upstairs.

"It's well past bedtime. No more noise."

"It's Audee, Mom," Jack Junior, her oldest, complained. "She keeps singing and trying to play with Tom."

Another sigh. "Come on, baby." Vera slid through the narrow opening and closed the warped door enough to lean over the end of Tom and Audrey's bed. Reaching as far as she could, she plucked her daughter from the bed. "Want to sleep with Mama tonight?"

"I don't want to sleep by myself," Tom complained immediately.

"Then get into bed with your brothers." Vera maneuvered back through the door, a tighter squeeze now with Audrey in her arms, and she pressed her lips into a thin line at the immediate complaints from eight-year-old Jack Junior and six-year-old Peter.

"He takes up all the room," Peter whined.

"It's crowded enough in here already," Jack Junior grumbled.

Vera poked her head back through the doorway as Tom pushed aside the sheet and hesitated at his brothers' complaints. "I'm sure Aunt Fay would love it if you two got up in the morning to milk the cow," she threatened sweetly.

The boys both clamped their mouths shut. Peter even reached a hand out to Tom to beckon him into bed with them. The smaller boy scrambled up next to Peter, who managed a smile for his little brother.

Vera adjusted Audrey on her hip and strode back through the living room, rolling her eyes. During the summer, the boys had taken turns with Fay to do the milking and, of course, hated it. Vera had thought keeping up the chore when school started in September would help the boys learn hard farmwork—she, Fay, and her brothers had done their fair share of chores during the school months growing up. But her mother had prevailed upon her to ease up and keep only the after-school chores. Her argument that little boys didn't need to work so hard and grow up so fast stopped Vera's own argument that her brothers had done the same chores at far younger. As a grandmother, Kathryn had softened when it came to the boys working on the farm. And when Vera had considered all that the war had taken from her boys' childhood, she didn't fight too hard against softening herself. Besides, they'd done their share of harvesting and cleaning tomatoes this evening. Her brothers were coming home tomorrow, but up until then it still took the whole family to keep the farm going.

Once upstairs, Vera settled Audrey on the bed she and Fay shared, hoping her sister wouldn't mind one more for the night. Vera blew out a breath that feathered the curls falling out over her own cheek. Fay hadn't minded the many other nights Vera had brought Audrey to bed with them.

"Are you all right until Mama gets done with her chores?" Vera asked, pulling the covers up under Audrey's chin.

Audrey nodded solemnly, her eyes already heavy. Vera leaned over and kissed the top of her head. "You be very quiet, sweetest. Grandpa's already asleep and he needs his rest, okay?"

"'Tay, Mama."

That sweet baby voice melted Vera's heart more than anything. She blew her daughter one more kiss before hurrying out of the room. When she got back downstairs to the kitchen, Kathryn was dicing up the tomatoes Vera had left behind.

"Sorry, Mom," she said.

Kathryn chuckled to herself and shuffled aside to let Vera resume her post. "You know, when you girls were small, I used to think that sometimes it might've been easier if I'd done all the canning myself."

Earlier that day, Tom and Audrey had "helped" them. Yes, things might have gone smoother and quicker without them. In fact, they might already be done.

"Hopefully you appreciate my help now." Vera winked over her shoulder at Kathryn, who grinned back.

"Of course, dear. We're so glad to have you. More than you know." Kathryn reached over and gave Vera a hug with one arm, leaning her graying head against Vera's shoulder for a moment.

Vera's parents had gotten the resident number at the farmhouse down to a manageable three people two years ago, then Vera had come back and added five more. But the truth was, the only thing she missed about California was the warmth. Their tiny apartment hadn't even had a bedroom. She fed her children far better here on the farm than she ever had on Jack's intermittent actor's paychecks and then his army pay. She smiled, like always, when she thought of him. He'd been so full of dreams, and Vera missed his unfailing optimism. It had meant more to her than money ever had.

When she'd gotten the telegram announcing his death in the Pacific, it had made the decision she'd waffled over since he'd left to fight. She couldn't get a job with two children still at home, and without a job she wouldn't have been able to pay the rent and bills, let alone get food.

Another giggle, which was quickly muffled, came from down the hallway. Vera shared a look with her mother and then they laughed quietly themselves. Vera was blessed to have the farm to come home to. Maybe some of Jack stayed with her in her ability to see the good among all the bad the world had offered her.

Yet another giggle tested Vera's patience.

"I need to remarry," she said. "I think perhaps Lewis Campbell. I'm certain he could buy me a nice, big house in town with plenty of bedrooms. One for each of my children."

Kathryn shook her head and transferred another bowlful of tomatoes to the colander that hung above the large pot on the stove. "Vera."

Vera didn't let the tone—stern but laced with humor—bother her. Lewis was a bit of a stick-in-the-mud, though. She supposed someone who ran a bank had to behave more seriously than someone who aspired to star in the movies. Rich or not, she still preferred the latter.

She went on joking anyway. "I think three or four bedrooms would be divine." Jack had always promised her a mansion on Roxbury Drive in Los Angeles. Not that she ever believed a word of that. But oh, she liked gazing into his starry-blue eyes when he said it. He had such a joy about his face and charm she couldn't resist—not at eighteen when he'd begged her to marry him and run off to California. Not every moment after when she'd begged him to be serious and get a steady job, and he'd laughed and told her not to worry. He'd hit the big time soon. With looks like his—broad, athletic shoulders, square chin, golden-blond hair—some part of her couldn't help believing he might be right.

Her mother half-heartedly snapped the towel at Vera, but Fay, Vera's little sister, interrupted whatever comment Kathryn had been about to make about Vera marrying for money. Fay strode into the kitchen and took off her hat. She surveyed the pile of tomatoes on the counter that Vera still had to clean and chop.

"You shouldn't have let me go," she said, scowling at her hands as she yanked her gloves off and tossed them inside the hat. "I ought to have stayed and helped."

"Don't be a goose," Vera said. "We'll be done in no time." She admired her sister's pretty navy and white-polka-dotted dress with its sweetheart neckline and ruffled short sleeves. Fay and Kathryn had sewn it to resemble one they'd seen in a magazine, and they'd done a marvelous job.

"How many still left out there?" Fay asked.

"Not many—but we'll leave them for the boys. Sort of our welcome home gift." Vera laughed and was grateful to see Fay smile too. Of anyone, she looked forward to their brothers coming home the most, it seemed. "How was your date?" Vera asked as Fay donned an apron over her pretty dress.

Fay shrugged and stepped up next to her sister, stifling a yawn as she did so. "I can't complain, I suppose. Haven't seen Joey in years. He asked me out for tomorrow night too."

"Sam and Andrew's train will be coming in at one," Kathryn said. "We'll be having a family dinner."

"I know, Mom." Fay sighed. "Joey is swell, but he's not going to break his heart over me."

Vera knew that tone. She'd heard it a lot since the boys went off to war and left Fay and Mom home to run the farm. Too much work for her and Mom to keep it up and not enough time for Fay to have fun. Vera's kids weren't the only ones who'd had to grow up too fast in the Larson farmhouse. Having the boys home tomorrow wouldn't change the fact that Fay had never gotten the carefree fun Vera had experienced at that age.

"Plenty of boys in this town have broken their hearts over you, Fay," Vera teased.

Fay snorted and picked up a knife to help chop the tomatoes. "Not really enough left to break their hearts over me."

Vera closed her eyes and grimaced. "I'm sorry, Fay. What an insensitive thing for me to say." Especially when one of their own brothers, Russell, wasn't coming home, along with too many Bellemont boys.

Fay shrugged. "You didn't mean it like that," she said. She forced a lively expression, despite succumbing to another yawn. "We've got so many beans to pick tomorrow, I don't want to think about it. Maybe this all won't seem like so much work when we've got a couple more hands around here."

"It will be nice to let the boys do the picking and for us to keep to the kitchen, like old times," Vera said.

"Sure. Remember when we used to beg to do the picking too?" Fay kept her face down, but Vera didn't miss the bitterness to the sentiment. Some tomato juice squirted at Fay, narrowly missing the exposed sleeve of her dress. "I'd better go change before I ruin this thing, not that I need it for much." Fay slipped the apron off and hung it over a chair, grabbing her hat and gloves before heading toward the narrow wooden stairs that led to two more small bedrooms.

"Audrey's in our bed," Vera warned. "If she's asleep you can bring her downstairs. Tom is sleeping with the older boys, so maybe she won't wake everyone up if she has her own bed."

Fay waved her off. "Why don't you leave her and sleep in her bed by yourself? I don't mind."

"You'll be up early, and I'm hoping she'll sleep in tomorrow. It would sure help me get some of those beans canned if she did. Besides, with all these tomatoes, I won't get much use out of it anyway."

"All right then." Fay went up the stairs, and Vera frowned over her sister's drawn expression. It was more than tiredness from the stress of bringing in the harvest.

"I bet Fay will be happy to have the boys home." Vera hadn't meant for her voice to catch. They'd gotten that telegram about Russell's death not long after Vera moved back to Bellemont. Two of the men from their family dead and Dad losing an arm. Reassuring themselves that it could have been much worse didn't ease the ache—nor did the knowledge that it had been worse for some of the families in Bellemont and all over the country, that some mothers sent their men off and didn't see a one of them again. Poor Dad. Poor Russell. Poor Jack.

"Mmm-hmm," was all Kathryn said. After a contemplative moment, her smile returned. "Emily stopped me at church on Sunday to ask if I would mind her coming along to welcome Sam home." Emily Holman was Sam's fiancée.

"Sam might mind a lot if she *didn't* come. Do you suppose they'll get married right away?"

"I do. Being away from each other so long will make them eager to make it official." Kathryn hummed as she pushed tomatoes through the colander.

"I hope Emily doesn't insist on waiting again, for Sam's sake."

"Me too." Kathryn laughed and Vera joined her.

"Dad went to bed awfully early tonight. He's not getting sick again, is he?" Vera asked.

Kathryn shook her head. "I don't think so. Pushed himself too hard today, I'm sure. He wanted Fay to be able to go out with her friends." She shrugged and concentrated on the tomatoes. "He's not as hardy as he was before. Bullet to the shoulder at that age . . ." Neither woman considered the rest of that thought. They'd come much too close to losing him as well.

Kathryn dumped the last bowlful of diced tomatoes into the colander and squished them through for several minutes in silence. "Why don't you go up and tell Fay to go on to bed? No sense in both of you staying up to put this soup into jars. We have a busy day tomorrow, and somebody ought to get some rest."

Vera wiped off her hands and detoured toward the stove to give her mother a kiss before she obeyed. The farm was small, a saving grace in a lot of ways. They'd escaped some of the worst of the Depression, and with all the men gone the past few years, she, Mom, and Fay had still been able to keep things afloat. Food on the table, some hay in the field. They had fared better than most. But living off the land still meant a lot of hard work, especially come fall. Lots of food to put back for the winter and hay to cut for the animals, and hopefully a little left to sell. Yes, having Sam and Andrew home would help a great deal.

≡ CHAPTER TWO ≡

ANDREW LARSON GRINNED TO HIMSELF as the familiar mountains of Wyoming flew past him in the window. Some green. Mostly brown. A lot of sagebrush. Home.

"I wouldn't be grinning like that if I knew Mom was going to skin me alive," his brother Sam leaned over and whispered.

His warning did nothing to kill Andrew's mood. He squeezed the hand of the beautiful black-haired woman sitting next to him, a pretty but plain and small diamond solitaire sparkling on her finger.

"Jo will win Mom over right off. Everyone will love her."

Josette still smiled every time he called her by that nickname. She'd spent one entire date at the beginning of their relationship trying to teach him the correct way to pronounce Josette, showing him how to soften the *j*, repeating her name over, and sounding like she was saying *Zshosette*. He could pronounce it fine now, after so many months of practice, but his English-speaking brain still saw the nickname "Jo" at the beginning, and he couldn't teach it otherwise.

"You can't be sure about how your mother reacted to our quick wedding ceremony." Josette squeezed his hand back and her careful tone betrayed her own worry.

Andrew leaned over and kissed her olive-toned cheek. "I can. I know my mother."

"And I know how spoiled he is," Sam broke in. "She'll forgive him anything."

"Even bringing home a French wife with only a telegram to precede us?" Josette said with hardly a touch of an accent. They had met in London, after all, where she'd lived for most of the war. And her father had been English. She teased Andrew that she spoke it better than him. Her disbelief at his words showed in the way she pressed her small pink lips together.

"He once burned down a shed and didn't even get a lecture. Mom might be a bit hurt she wasn't at the wedding, but she won't hold it against him—or you," Sam said with a wry smile.

"See, Sam would never lie to you about the amount of trouble I may or may not be capable of getting into." Andrew grinned at his bride, hoping to chase away her insecurities. Her shoulders relaxed a little more.

Houses started to dot the view from time to time. Andrew's and Sam's eyes met automatically after they spotted the Larson farmhouse off in the distance, huddled right up under the mountain. They'd be pulling into the Bellemont station soon. Real soon.

Josette leaned over Andrew to peer out the window, and he watched her expression. What would his French bride think of Wyoming? Of brown. Of a lot of sage brush. Of surprisingly beautiful farmland for such a dry place.

"Well?" he asked when she didn't say anything.

"I'll be with you, so of course I'll love it." She sat back and reached up to trail her thumb across his cheek before planting a kiss on his lips. She wiped the lipstick off a second later and smiled.

"I hope you will," he said. He wrapped an arm around Josette, pulling her close to him so she could rest her head on his shoulder and watch with him as the town of Bellemont drew closer. As the sagebrush gave way to trees, his mind wandered back to the day nearly a year ago when he had opened the door to the OSS London headquarters on Grosvenor Street for a tall, lithe young woman with hair the color of midnight. He'd seen her around and heard the name Josette Beauchamp talked about as an intelligent woman SOE had sent over to help train the operatives the OSS was sending back into France. The day he opened the door for her was the first time he'd gotten a look at her up close, and he was gone for her from that second onward.

It had taken him a few more weeks, and a few more "chance" encounters, for him to work up the courage to ask her to dinner. She'd told him later how relieved she'd been when he'd finally done it. They'd chatted like old friends that night, barely taking the time to finish their meal—Andrew going on about home and the farm, Josette opening up about growing up between both England and France, with a diplomat father. On the slow walk they'd taken home, he'd coaxed out of her the harrowing tale of her escape from France after being betrayed to the SS, as well as a promise for a second date.

"There's the station," Sam said, interrupting Andrew's thoughts.

Josette lifted her head off Andrew's shoulder to watch the small brick station grow closer, and his heart rate picked up. He couldn't wait to see Mom and Dad, and Vera and the kids, and Fay. He couldn't wait for them to meet Josette—to discover the brave, intelligent, loyal woman he had that night of their first date when they'd stretched it out as long as they could, the same way they did every night after. His family would fall in love with her as quickly as he had, and he could give her a family again.

A few minutes later the train rolled into the station, slowing and then halting with a jerk. Andrew and Sam gathered up their luggage—mostly Josette's. Andrew adjusted so he had it all in one hand, then he reached for Josette's, holding it firmly as they disembarked.

"Sam! Sam!" The voice of Emily, Sam's fianceé, rang above the others.

Andrew had to swallow a laugh at the way his mother not-so-gently nudged Emily out of the way and charged past her, arms out wide to grab both Andrew and Sam in one big hug. She didn't notice Josette clinging to Andrew's hand behind him.

Vera and Fay joined the hug, both of them sliding their arms into wherever they fit. Over his shoulder, Andrew saw that Emily had grabbed one of Sam's free hands and clutched it in both of hers, tears shining along with the joy in her eyes.

A hand rested on his shoulder and Andrew looked up into his dad's gaze. More wrinkles lined the skin around his eyes and mouth than the last time Andrew had seen him, and the gray that used to peep through among the dark hair at his temples had spread to include most of his head. Though Mom had written about Dad losing his arm, it still shocked Andrew to see it missing. To see a thin, old man when he'd left a still-strong farmer before they drafted Dad too.

Dad nodded to Josette. "Kathryn, have you forgotten something?" he said.

His mother raised her head from where she'd rested it against Sam's chest and cast Dad a confused look before her gaze alighted on Josette. "Oh my!" she said. "Forgive me, dear, we just got the telegram yesterday, you know!"

As Andrew shuffled Josette forward to greet his mother—in a hug as ardent as the one she'd greeted her boys with, of course—he caught sight of a girl standing a few steps away from their group, lace-gloved hands crossed primly in front of her, holding a clutch that matched her pale-blue dress. His throat went dry.

Susie Brandenburg's black hair shimmered in the sunlight where it hit her head from over the top of the train station building on its way to slipping behind the mountains, and she smiled in her polite, Princess of Bellemont way. Andrew tore his gaze away and cleared his parched throat, trying to concentrate on what his mother was saying to Josette. But he couldn't help thinking of how Susie had Dear John'd him months ago. What would bring her here today? Hopefully some other fellow or a family member Andrew didn't remember.

His mother gathered him back into her arms, flicking away his worried thoughts in an instant. "Imagine, my little Andrew with a wife," she said, and the word *wife* seemed to ring through the air.

"I'm the luckiest fellow alive," he said, drawing Josette closer. She had relaxed in the presence of his family, beaming at them as his sisters began peppering her with questions. Over her head, Andrew couldn't help glancing at Susie one more time. Her mouth had dropped into a surprised *O*, but she snapped it shut, and to Andrew's dread, her wide-eyed shock was replaced with pure fire.

≡ ★ ≡

Dominick Whitaker should have known better than to let the school secretary, Mrs. Hogarth, talk him into picking up the new teacher at the train station. Not that the woman ever took no for an answer from anyone, but he should have tried harder. He leaned up against the depot building and folded his arms. A handful of soldiers had come in on today's train, most of them young, and so far as he could tell, every one of them with at least a girl there to meet them—if not a whole pack of people like in the Larsons' case. He didn't know the two men's names, surrounded by Mr. and Mrs. Larson and their pretty daughters, Mrs. Trumbell and . . . what was the younger one's name? Then there were Mrs. Trumbell's kids. A couple of pretty girls were part of the group too, although one stood apart and then left without saying a word to any of them.

He knew that one of the Larson boys wasn't coming home. Hard not to know in a small, interconnected community like Bellemont, even as new as Dominick was to the town. Plenty of Bellemont boys weren't coming home, just like everywhere else. How did they stand it? How did they smile like that when they'd left friends, brothers, sons, whomever back in Europe or in the Pacific? Left them there forever.

He swore under his breath and shook his head. They hadn't seen the things Dominick had or lost as many men as him, he guessed. That's why he hated the train station. These days soldiers came in on almost every train. Every time he saw one come home, it reminded him of the men—and the woman—that weren't coming home, thanks to him.

"Hey there, Mr. Whitaker."

Dominick looked up. The Larsons approached, with young Jack Trumbell Junior, one of Dominick's students in the third-grade class he taught, and Jack's little brother running out in front of the pack. Jack waved at Dominick with a grin, and Dominick acknowledged him with a wave back.

"Mr. Whitaker." Mr. and Mrs. Larson each nodded at him, and even Jack's mother, Mrs. Trumbell, cast him a grin. He saw her around town from time to time. Occasionally she brought the boys in to school when they missed the bus and he'd catch a glimpse of her as she dropped them off. Given the age of her oldest and the stories he'd heard about her marrying at eighteen and moving to California with her new husband, Dominick would guess she must be around his age, thirty, or maybe a bit younger. The army had kept him too busy, even before the war started, to worry about starting a family. Considering his past, he didn't intend to get to that anytime soon either.

He couldn't help but notice that Mrs. Trumbell was always smiling. That was something else he didn't get. She'd lost her husband and a brother to the war, and half her father as well. Those women had worked themselves to the bone keeping the farm going while all the men were away. Dominick hadn't been around, of course, but everybody in town talked about the Larson women with pride. Maybe Mrs. Trumbell could smile because it'd been close to two years now, near as Dominick could figure, since her husband died. Shoot, though. How could a woman left alone with a pack of kids like hers smile about anything?

His attention still followed the family as they piled into a couple of cars—the younger boys jumping into the back of the farm truck, with Mrs. Trumbell at the wheel and her younger two children climbing in beside her. The rest squeezed into a red Chevy sedan, all of them laughing, joy shining off their faces. Old Mr. Larson had a spring in his step, and he kept patting Mrs. Larson's hand. Lucky folks. How did they do it?

"Are you Mr. Whitaker?" A voice broke Dominick out of his thoughts and drew his gaze toward a tall, slim young man walking toward him, swinging a worn suitcase in one hand. "Must be. Looks as if we're the only two fellows here without a girl to kiss." He chuckled and stopped in front of Dominick, waiting, Dominick supposed, for him to reply.

"That's me. I guess you're George Preston, the new teacher?" Dominick straightened.

"Yes, sir." George Preston held out a hand for Dominick to shake, and he obliged the younger man. *My, he is practically a boy. Must be fresh out of college.* An unexpected blast of anguish nearly choked Dominick up right there. Same age as Laurent Alleman, the boy Dominick had—

He stopped himself before the memory overwhelmed him. "My car is this way." He hurried off the platform steps, out ahead of George, hoping to get his wits back in order before the other man questioned him too much.

"I've been home a few months, but I still remember that hug my mother rushed to give me the second I stepped off that train," George said wistfully. Dominick stopped his hurried march away at the driver's side door of his Ford sedan. "I suppose you were a soldier too," George said, his hand on the door of the passenger side.

"Yes," Dominick snapped, pulling his door open and sliding inside.

When George followed suit, pulling his suitcase onto his lap, his expression held understanding—the way any soldier knew when a fellow couldn't talk about things. Dominick didn't like the pity of it, but he was grateful for the silence it brought anyway.

"You oughta put that in the back," he said, jerking a thumb toward the back seat.

"In a small town like this, my lodgings can't be far, can they?" George asked.

Dominick shook his head.

"This is fine." George patted the banged-up suitcase that had probably belonged to a few Prestons before him. "Don't need much anymore, you know?"

Dominick met George's gaze. "I do."

≡ ★ ≡

There wasn't much time for talking until the Larsons had all finished dinner. Vera and Fay had plopped Josette on the couch to bombard her with questions. Andrew's wife wore a pleased smile, and her expression shone with nearly as much happiness as the day they had married. Like Sam had guessed, everyone had gotten over them not waiting even a few more days so they could get married in Bellemont with the family.

"Oh, that's Andrew for you," Dad had grumbled with a mischievous grin of his own.

So Andrew joined his mother, Sam, and Emily in the kitchen to clean up. He supposed Emily and Sam wouldn't mind a few minutes by themselves, but Mom didn't want Sam going anywhere and Emily didn't want to be anywhere Sam wasn't. They chatted cheerfully as they worked through the pile of plates, cups, silverware, and pans filling the counters around the sink.

His mother looked up when he came into the kitchen and rolled up his sleeves. She swatted at him. "Where's Josette?"

He shuffled his mother away from the sink and took over. "Vee and Fay have got her taken care of."

Kathryn eyed him. "Well, I thought you two might live in Grannie Mae's old place," she said, speaking of the one-room house down the road that Dad's farmhands used to live in, back when they farmed enough land to need extra hands. Andrew supposed that now, with the war over and more of them around, they might start planting some more fields and eventually hire some hands back on.

"That sounds fine," he said with a glance at Sam. He wondered if his brother had expected to set up house there. With him back, he and Emily would probably tie the knot as soon as they could. She'd been waiting for years now. They'd been going steady since Emily moved to Bellemont back in '39. Well, Sam ought to have married Emily during leave some time.

"It's going to take us a day or two to get it cleaned up," Kathryn went on. "Nobody's lived there for ages. Vera said Tom and Audrey could sleep in the room with her and Fay. You'll still have to share with the boys, but Vera's got that curtain up. That'll give you a little privacy. Not what you want, I suppose, being newlyweds, but you'll have to make do."

Andrew smiled at the water before daring a peek at his mother's face. "I know I didn't give you much warning, Mom."

Kathryn huffed a not-too-angry sigh and swatted at him again. "I suppose I would have liked to see you married, son."

"Me and Jo were going to wait, but when it came down to it, Mom, I'd already spent enough time away from her. I made her come out to Washington, and we thought we ought to get married quick as we could."

"Ahhh, young love." Sam mooned at Andrew, so he flicked some suds in his brother's face.

"It's romantic," Emily offered with a decisive nod.

Sam quirked an eyebrow. "Now don't you go all soft on me, Miss Holman. Didn't I offer to make your dreams come true a year ago? Now who was it that insisted she wanted a big church wedding and the whole thing, and of course a wedding done up in a day or two like all those other war brides wouldn't do for her?"

Emily rolled her eyes and dried another dish. "You're just lazy, Sam Larson. You didn't want to get all dressed up and have to shake people's hands."

"So long as you invite me, I don't care how slowly or quickly you get married, Sam," Kathryn chided with a pointed look at Andrew, but it softened right away and Sam groaned.

Kathryn shuffled back into her spot washing dishes, pushing Andrew out of the way. "Go save that girl from Fay and Vera, dear. Hurry now. It's your honeymoon, after all."

Sam shook his head at the soft treatment the younger brother got, and Andrew saluted him with a chuckle before heading back to the living room for Josette. If they had to share a room with his nephews tonight, he'd better take Josette on a drive up to Eagle Point.

☰ ★ ☰

Once Andrew parked his father's car at the top of the local lookout, he curled his arm around Josette's shoulders and pulled her closer. The night was clear enough and moon full enough that it offered enough light for him to gaze adoringly at his wife. He let out a contented sigh.

"What is it?" Josette asked, resting her head on his shoulder like she had on the train ride. He rested his head against hers, enjoying the way her soft hair brushed against his cheek and the gentle scent of something flowery.

"Just happy. I must be the luckiest fellow on this earth. To come home from the war well and whole and with a beautiful bride at my side, a warm place to sleep, and plenty of beans to eat."

Josette giggled at his joke about the beans. Fay had insisted that Andrew and Sam would pick every single green bean out of the garden despite Kathryn's protests that they ought to allow the boys some rest after all that fighting the last few years.

"Well then," Josette said. "We're quite a pair. I happen to be the luckiest girl in the world."

He tilted her chin up to plant a kiss on her small, heart-shaped lips. Combined with her narrow nose, high cheekbones, and wide-set eyes, they gave her face the look of a beautiful doll—rosy pink cheeks and all.

"Not many girls get to spend their honeymoon sleeping in the same room as two little boys," he teased.

"That's true." She giggled again, but when she leaned her head back against him, she let out her own contented sigh. "Not many fellows bring their bride home to more family than she knows what to do with."

"I did warn you," he murmured, trailing kisses along her forehead.

"And it's as heavenly as I expected."

"You think so?" Andrew couldn't help his grin. He'd told Josette all about his family right away. She'd leaned her elbows on the table in the diner where they had their second date, and her eyes had gone all dreamy when he talked about how his mother had kept the farm going all those years, how she made dinners that had danced through Andrew's dreams for going on three years. How bossy Vera was, how much fun he and Fay got into. The nights he'd spent sleeping under the stars with his brothers. He'd wanted Josette to love them as much as he did.

"They're wonderful. I've never had sisters before, and I can't imagine there are any two better than Vera and Fay. And to be an aunt! Audrey is the most adorable child I've ever seen—mind you, her brothers have a tough job ahead of them keeping away the boys. Gosh, your mother just dotes on you all and even me. I'd forgotten how wonderful it is to have a mother wrap you up in her arms, but I remembered it all again when yours hugged me." Her eyes shone, but the joy in her expression outweighed any sadness Andrew detected in her tone. He hugged her closer all the same and then kissed her again. He wouldn't ever tire of kissing Josette, not in a hundred years. Andrew had known it from the first time, outside the door of her flat. Staying beside her seemed the best thing in the world he could do.

Outside the car, a coyote howled from far off and it turned their attention to the view out the windshield. A few lights from the houses in town sparkled at them, and even some from the homesteads dotted the countryside around it—farms that were the breath and air of Bellemont. It did Andrew's soul so much good to come home, especially with Josette beside him to share it all with.

⹀ CHAPTER THREE ⹀

"Well, how on earth did you escape the farm in the middle of the day, Vera?" Eleanor Pendley slid forward on the bright-red vinyl seat of their booth at the local diner and took a sip of her soda.

Vera pinched the fingers of her gloves and slid them off her hands, setting them on the spotless, white-with-speckled-silver table between them. She shrugged out of her fading blue wool coat before reaching for the soda Alice, the waitress, had set before her.

"Mom said we all worked so hard getting that ratty old house shipshape that we deserved an afternoon off. I think she did it more for Fay than anyone else. All those feelings she's got bottled up inside of her and none of us know how to help her. She was only eighteen when the boys left, and she never got to be the social butterfly she wanted to."

"Poor Fay." Eleanor stuck her elbow on the table and frowned.

"Mmm-hmm." Vera paused to take a long drink and cast a glance around the sparsely inhabited diner. A couple of teenage girls sat at the counter, drinking malts and chatting with the young man working there. Vera should know them—Bellemont was too small not to know most everyone—but she'd lived in California a long time and spent the two years back in town working out on the farm. She turned back to Eleanor. "Well, of course I waited far too long to come home. Should've come as soon as Jack shipped out."

"I'm sure having the boys home will help things, won't it?"

"Of course, but we'll still have to pitch in more than either Fay or I would like. The boys want to expand again, but we can't afford to hire a new hand since all the profit from this year will be just enough to get us all through winter. And there's Dad. It's not that he can't still work hard, even without his arm, but he's old and tired. Must be hard for a man his age to recover from something like fighting in the war."

Eleanor's expression dropped to her soda and she swirled her straw around, knocking bits of ice askew in the dark liquid. "Must be hard for any man."

Vera reached across the table and grabbed Eleanor's hand. Guilt sparked in her stomach at unloading everything on her best friend when who knew how she was adjusting to having her husband home. "Oh, El. Here I've been going on and on about me. How are things for you? How is Alvin?"

"Real well, I think." Eleanor waved off Vera's concern. She sat up and adjusted her seating, pushing herself back to the rear of the bench. Alice always kept everything in the diner so clean, including the benches, Vera usually had a hard time as well staying anchored in one spot. "It's like a honeymoon all over again—of course, we never actually had a honeymoon in the first place," Eleanor said. "He says he might take me to Yellowstone. Wouldn't that be neat?"

Eleanor's cherub-cheek beam brought joy bubbling up from inside Vera. Her friend had waited an awfully long time for the kind of happiness she deserved.

"Sounds like an excellent idea," Vera said.

"It's so nice to have him home, but my, the housework has picked up. How do you girls do it—keep the farm up and all and still have a clean house?" Eleanor turned back to her drink, the wattage of her beaming expression dimming somewhat. But Vera couldn't blame a girl for not getting excited over housework. "You're all saints. Of course, I'm putting in my notice at the bank now that Alvin is back." She laughed to herself. "I swear, I spend half my day trying to come up with something he'll want to eat for dinner."

But maybe this was more than disappointment in the true nature of being a housewife. Vera placed her elbows on the table and leaned forward as she caught the forced lightness in Eleanor's tone. She wouldn't be the first war bride to get a shock at what married life was like when her husband got home.

"Must be difficult going from being on your own and having your own schedule to watching after Alvin now too."

Eleanor took another sip of soda and then her face broke back into a grin, a real one too, as far as Vera could tell, and having known Eleanor for all her life, she considered herself a competent authority on the subject.

"But it's great having him home. It feels like we only had a few minutes together after we got married before he shipped off. I'll happily do his laundry every hour for the sake of staring at him in the face instead of his picture." Then she checked her own smile and bit her lip as sympathy filled her expression. "I'm sorry, Vera. It must sound like I'm gloating."

Vera laughed. It'd been a long time since she missed Jack. She'd had two years to get used to the idea of him never coming home. And though picking up her brothers from the train and seeing a dozen or so men—some of them she and Jack had gone to school with—had twisted her insides a bit, it didn't hurt so much anymore. Maybe she should feel guiltier about that.

"No, you're not gloating." Vera took Eleanor's hands back in hers. "It's not so hard when I've got my family and people like you to take care of me." They ducked their heads together over the table for a moment, and Vera relished in it. They'd sat in this diner plenty of times during school, whispering to each other—mostly about that handsome Jack Trumbell and any boy Eleanor might have eyes for at the moment. The memory was so real that when Vera looked up, she almost expected Jack to walk through the door of the diner, scanning the room for her. Maybe she hadn't missed him in a while, or maybe missing him had been so constant for her she'd become used to it.

The women pulled apart, and they sipped on their drinks until Eleanor spoke up and changed the subject. "Who's got the kids?" she asked.

Before Vera could answer, the bell above the door rang, and both women glanced over to see Fay marching in with Audrey on her hip and Tom in tow. Vera shared a grimace with Eleanor. "Well, Fay, obviously. Said her girlfriends would love to see them and that she got to go out by herself all the time." Vera stood without waiting for a reply from Eleanor as Fay marched toward their table. "What's wrong?" Vera asked Fay as she drew up to their booth with the children. Tom, though out of breath, didn't seem upset. Neither did Audrey, and Vera couldn't see any obvious injuries on either child.

"Susie Brandenburg," Fay snapped, slapping an envelope down on the table. "Look at that."

Vera leaned over and inspected the curly, perfect handwriting. "Mrs. Samuel Larson, Mrs. Jack Trumbell, and Miss Fay Larson." She shared another look with Eleanor, who shrugged in confusion. "And?" Vera questioned.

"It's for an afternoon party. She's forgotten a certain lady in our household, have you noticed? Mrs. Andrew Larson?" Fay vehemently swung Audrey to her other hip, causing the little girl to grasp her aunt's sweater in fear. Vera reached for her, to save her any more discomfort. Fay complied.

"I'm sure it was a mistake. After all, not everyone knows about Andrew bringing a wife home," Vera said.

Fay's expression turned stormier. "Oh, that little—well, she knew. She gave me the invitation when she saw me walking this way to meet you, and when I said, 'Oh, I'm sure you won't mind if we bring Josette along—Andrew's wife,' she said, 'Oh, that's not necessary. She won't know a soul and she'd feel out of place.' And then she pranced off in that silly way she does with her nose straight up in the air."

Vera covered a laugh with her hand because she certainly did know the exact way Fay meant—though her little sister had exaggerated.

"I say we bring Jo along anyway," Fay went on, and Vera had to reach over and slip Tom's hand out of Fay's since he kept tugging on it and she just kept squeezing harder. "And see what the little—well, *sweet* Miss Brandenburg," she sneered the word *sweet*, "—thinks about that."

"Mama, can I have some ice cream?" Tom asked, pointing to a family sitting a couple of booths over. Two little boys sat on one side with their mother, both of them with bowls containing bright-pink scoops of fluffy-looking ice cream.

"Of course," Vera said to avoid answering her sister, and she took her children to the nearby counter. Fay dropped into Vera's unoccupied side of the table so passionately she nearly slid right off and under the table. With a huff, she straightened and helped herself to a large drink of Vera's cream soda.

When Vera reached the counter, the two young women sitting there hastily started a conversation of their own, probably because they'd been caught up in Fay's dramatic entrance to the diner. The young man came and took Vera's order: two single scoops on cones, one strawberry, one chocolate. He had the treats ready quickly. Vera handed Tom his chocolate cone and directed him back to the table, holding Audrey in one hand and her strawberry cone in the other.

"Maybe we should all stay home," Vera said when she returned and settled Tom in the booth next to Fay. Eleanor scooted over, and Vera sat next to her, Audrey in her lap.

"That would teach her," Eleanor chimed in, "since folks around here think as much of the Larsons as they do of those uppity Brandenburgs."

"And I don't think Josette would like the idea of crashing a party she isn't wanted at. That's more your style, dear," Vera said.

"Oh, Jo's got some spunk in her. She's French, remember."

They laughed and Vera snatched her cream soda from Fay's grasp.

= ★ =

The pointed lack of invitation for Mrs. Andrew Larson was only the first of many darts Susie Brandenburg aimed in Josette's direction, and Andrew's blood boiled over it. The latest concerned dresses. Andrew had insisted that Josette buy a new dress for the reception his mother planned to have for the couple, since she'd been deprived of planning the actual wedding. The problem came when Josette's French sense of fashion had led her to Mrs. Starry's shop. The seamstress kept the ladies of Bellemont trimmed out in the most fashionable designs she could convince them to wear in rural Wyoming, better than any seamstress for miles. Her loyalties unfortunately lay with the Brandenburgs, who, between their own overrated social status and their insistence of keeping up good society, controlled well over half of the seamstress's earnings. She had politely informed Josette that she couldn't take any orders from her.

Josette leaned over Andrew's chair—a piece of furniture borrowed from his parent's house, and the only piece of furniture in their sad living room for now—and kissed him on the forehead. "I can tell from the red in your cheeks that you're stewing over Mrs. Starry again."

"Mrs. Starry and Miss Brandenburg," he said, reaching for Josette's hand. "How dare they treat my wife that way?"

"It's nothing, dear. This little girlfriend of yours will stop throwing her tantrum soon, and all will go smoothly. In the meantime, Vera said she would help me make a lovely dress and we found some fabric that is wonderful. *Ne inquiète pas.*" Her favorite phrase to ease his mind about anything—*Don't worry yourself.* She plopped down into his lap and planted a long kiss on his lips, meant to soothe him, no doubt. He didn't argue with her methods, at least not for several minutes.

"This little *former* girlfriend of mine needs to learn her lesson," he said when Josette had finished.

She laughed at him. "You sound like Fay. She insists that the Brandenburgs will not be invited to our reception. When Mother Larson scolded her for it, she told me she'd deliver the invitation herself—right into the fire."

Andrew and Fay had been partners in crime growing up, so it didn't surprise him that his sister felt the spurn as keenly as he did. He couldn't help that Susie deserved all their ire. After all Josette had gone through during the war—to think she had to come to Bellemont and deal with schoolroom rivalries. The whole thing was laughable, except that it hurt Josette's feelings in any case, schoolroom or not. He wished Susie knew more of Josette's heroic background—the number of pilots she'd managed to get into the hands of the resistance and back to London, the information she'd gathered, the fake ration cards and identity papers she'd risked her life for. Maybe if Susie understood that, she'd make a way to include Josette in her society. Or maybe it would show Susie she'd met her match. Josette could work circles around Susie. She'd been training operatives, for heaven's sake!

"I agree wholeheartedly that she shouldn't be invited," he said.

"Would it really make you feel better?" Josette asked with an arched brow.

"Very much," he insisted.

She patted his cheek and stood, walking back to the kitchen to finish making dinner. It was the first dinner in the few days since they'd moved into the small house that they'd had alone. His mother had insisted they come down to the farmhouse every night so she could feed them. Everyone in the family loved Josette, Mom especially, but she didn't seem to trust his wife's ability to care for him. Josette had said, "Who can blame her, darling? She hasn't seen you in years."

Back before the war, when he'd begun going steady with Susie, Andrew had been quite proud of himself for capturing her heart. Though Bellemont was small, and Susie's choice of beaus thin, it had been something of a victory. She'd gone on in letters—before her Dear John, of course—of how her children would come from such respected Bellemont stock. A thread of condescension had run through her words about how the Larsons were "only farmers" yet still so highly regarded in the community. "It will be nothing at all for Father to really make something of you," she'd said in one letter. Andrew shuddered at the thought now, but when Susie had been making all the plans, her ambitions for him to wear nice suits and work for her father's real estate firm hadn't bothered him. She'd always waved away ideas about him working on the farm. "Sam will take care of that," she'd say. "He's perfect for it."

"Not inviting Miss Brandenburg will only goad her more," Josette said, breaking into his thoughts. He looked up to see her standing in the archway that separated the small kitchen from the living room, wiping her hands on a dishtowel. She waved it at him sternly.

If Andrew knew one thing after going steady with Susie Brandenburg, it was that whether goaded or not, she meant to make life miserable for Josette, if only to punish him. He couldn't say why Susie had changed her mind and made such an issue about him marrying Josette, but she wouldn't take seeing her plans thwarted lightly. In fact, Andrew was hard-pressed to remember a time when she hadn't gotten exactly what she set out to have.

He couldn't allow Josette to know that though. He pushed himself out of the chair and wiggled his eyebrows at her. "*Ne t'inquiète pas, mon amour.*" In a few steps, he crossed the room and drew his laughing wife into his arms.

"Come in for dinner," she said when he'd finished kissing her, and she took his hand to lead him to their small wooden table tucked into a corner of the kitchen. "I made soufflé."

Andrew made a show of pulling out a chair for her, eliciting more laughing. Considering all the heartache she'd suffered in the past, he insisted on making her smile as much as he could manage. He sat down across from her and took a deep breath of the rich smell of the dish.

"Tomato and cheese soufflé," Josette explained, dishing some out on a plate that his mother had loaned them. They had only two of everything, all mismatched, to make do until Josette could "set up a proper household," as his mother had put it.

"It looks delicious." Andrew cut off a piece of his soufflé, his fork sliding through the airy, porous dish. His suspicions about its taste proved correct after a single bite. "You are a dream," he said around a mouthful of his second bite and while already preparing his third.

Josette cast him a proud smile—lips closed as she too chewed. "Thank you. My skills have vastly improved thanks to the fact that we have no rationing and a wealth of eggs."

"Those chickens might be the most productive things on this farm," he said. "Besides you, of course."

Having already finished off his soufflé, he stood to help himself to another piece from the dish in the middle of the table. "I make no promises of that, Mrs. Larson. I may find any excuse I can to stick around this old house to admire you all day." The table was small enough that after adding the second helping to his plate, he was able to lean over it and kiss her on the nose before sitting back down again.

"You're quite romantic, but I suppose Sam would drag you off sooner or later—or Fay, for that matter. She's very insistent on getting out of as much farmwork as she can as soon as possible."

"I cannot blame her. I feel the same." Andrew winked. They both laughed since he had too much farming in his soul to mean that. "At least until I get a proper honeymoon," he amended.

"Those two nights we spent in that pretty room we shared with your nephews were quite lovely, and I'd thank you not to complain." Josette finished off her portion of soufflé, dabbed her smiling and alluring lips, and then put her napkin over her plate.

Andrew could not help bursting into laughter. The room was stuffy with so many people squeezed into such a tight space, and the bed was so old he wasn't sure if he'd slept a wink. But Josette had been in his arms, and so he found himself agreeing.

He grabbed her hand as she stood to clear her plate and pulled her toward him and into his lap. "You are probably right, *mon amour*. Everything is lovely with you."

She placed her hands on either side of his cheeks and lowered her face toward his. "You know you sound quite silly when you speak French, don't you? Just like an American."

To which Andrew replied by speaking a string of nonsensical French words as poorly as he could and forced Josette to stop him by kissing him. And the rest of dinner was forgotten.

꞊ CHAPTER FOUR ꞊

SAM LARSON CARRIED HIS PLATE of food and Emily's as he wound his way through the crowd at the community picnic, held every year to commemorate the harvest time. He'd prepared both plates with his mother's potato salad—famous in Bellemont for being the best—cold ham, buttered rolls, and cake, of course. When he reached the spot underneath a cottonwood tree that Emily had saved for them, he laid her plate in front of her before sitting next to her. He relaxed against the trunk for a moment, watching Emily adjust her position—legs out to the side, spreading the pale-pink, embroidered skirt of her dress, her face hidden for a moment by the brim of her hat. She tilted her head to flash him a smile of gratitude as she picked up the plate and fork.

"All my favorites. You must know me well."

"Well enough to marry you." He reached for her free hand and pulled it to his lips to kiss it. "What do you say to next week?"

"Next week?" Emily chuckled. "I can hardly plan a proper wedding in one week. There's invitations to be sent out. I'll need to get a dress—that is if Mrs. Starry will deign herself to serve me considering my close connection with Josette . . ." She shook her head and sighed, focusing a moment on a bite of food as her gaze roved over the guests of the community picnic. Many families sat at the wooden picnic tables nearby; those that hadn't had been drafted for food service. Four valiant picnic tables stood in a tight line and bore the enormous burden of dozens of delicious dishes prepared by some of the best cooks in Wyoming, most of it made from food that had likely been in the ground that morning. Many other groups of friends, couples, and older children had found seats in the grass, like he and Emily had. Fortunately, though, she had secured a spot away from the crowd.

"And besides," she continued. "September is a busy month at the office. I couldn't possibly plan a wedding when I'm up to my neck in contract paperwork."

"It's about time you quit that job anyway. Then you would have plenty of time to plan a wedding. I can't wait much longer." Sam sat forward and kissed her cheek before reaching for his own plate. He would have liked to have married Emily Holman two years ago after he convinced her to accept his proposal. His consolation in going back to Europe without a wife had been that she was too stubborn to accept anyone else in so short a time. He'd spent near three years himself. He was almost thirty years old. High time to have a wife and a home. High time to have Emily as his wife.

By the arch of her eyebrows and the way her bottom lip dropped into an *O* shape, he would have thought he scandalized her somehow. The heat rushed to his face. Did she think he'd meant something lewd in his statement that he couldn't wait?

"What I meant was—"

"Quit my job?" She gasped over his attempt to explain himself, confusing him. "Why in the world would I quit my job?"

He straightened his shoulders, fixing her with a stern expression he'd practiced on many enlisted men. "To be my wife, of course. True, the farm won't provide a living for both me and Andrew for a year or two, but Mom and Dad always did all right, and we'll be expanding next year."

His stern expression had never intimidated Emily to the least degree and it didn't now. "What does that have to do with anything, Samuel Larson?" she demanded.

The heat in his face rose, a mixture of embarrassment and anger. "It means I can provide well enough for my own family, and there's no cause for you to work once we're married."

"Lower your voice, *dear*," she snapped. "I like my job very much, and if you were the richest man in Bellemont, I'd keep it anyway. Plenty of women work these days, and I intend to be one of them."

Now Sam's mouth dropped into a flabbergasted *O*. "I have never heard of anything more ridiculous. It might have been necessary for women to work during the war. It was their patriotic duty with most of the men off fighting— but there's no cause now."

Emily pressed her lips into a firm line and turned away from him, studying the children playing in the grass and those still in line for food, including Miss Susie Brandenburg and a gaggle of girls Sam recognized as being Andrew's age, and Josette and Andrew as well.

"Now that's really unkind," Emily said under her breath.

Sam, already regretting his outburst, reached for her shoulder. "Emily, don't be—"

"Every single one of them is ignoring that delicious-looking quiche Josette made. So childish." She grabbed his hand—and knowing her as well as he did and considering the urgency in her expression, he knew she'd forgotten all about their argument for the time being. "Oh, Andrew is going to say something. You'd better go stop him before he makes a scene. Those girls are quite rude."

Sam stood up with a grumble. Not only had his goal to get Emily to commit to a wedding date been derailed, but now he had to go rescue his little brother from further social disaster for his poor wife. "This will just be the beginning of rude if Andrew embarrasses Susie in front of everyone."

Emily abandoned her plate and stood with him. "I don't see why everyone in town thinks they have to kowtow to those silly Brandenburgs."

"As the owner of plenty of businesses and real estate in Bellemont, there are more than enough people that do have to kowtow to them, unfortunately. And Mrs. Brandenburg came from New York City, so of course all the women think she knows everything there is to know about society."

"Yes, I've heard them talk." Emily huffed and reached for another plate as they neared the table. Sam peered at her questioningly, but she paid him no mind as she marched right up to the quiche and dished herself a large helping.

"Oh, Josette, dear, did you make this? It looks delicious," Emily said, her voice loud enough to carry over the giggling girls and earn a few glares as well. "I can't tell you how glad I am Andrew brought you all the way from France and injected some real *culture* into this backward place."

"Thank you," Josette replied, her cheeks rosy. Her eyes danced with mirth and gratitude.

Sam leaned over his future bride. "You might rein it in, or you'll be the next target of Susie's wrath."

"Oh, fiddlesticks. What do I care about nonsense like that? I'm no socialite."

"Mr. Brandenburg owns your apartment building and you'll care when he evicts you. I won't, mind you. It will mean you'll have to marry me sooner rather than later. So please do go on and defend Josette's honor. With vigor. Andrew will surely appreciate it as well."

Emily pierced him with a glare and whirled back on Josette and Andrew, who was heaping Josette's quiche onto his plate and ignoring the tantalizing dishes around it. Sam stepped back and folded his arms. Why had Emily called him to action if she intended to fight the battle by herself?

"Where did you get that superb dress, Josette?" Emily said, moving into line right behind them. "It's fabulous. Isn't it fabulous, Sam?" She cast him a look over her shoulder. With a glance at the girls trying not to pay Emily and Josette any mind, he followed his fiancée.

"Yes, it is," he said obligingly.

"Did you bring that from Paris? You must have. I'm sure I saw it in a magazine."

Sam rolled his eyes at Emily's dramatics, but Josette smiled, amused. "Oh, I haven't been to Paris for a very long time. I bought it in New York on my way here."

Emily turned the battle toward Susie before Sam realized what she was doing and could stop her. "New York, you say? Miss Brandenburg, isn't that where your mother is from? Everyone says she knows everything about clothes there. I'm sure she would love Josette's dress, don't you think?"

Susie, who had only condescended to acknowledge Emily over her shoulder, turned away with a huff. "I doubt it." She marched away from the table with her plate, her gaggle following behind, whispering and some daring to stare at Josette's dress in awe for a moment.

"Come now," Sam said, taking Emily's arm. "You'd better come over here and sit down with me. You're going to need quite some time to finish all this food you've gotten for yourself—and the plate you left under the tree."

Josette laughed with Andrew and waved goodbye as Sam steered Emily away, back toward their private seat under the tree.

"Don't wear such a long face," she said, wrapping her arm around his. "Wasn't it fun to put that child back in her place?"

He turned and observed the picnic table Susie Brandenburg and her parents lorded over, and the not-inconsequential crowd of people gathered there and at the tables surrounding it. "I know you haven't been in Bellemont long, but I'm afraid you've stirred up a hornet's nest."

Emily followed his gaze and then shrugged at him. "Well, Fay would have done it sooner rather than later anyway. She's refusing to invite them to the reception."

He helped her sit back down in the grass. Any more talk of their wedding and a possible date was futile. "Well, the battle lines have been drawn. It remains to be seen which family will be left standing when it's over."

The proud, pioneer-stock Larsons? Or the rich, influential Brandenburgs?

☰ ★ ☰

"Another eight quarts, Mom. What do you think of that?" Vera put her hands on her hips and surveyed with pride the table full of canned potatoes.

"I think you two ought to put your nose back to the grindstone," Fay said, coming into the kitchen with another basketful. She laughed and went to the sink, carrying the basket along with her.

Vera sank into a chair at the table. "You couldn't let me have a moment to enjoy my labor?"

"You can enjoy your labor all winter, Vee." Fay dumped some of the potatoes into the sink and began scrubbing. Their mother went to help, and so Vera pushed herself to standing, although she would have welcomed another moment or two off her feet.

The front door banged open as Vera began peeling the growing pile Mom and Fay set before her on the counter. "Jack, Peter? Is that you, boys?" she called.

"It's us," Peter said from the living room.

"How was school?" She set the peeler down and wiped her hands on a towel she had tied around her waist, then headed for the living room. Jack Junior had sprawled on the couch, face down, but Peter hovered near the door. They both had chores to complete with their grandfather after school every day.

"Terrible," Jack Junior answered while Peter simply shrugged.

Vera waited for Jack Junior to continue, but when he didn't explain his muffled reply any further, she turned to Peter. "Why don't you take Tom with you to check for eggs?" She nodded toward her four-year-old, who was playing with some blocks on the floor.

"Yes, Mom." Peter hurried across the floor and bent over Tom. "Wanna come see the chickens with me?" Tom didn't need asking twice. He abandoned the blocks for Peter's outstretched hand and hurried out the door with him.

Vera sat on the arm of the couch near Jack Junior's head. He had his father's golden hair, and a section in the back stuck up where he had a cowlick. She brushed her fingers over the stubborn pieces, though it wouldn't do any good.

"Well, son, what was so terrible about school?"

"Mr. Whitaker. I hate him. He's the worst teacher I ever had. I want to go back to California where at least the teachers knew something."

"Jack!" Vera gasped. "You know better than to talk about a teacher like that." She frowned. "What has he done?"

"Made me sit in the corner while everyone else went to recess—and Bobby said Paul Allan was his new best friend since I was too dumb to come out. And he's the reason I had to sit there in the first place. Him and stupid Mr. Whitaker."

"First off, if you call Mr. Whitaker one more name, I'm going to wash your mouth out with soap." Vera folded her arms.

In such a small town, Susie Brandenburg's feud with Josette was bound to trickle into the younger set sooner or later, and since Jack Junior had, until today, been best friends with her cousin Bobby, it only surprised Vera that it had taken this long. She bit back a huff of frustration. It had been months since Jack Junior talked about moving back to California, and she had counted her lucky stars. He kept to himself more often than not, or preferred the company of his younger brother, and that had led to some difficulty for him in making friends since they got to Bellemont. He and Bobby had been nigh inseparable all summer. Now those snooty Brandenburgs had to up and ruin it. "Now tell me, how is it Bobby's fault you ended up sitting in the corner? And kindly take your face out of the pillow so that perhaps I'll understand you."

Jack Junior pushed himself up on his elbows. "He said my new aunt was a yellow-bellied Frenchie and that she ran away and stole Uncle Andrew from Miss Susie because she was too scared to stay and fight the Germans. So of course I had to punch him in the face for saying something like that about my Aunt Jo. She's no coward. Uncle Andrew said she used to hide ration cards in the hem of her skirts to help people hide, until she almost got arrested and had to go to London."

Vera fought a smile hard. Her three boys were half in love with Josette themselves, and Jack Junior most of all once he'd heard she'd been part of the resistance. "You were right to stand up for your aunt, but you weren't right to punch Bobby Brandenburg."

"Awww, Mom. You're just like Mr. Whitaker. Are you gonna make me sit in the corner too, for defending my family? I bet Mr. Whitaker doesn't understand that one bit." Jack Junior dropped his face down into the pillow again.

"You're jumping to conclusions as bad as Bobby, Jack Trumbell," Vera said. "Mr. Whitaker was a highly decorated soldier; didn't you know?" Not that it had surprised Vera. Not many people in town knew much about Dominick Whitaker, nor had they found anything out since he came to Bellemont to teach the year before, but Mrs. Asbury, head of the Women's Club, had talked him into marching in the Fourth of July parade with some other soldiers. Vera had seen his stripes, and so had everyone else. The way he wouldn't say a word about it had everyone talking twice as much about him.

Jack Junior lifted his head enough to scowl. "What? How come he never said anything about it, then? All the soldiers I know like to talk about how they fought for our country."

Vera scooted down onto the couch to put a hand on his back. "Not all of them. Your grandfather doesn't say a whole lot, does he?" she pointed out.

"Nah, but Pop lost an arm. 'Course he doesn't want to talk about it."

"Some of those men lost things we can't see, Jack, and it hurts them just as bad. Please don't talk badly about Mr. Whitaker, and you ought to apologize to him for your disrespect." She rubbed her hand over his back soothingly and he sat up, his scowl more chagrined than anything else.

"Is that all I have to do?" he asked, leaning into her.

"Well, you should apologize to Bobby too, if you want him to stay your friend. Maybe you can tell him the story Uncle Andrew told you about Aunt Jo walking right past those German soldiers on the bridge with a skirt full of ration cards."

"Can I ride my bike to his house now, Mom?" Jack Junior jumped up from the couch, and his countenance changed from gloomy to excited at the prospect of making up with his friend. Amazing how only a few minutes before, his life had been terrible.

"Finish up your chores, and then you can go," she said, scooting off the couch. Audrey began crying from upstairs in Vera's bedroom, where she'd lain the little girl down for her nap. Vera bent over to plant a kiss on Jack Junior's head. "And if he doesn't want to accept your apology, it's not the end of the world, okay? There are plenty of boys in your class for you to play with."

"I bet he won't care a lick after I tell him about Aunt Jo." And he lit out of the house to finish his chores, screen door slamming behind him, before Vera could argue that Bobby might still reject his offers of friendship. Should she call Bobby's mother first, smooth out—or test—the waters before Jack Junior got his feelings hurt?

She shook her head and climbed the stairs. Temper like his father. Barreling head-on into whatever anger or enthusiasm drove him for the moment. Too much Larson mixed in there as well, though Vera was hard-pressed to be anything but proud that he had stood up for Josette. And anything but anxious about the latest clash and how it would affect her son.

≡ ★ ≡

Vera's anxiety had been short-lived. Well, her anxiety over what the latest clash would be and how it would affect Jack Junior. Within thirty minutes he had returned with a bloody nose and the news that he would never so much as look at Bobby Brandenburg again.

She hurried a little faster up the dirt road, trying to cover the two miles between the Larson farm and this branch of the Brandenburg clan before Arlene Brandenburg got too worked up about the fight. Jack Junior had insisted that Bobby threw the first punch when Jack Junior called him cowardly for picking on a girl, but in truth, Vera had spent little time waiting for her son to recount the story before rushing out the door to do damage control. In her opinion, Susie had taken this feud far enough when it affected the friendship of eight-year-old boys.

To her surprise, as she approached the edge of the lush lawn that stood out against the brown and sage brush that surrounded it, Mr. Whitaker, the boys' teacher, came down the front steps, hands in his pockets and, for all intents and purposes, tail between his legs.

"Evening, Mrs. Trumbell." He nodded at her as he approached. Vera's heart did the thumpity-thump that had gotten her into trouble with her husband, Jack, in the first place. Only where Jack had been all golden-boy charming, Dominick Whitaker was irresistibly dark and rugged, complete with a thin scar running an inch or two along his square jawline and almost hidden by the stubble of a day's growth.

She shook herself. She might wish for marriage so she could stop having to take care of everything by herself, and Mr. Whitaker might be gosh-darn handsome and mysterious to boot, but he was the last man in Bellemont looking for a wife. More than one available woman in town had tried setting her cap at him, and every single one had failed in getting so much as a smile from him. Besides, Vera had her family. Her situation wasn't so desperate yet that she needed to humiliate herself over him.

Even if those brown eyes had her feeling like she *was* that desperate.

"Mrs. Trumbell?"

Heat swathed Vera's face. "Oh, um. Good evening, Mr. Whitaker. What are you doing here?"

"Mrs. Brandenburg summoned me about today's incident at school—and apparently the one after school." He raised an eyebrow and Vera shrugged. She'd spent the whole walk trying to work up the proper chagrin when she really thought that someone ought to punch every last Brandenburg in the nose. "Don't bother going in there," Mr. Whitaker went on. "She's phoning Principal Eubank to get the boys into different classes."

Vera glanced at the house and slumped. "That is too bad," she said as she turned and fell into step beside Mr. Whitaker, walking away from the house. "Bobby was the first good friend Jack Junior has had since we got here."

"Friends come and go. A boy ought to learn that," Mr. Whitaker said gruffly, staring out across one of the fields.

Vera's heart ached, both for the truth in that for her son and for whatever Mr. Whitaker had suffered to feel it so keenly. She had to adjust her stride to keep up with Mr. Whitaker's quicker pace. "Forgive me, but a boy ought not to have to learn that too soon—the war made too many boys into men too fast, and I'd like my son not to have to live any more of that."

Mr. Whitaker regarded her, startled, but Vera refused to feel guilt for what he might have suffered to make him so callous about the situation. Jack Junior had faced rough times too. He was the only one of her children who really remembered his father, and he felt his death the hardest because of it. Then she'd brought him to the farm and circumstances had forced him into the work of men twice his age.

"Of course not. It is too bad that it's come to this over—" Mr. Whitaker stared hard at Vera a moment. No wonder the children in his class were normally so well-behaved. He wasn't even angry, and a shiver ran down her spine. Of course, it could have been something quite different from fear . . . "I guess I don't know why the Brandenburgs are fighting with the Larsons."

"Oh, Susie's in a twist over Andrew bringing home a French wife instead of marrying her. Andrew was one of the most popular boys in school. I'm sure she had a lot of plans to settle down with someone as eligible as him and preside over her own little circle the way her mother presides over everything in town."

"Is that it?" he asked disdainfully.

Vera nodded, staring at the road and the small swirls of dust their feet kicked up as they walked. "And it's her own fault too. Stopped writing Andrew last spring so she could date the Bidwell boy, only he up and went to college and left her here."

Mr. Whitaker grunted and they walked several feet in silence. He paused as they came to the lane that led to the Larson farmhouse; he would continue on into town, a three- or four-mile walk. Vera wondered if he had a bicycle.

"I'll speak to Principal Eubank in the morning. I'd like to keep Jack in my class. He's a good boy. I did feel bad about punishing him. He was only standing up for his aunt." He cleared his throat. "I know a good deal many brave French men and women, and I hate to hear the kind of nonsense Bobby's been taught because his cousin is jealous."

"Thank you," Vera said. "For looking out for Jack. He is a good boy, just . . . passionate. Like his father. So much like his father."

Mr. Whitaker nodded. "Folks say he was an all-American football player."

"Yes." She chuckled, snatches of memories of those days twirling through her brain. Seemed ages ago, the night Jack first asked her to wear his letterman's jacket. "I'd forgotten about that."

"Good night," Mr. Whitaker said abruptly and hurried on down the road without waiting for a reply from her.

Had she said something to offend him to make him leave so suddenly? She watched him, wondering what she'd said. It could be anything these days. Pain seemed to linger in his eyes. How much had Dominick Whitaker lost, and would he ever heal from it?

⹀ CHAPTER FIVE ⹀

THE NIGHT OF THE RECEPTION had turned out superbly, as though the perfect fall afternoon had been made to order. The homey smell of roasted vegetables drifted over the guests, who stood in groups of twos and threes and fours around the Larson's yard, chatting. And everyone had been kind enough. Thanks to Susie's campaign against her, it might take some time for Bellemont to warm up to Josette. Heaven knew she'd faced much worse. Like the night the Gestapo came within an inch of finding her secret cupboard full of ration cards and false IDs.

And her resistance work had led to amazing things. Moving to London had brought her into Andrew's path, and to America and a family again. At least *Maman* and *Papa* hadn't had to see France fall to the Germans, but the last eight years had been awfully lonely anyway.

Josette leaned farther into Andrew's side, listening to him talk about the evening with Fay, who stood on his other side. The reception was winding down. They had greeted all the guests and no new ones were in sight of the Larson's large front lawn. Soon she'd need to help Mother Larson and the girls pack things away, but not yet. She sighed.

Andrew tightened his arm around her waist. "It was a good party, *ma chère*, wasn't it?" he said.

"Lovely. I'm so glad it wasn't spoiled." At least Susie's continued snubbing had given Josette this. She laughed to herself. Her husband grew quite upset every time Susie did some mean thing, but in reality, it was a relief to Josette that social snobbery was her biggest worry, and she was happy that the days of far greater worries, such as rationing, bombing raids, avoiding arrest, and training operatives for the OSS were behind her now.

"Thanks to a 'lost' invitation," Fay muttered under her breath to Andrew.

"Lost?" Josette said, though she knew by the way Andrew and Fay colored that they hadn't meant for her to hear. Josette frowned. "I thought you must have been teasing when you said you wouldn't invite her." She lowered her voice and turned to Andrew. "Really, how could you—you've broken up Jack Junior's friendship over this nonsense."

"Me?" Andrew said, his eyes wide with disbelief. "I didn't have anything to do with that."

"Snubbing them back makes you just as bad." She regarded him with disappointment, and he had the decency to pull at his collar guiltily.

"I'm sorry, Jo. You're right," he said. Fay rolled her eyes and walked away. Andrew watched her before turning back to Josette. "She's only looking out for you."

Josette hadn't meant to chastise Fay. Her new sisters-in-law had been so welcoming to her—every member of the family had, making her feel as though she'd been part of it for much longer than she had. She wouldn't want Fay to think she was ungrateful of their loving treatment.

"I know, and I'm sorry if I was rude," Josette said. "I'll talk to Fay. But I don't want to be as childish as Susie."

He pulled Josette closer, putting his other arm around her. "I understand. We shouldn't have done it. You have to admit, though, that this party wouldn't have turned out half so great if Susie had shown up to stir everyone up." After a moment, he let go and slid his hand down into Josette's. She'd missed him those months after he'd had to leave London for Washington, and still, after a month of marriage, holding his hand stirred up those same girly daydreams and butterflies that had plagued her from the first time she saw him at the door of the OSS office in London. He'd looked so sharp in his olive-colored uniform, and she'd been struck by his good looks. A few moments of conversation, however, had shown him to be down-to-earth and thoughtful. She'd eagerly accepted his offer of a date a few days later.

"I don't think she would have come, and then we might have said we had done the right thing," she said.

"Perhaps." He shrugged. "But I couldn't risk her coming and ruining your special day out of spite. Yes, it's all petty, but if it gave you a chance to feel welcome here, I don't regret it."

"You're a scoundrel." Josette laughed. He was anything but. At twenty-two he still had the face of an innocent boy—most of the time. Those same, young features could turn as mischievous as any expression of Jack Junior's or Peter's. She was a few years older and had often taken on the adult role in their relationship, and when Andrew stared at her the way he did now—adoring and protective—she didn't mind it one bit.

Vera came over to join them, and Josette took note of the direction she'd come from—chatting with Dominick Whitaker. No doubt they'd been discussing Jack Junior, but pink stood out in Vera's cheeks and the satisfied smile on her lips told Josette she'd enjoyed the conversation no matter what the topic.

"Another important parent-teacher meeting?" Andrew teased.

The pink in Vera's cheeks deepened to a flat-out blush. "He wanted to let me know that Jack and the Thompson boy have struck up a friendship at school, and Jack seems to be all right with this whole mess with Bobby."

"Well, and so what if you were flirting with him, Vera." Josette nudged Andrew with her elbow.

"I wasn't flirting," Vera said, then she broke into a nervous laugh. "I wouldn't know how to anymore. It's been so long."

"That can't be true," Josette said. "Everyone tells me your husband was quite a charmer. Did he quit flirting with you because he married you?"

Vera's blush faded back to an attractive, pleased pink in her cheeks. She smiled fondly. "Oh, no. He was a charmer. But he's been gone a long time too. Over two years since the last time I saw him. Almost three before that. He joined up in '40, just waiting for his chance to serve his country. He was passionate like that. Diving head-on into whatever took his fancy at the moment. He was still just as over the moon about being a soldier in every letter he wrote me too—it helps that he loved what he was doing and that he believed in the cause he died for."

Josette reached to hug her. "Yes, it does."

Though her eyes shone, Vera laughed at herself. "I'm sure I could use the practice flirting, though Mr. Whitaker is hardly the best man to practice on."

"Well, I agree," Sam said, joining the conversation. "I've heard enough about his unit to advise you to steer clear of him. Brave, but dangerous. That's what everyone said about him."

Vera turned to study Mr. Whitaker for a moment and mumbled to herself, "All the more reason . . ." Then she said to Sam, "Now, I don't need you to play the part of my protective older brother. You've tried that tack before and look at where it got me—I ignored everything you said and ran off and married Jack Trumbell despite you. Maybe *to* spite you." They all laughed and Vera continued. "Leave off Mr. Whitaker. He's a good man. I can tell."

"Well, I know plenty of good men if you're looking for a husband, Vee, and who would suit you a lot better," Sam said.

"Quite arrogant of you to think you know my type," she shot back with good-natured sternness.

"Andrew, Josette?" Kathryn hurried toward them. "The governor is leaving. You two ought to go and say goodbye—thank him for coming all the way from Cheyenne when he must be awfully busy."

"Of course we will, Mother." Josette tugged on Andrew's arm. That had been a bright spot in the evening. The governor's son and Andrew had gone to school together, and he had come for the reception and brought his parents with him. Despite having scolded Andrew for their pettiness, Josette couldn't help the smug feeling that Susie Brandenburg would hear about the governor coming—and to a function she hadn't been invited to!

"Oh, you little sneak," Andrew whispered to her with a laugh. "I know that satisfied look of yours when I see it."

"Well, it is nice that he came, isn't it?" Josette couldn't help laughing. She may not approve of engaging in this silly war with the Brandenburgs, but she wouldn't be beaten by a spoiled socialite either, not when she'd beaten her share of much tougher foes, and more dangerous circumstances to boot.

≡ ★ ≡

Dominick walked in silence along the dirt road from the Larson's into town. With summer dying and another cold Wyoming winter hovering somewhere in the wings, he liked to enjoy every moment of the brief fall. Soon the weather would turn too cold to stroll along the peaceful roads here and up and down the mostly quiet streets of quaint Bellemont. He'd wanted to come teach here for all those things. Sure, he wasn't the only man to have lived through more than enough war for a lifetime. He needed the calm, quintessential small-town life that he'd found from the first time he visited. It would help him settle his soul. He would never again be the man he was before the war—too much had happened to change him—but living this quiet life might get him closer to being at peace with the man he'd become.

And he didn't need the attention of Mrs. Trumbell. But considering how he liked the easy sound of her voice and the unworried way she took everything in, what he actually didn't need was trying to figure out Mrs. Trumbell's attention.

Not that she meant anything by it. She wanted to hear about Jack Junior and how he was doing. Dominick had been the one to find her at the reception and give her reasons not to worry about her son. She had a way of blushing every so often when she met his eye that didn't get past him. She liked him too, though he couldn't for the life of him figure out why she might.

From everything he'd heard in town—and people liked to make sure he heard things, probably because they were all curious about him and hoped their opening up would lead to him opening up—Vera's husband had been Dominick's opposite. The town hero. A football star. He'd married Mrs. Trumbell young and they'd gone to California for him to take a stab at acting. Mrs. Asbury made sure Dominick knew that Jack Trumbell had the looks. A regular Gary Cooper. Dominick had never known him, and the man was dead, so why the blasted itch to bring him down a peg or two?

Not because Dominick really wanted Mrs. Trumbell to like him . . . well, he hoped not, but that was probably the case. He'd have to squelch any encouragement, anything that might seem like encouragement. Another thing people made sure he heard was that Mrs. Trumbell needed to get remarried.

Everyone knew the Larson farm did just fine even if they had downsized quite a bit while the boys were away fighting. Old Mr. Larson was known for his economy and good sense. They might not be as rich as the Brandenburgs, but the Larsons had weathered far more harsh Wyoming winters and bad crop years and come out on top every time. That garnered respect greater than anything they could have earned from riches.

But she had *four children*, Mrs. Sluiss had informed him. A woman with *four children* needed a husband. Though he'd busied himself too much with his army career to work on a family of his own, it had been something Dominick wished for in the future. Now, more than ever, a wife and children fit into his idea of a quiet life. But in all honesty, he was in no position to be a husband to any good woman like Mrs. Trumbell, let alone the father to four children. His mistakes in Europe would follow him all his life. He couldn't taint someone as sweet as her—she wouldn't have a man like him if she knew the things he'd done. He had to face that he may never have the family he'd always assumed he would.

It surprised him when he looked up and realized he'd made it to the highway. He'd intended to enjoy his walk. Bask in the crisp autumn air and slight chill to the breeze now that the sun had begun to dip. Instead, he'd spent half his walk already with his thoughts far too much on Mrs. Trumbell.

He hurried his pace into town and the small house he rented from Mrs. Sluiss. It wouldn't be hard to not encourage Mrs. Trumbell. He didn't have to seek her out at functions to discuss Jack Junior. A note or two would suffice. Then he wouldn't smell her perfume, something with roses in it, or wonder about how she could talk about her husband with such ease—how it didn't bowl her over when someone brought up what a good football player he was. He'd felt so stupid that night they walked from the Brandenburgs together. He'd expected her to get emotional on him, but she'd smiled. *Fondly.* As though she liked remembering him.

Again, the fact that Dominick had arrived somewhere, namely his house, surprised him. He opened the door rougher than he needed and flipped on the light in the front room, though it did little to brighten the dreary place. He had a small couch and an old radio. He dropped down onto the couch and turned the radio on, fiddling with the dial until he found something upbeat.

It would be easy, he assured himself, to not think of Mrs. Trumbell anymore. Even if he had spent an hour just now thinking of nothing but her.

⫶ CHAPTER SIX ⫶

"OH, YES. JUST PERFECT," JOSETTE said to herself as she stood up and inspected the deep-purple rug, making sure it sat straight in front of the rose-colored couch. It changed the room immensely. She whirled on the old chair that she arranged opposite it. She'd bought a beautiful rose fabric to sew a cover for it. She'd have this house in order in no time.

A knock broke her out of her thoughts, and Josette hurried to the door. When she peered through the screen and saw three ladies standing on her porch, she slipped on the black heels she'd left by the door before she answered.

"Good afternoon, ladies." Josette held the door open wide, disguising her surprise at Susie and two of her closest friends standing on the steps, Susie with a pie in her hands. "Please, do come in."

"Thank you." Susie beamed at her, and for a moment, the way the single light in the living room hit her hair gave her a halo. She strode in, more comfortable than Josette ever would have been in a room with a person she had been working against for the last few weeks. The other two girls followed, keeping their gazes on the carpet.

Susie turned to hold the pie out to Josette, her gaze falling over the old chair for the first time. Her nose wrinkled in disgust, but she covered it. Josette's face flamed, and she took her time closing the door behind them. She vowed to get that cover done as quickly as she could, although she hadn't cared so much about how it looked until Susie came. In truth, the old chair was the best piece of furniture Josette had owned in the last few years until Andrew insisted they buy this new couch.

"Where should I put this?" Susie asked, her radiant, and condescending, smile returning.

"I'll take it into the kitchen." Josette held out her hands and Susie gave her the pie. "Oh, it's strawberry. How delicious-looking." She poured every bit of genuineness she could into the statement. Susie had sculpted the fluffy whipped cream into careful peaks, and the strawberry mixture underneath didn't move an inch as Josette took it, betraying how perfectly set it was. It almost made her jealous.

"Yes, Andrew's favorite." Susie shrugged as though she made Andrew's favorite meals in her sleep.

"I kn—"

"You probably didn't realize," Susie spoke over Josette. "You haven't known him near as long as I have." Then she added a giggle.

Josette blinked. She'd known Andrew for almost nine months, and he'd told her his favorite pie was strawberry on their first date. It wasn't exactly classified information. In an effort to be gracious, Josette bit her tongue against telling Susie that. Instead, she hurried through the doorway to the tiny kitchen and slid the pie into the refrigerator.

It was silly to worry about such a small thing as what Susie or anyone in town thought of her. She'd risked her life on multiple occasions back in France and faced much scarier things than a girl bent on revenge for someone stealing her beau. She put her hands on her hips and marched out to face the enemy.

When Josette returned to the room, the three girls had taken seats on the new couch, leaving her the ratty chair. It looked so much rattier now that Josette thought about it. Was it the new carpet and couch or the company that made her think that? She fell back into the old thing, where the stuffing had worn down to the springs in the back from too many years of use. She scooted to a more ladylike position by perching on the front of it, facing down her guests with the best smile she could muster.

She opened her mouth, waiting for something kind to come to her, but Susie saved her from speaking by piping up first. "I suppose you'll find something more . . . comfortable later," she said with a glance around the room. Spic and span and gleaming, thanks to Vera, Fay, and Mother Larson—but yes, worn, now that Josette really scrutinized it. Rough wooden floors and walls. The paper peeling and paint faded. "I mean, I suppose everything was very last-minute, considering your elopement."

She said it like it was a bad word and insinuated more with the little cough she tagged on to the end of it. "No, we didn't give them much warning," Josette said. "But Andrew plans to work with his brother on the farm, and this house is convenient for that."

There came that condescending smile again. It made Josette want to stuff her handkerchief down Susie's throat. "Oh, well. Andrew always said he would build me a nice big house up on the hill overlooking the farm." She giggled again. "But things change, don't they?"

"Yes, they certainly do," Josette said through gritted teeth. She surveyed the other two girls, wondering when they'd join the conversation, but the carpet held all their attention.

"So exciting that you came all the way from France. Everyone's talking about that. It was good of Andrew to marry you so you could get to America, wasn't it? We Americans are good at that. Saving the French." She tittered again.

Josette had no reply for this latest attack. Her face burned and her blood boiled. She hopped to her feet. "It was nice of you to bring the pie. I'm sure Andrew will be eager to eat it." She could muster no more politeness than that. *Be gracious, be gracious,* she said to herself before she blew her top.

And Susie had the gall to tip her nose up, her eyes shining in triumph. "Yes, he will. It's probably been ages since he had one." She stood as well, leading the other two to the door and out without any other farewell than that.

Josette fell into the chair, determined not to dissolve into tears over such a little thing. She jumped out of the chair and marched into the kitchen, then took the pie out of the fridge and dumped it resolutely in the trash. And when she realized whether Susie had made it or not, Andrew would have liked to eat it, she sat at the kitchen table and cried.

$$\equiv \star \equiv$$

Josette tried to keep herself distracted that afternoon by starting the cover for the old chair. She was in their bedroom doing just that when Andrew came in. At the sound of him calling, "Hello, *ma chère?*" in that ridiculous, and surely exaggerated, American accent, something in her chest pinched. Guilt. Guilt that she'd thrown away that whole pie in a fit of anger at Susie and her smug insults.

"In here," she called back from the small bedroom where she'd set up the sewing machine Mother Larson had lent her.

She didn't start up the machine again as she listened to Andrew's booted feet come down the hallway. A few months ago, the memories that a sound like that conjured up might have sent her heart racing. It was too easy to close her eyes and forget that she was safe in America, that Germany had been defeated, and that the Gestapo wouldn't barge through her door again.

"I thought I saw Susie Brandenburg's car driving down the road from the house," Andrew said when he appeared in the doorway.

For no good reason, a surge of jealousy swept through Josette at the thought of him recognizing that ostentatious, cherry-red Hudson convertible Susie drove. "Oh, did you?" she said, sliding the fabric back under the foot of the sewing machine and whirring away again, even though she should have gotten up and welcomed Andrew with a kiss.

He strode across the room and laid a—quite dirty—hand upon her shoulder. "What's she done now, Jo?"

"Nothing!" Josette cried shrilly, abandoning the machine again and standing so quickly the rickety wooden chair she'd dragged in from the kitchen wobbled and screeched as she sent it backward. "She's been ever so kind. Brought you a strawberry pie and everything—but I'm sorry, I threw it in the garbage." She whirled to face Andrew just as she pronounced that and caught his eyes widening in shock and then disappointment flitting through his expression before it fell into something far too sympathetic for Josette's taste at the moment.

"Did she do something horrible?" he asked gently, coming toward her, his arms open in that sweet way. He could never resist holding her when she was hurting, and right now it irritated Josette beyond reason.

"Good heavens, Andrew. I've thrown away a perfectly good pie. Your favorite. What a silly and ridiculous thing to do. Would you stop being so understanding and let me throw a proper tantrum over it?" She stomped her foot, still clad in the black high heels she'd worn for Susie's visit.

Andrew chewed on his bottom lip, but she knew him well enough to see he was trying to cover up a smile at her outburst. "You're quite right, *mon amour*. Throwing away strawberry pie is unpardonable. I've half a mind to take you over my knee and spank you." He added on some improper things in French that made Josette blush.

"Andrew!" she gasped, and he held back his smile no longer as he came and took her into his arms.

"How was my accent just then, Jo?"

He'd made such an effort at giving his nickname for her the proper French pronunciation that she couldn't help dissolving into giggles and tears. "Horrific. *I've* half a mind to wash your mouth out with soap."

He brushed away some of her tears with his thumb, kissing her cheeks where he'd wiped them. "Was she very terrible?" he asked in a soft voice, studying her with serious concern.

"She said some awful things," Josette admitted in a small voice.

"Her strawberry pie is no good anyway," he said, and she knew he was lying. She'd licked off a bit of whipped cream that she'd gotten onto her fingers as she tossed it. It had tasted divine—sweet with just the right amount of vanilla.

"Oh, Andrew." The giggles faded into more tears. "I've ruined that beautiful pie."

"She deserved it," he said, kissing away those tears.

"You didn't." She sniffled and laid a head against his shoulder, picking it quickly back up again when she smudged her cheek with mud.

"Don't worry over it." He fished his handkerchief from his pocket, but Josette had to push it away with a hiccupping laugh. It was as covered in dirt as he was. She pulled her own from the pocket of her dress and mopped up her face.

"I'm better now. You ought to get back to work. Sam will miss you. It was so kind of you to come check on me after you saw her car. *Je t'adore.*" She kissed him fervently to show her gratitude, a kiss that Andrew prolonged. "Now you're just trying to get out of work," she accused in a laughing whisper.

"What better excuse? I am practically still on my honeymoon." He swept Josette into his arms. "I have half a mind to take the rest of the afternoon off."

Josette wrapped her arms around his neck to kiss him. "I have half a mind not to argue with you—not even one tiny bit."

≡ ★ ≡

Andrew insisted they go to the farmhouse for dinner that evening. It seemed unfair to ask Josette make dinner after all that had happened with Susie that afternoon. She admitted she wasn't up to making anything, and he couldn't blame her. Nor did he blame her for tossing that decadent-looking pie, with Susie's fresh whipped cream, into the trash. Not after what Susie had said to Josette. He'd tried not to think too much about maybe spooning out one bite.

"Jo, won't you let me go talk to her?" he said. They'd spent a happy afternoon together, but the episode hadn't been far from his mind. "What she said today was plain rude. She may be spoiled, and people may treat their family like royals, but I guarantee her mother would be ashamed that Susie had stooped so low to hurt your feelings."

"It's okay. Really, I'm fine. People much worse than Susie have said much worse things." She sighed and leaned her head against his shoulder. The fact that his sweet Jo compared social snobbery to some of the horrors she faced during the war made bile rise in Andrew's throat.

He stopped and turned her to face him, hands on her shoulders. "You shouldn't have to hear it now. I wanted Bellemont to be your home. I wanted you to be happy here."

She let a smile through as she threaded her arms around his neck and leaned into him. "She'll stop soon, I'm sure. I'll have to weather it."

"I don't want you to have to weather it, *mon amour*," he murmured and stroked her cheek. "Shall I take you back to France or England? I'd go anywhere to make you happy, Jo. I would."

She shook her head, and her smile turned more genuine. "Sam needs you here. And you need you here. This place is in your blood. I remember how you talked about it back in London. Susie bragged about how she knew your favorite dessert, and when I thought more about it, it comforted me to think that your favorite dessert is the least of the wonderful things you've confided in me. Like the kind of pride you feel when you sit down to a meal that you've provided off the farm. Or how much you like the way a field looks right after you till it up."

Andrew pulled Josette tight against him. "I love you."

"I love you more," she said into his shoulder.

They continued on in silence again, this time more comfortable, though the sting of her hurt feelings stayed with him still. When they reached the house, Josette joined the girls in the kitchen to finish preparing the meal, and Andrew sat down in the front room to listen to *The Lone Ranger* on the radio with his father.

"Evening, son."

"Evening, Dad."

Dad turned his attention back to the broadcast, and Andrew found himself listening in on the conversation in the kitchen. Fay had turned it to Susie's despicable behavior, and Josette filled them in on her latest attack.

"She has some nerve," Fay said, the anger filling her voice with an edge. "You wouldn't believe the nonsense she's spouting in town." Her statement was followed by the clamor of a pan lid going back on a pot with more force than necessary. "Telling everyone the governor only came to your party because Andrew called Teddy and begged him to bring his father."

Heat shot into Andrew's face faster than a brand seared a cowhide. How had Susie even found out that he'd asked Teddy that? Well, Andrew never could trust him with a good secret. Though he would have thought that Teddy could manage to not broadcast to the world that Andrew wanted someone important to show up Susie for Josette. Now it turned out he'd only made it worse.

"Is that true?" Dad asked.

Andrew slumped back against the chair. "About me asking Teddy to bring his father? Yeah, it's true. I wanted to help Jo."

"I suppose if you kids would leave it alone, it'd blow over soon enough."

"I can't sit back and let Susie make Jo miserable. She came to the house today on the pretense of welcoming Jo, when really she came to say rude things and hurt Jo's feelings. She was out of line, Dad. Jealous or not, she had no right."

"No, I agree with you there. Don't know what you can do to help it though, with a girl like Susie. She always did want her own way over everything."

Andrew rubbed a hand over his face. "I don't see why in the world that ought to be me right now. To tell you the truth, I never guessed she cared that much. Only that she thought I looked neat in my uniform and that she liked telling her girlfriends how she was dating a G. I. She made all sorts of plans about us getting married, but I never took it too seriously—I was fighting a war!"

"Girls can act funny sometimes about things they can't have."

"I suppose so." Andrew sighed.

"You boys thinking we ought to plow the west field?" Dad asked, switching the subject. He probably had no more wisdom to add—and no more ability to understand Susie than Andrew.

Andrew nodded thoughtfully. "That's a good idea. Might make things easier in the spring."

"Not a lot of extra hands around here." Dad waved what remained of his severed arm in the air and both men laughed. Though the jokes came few and far between these days, it always brightened Andrew's day to see an old spark of the man he'd known come back.

"You could take Jack Junior and let him steer for you," Andrew suggested. "I'm sure he'd like that a lot better than picking beans."

Andrew grinned, but more because of the smile on his father's face than anything else. He'd come upon Dad and Jack Junior and Peter in the barn the day before and listened for a moment as Dad taught them about the tractors. His face had held all the love Andrew remembered it having when he'd taught Andrew at that age. Dad lived for farming. It was deep in his blood, and losing an arm couldn't take that from him. It lightened Andrew's heart that Dad could still find joy in it, amid the frustrations he experienced now every day thanks to that missing limb.

"Practically anything is better than picking beans," Andrew said, resting his head back against the chair and thinking back to what Josette had said about them needing him here. He couldn't leave the farm. This farm brought life back to him, the same way it brought it back to his father. The soil his family had worked and lived on for decades healed more of the broken parts of him from the war than anything else could—except maybe Josette. And without Andrew, they'd be short the people they needed to start planting all the fields again.

But how could he ask his wife to stay in a place that had made her feel so unwelcome?

⹀ CHAPTER SEVEN ⹀

SAM LEANED BACK INTO HIS seat at Alice's diner, his arm over the top of it, fingers brushing Emily's smooth, auburn hair laying in curls against her shoulders. The diner was quiet, just a few other couples seated among the brightly colored booths and the few tables that sat near the counter. Boy, Sam needed someplace quiet. With Vera and her kids living at home, he slept on the pullout couch in the living room. Sure, he'd been in much worse conditions, but after coming home from the war, was it too much to ask for some peace and quiet? All the more reason to convince Emily to get married as soon as possible. He couldn't quite justify the expense of renting a place in town as a bachelor, especially when he expected to be married shortly.

"I always get the country fried steak when I'm here. I should get something different, shouldn't I?" Emily said. Sam watched her as she bent over the menu she must have memorized by now, considering all the Friday night dates they spent here. Emily still sat as close as she could to him, the way she had when he'd been in Bellemont on leave two years before. The knowledge of the many things that could happen to prevent him from coming home had nearly convinced her then to marry him right away, but her pragmatism had held out in the end. "I don't want to be a war bride or a widow," she'd said.

"It's so good," she murmured from beside him, bringing him back to the present.

Sam chuckled to himself. "I haven't had the chicken fried steak in a while. Maybe I'll get it and you can eat some of mine."

"Excellent idea." She beamed at him and turned back to the menu. "But then what should I get?"

Alice came by with their drinks, but Emily waved her off since she hadn't decided yet. Sam didn't mind. The soft music coming from the jukebox and the low murmur of the others in the diner beat the constant noise at the house.

How did Dad handle it, cooped up there with all of them? He helped as much as he could on the farm, but he tired quickly, retreating home to rest up—and how did he rest up, with Tom and Audrey playing and Mom and Vera knocking around in the kitchen, trying to keep up with all the food they kept bringing in from the harvest of the huge garden? Sam's back ached thinking about all the peas and beans and carrots he'd picked over the last few weeks since he'd been home. He leaned his head back on the slick vinyl of the booth and closed his eyes.

"I had forgotten how often I had to convince you to stay home on some Friday nights and that it wouldn't hurt my feelings."

His head snapped up at the sound of Emily's voice. "What? Sorry, Em."

She laughed quietly. "You were sleeping, Sam. Alice already came and got our orders. You should have stayed home and slept. You must be exhausted after all the hard work you've put in at the farm." She ran her fingers softly through the buzzed hair over his ears, making keeping his eyes open even more difficult.

"Sleep? At the house? Not likely. If you don't mind watching over me, I'll finish my nap here." He winked and then sat up to take a long drink of the ice-cold soda in front of him, hoping it would kill his exhaustion, at least long enough to enjoy his date. No matter how much he wished for a good night's rest, he never wished for it enough to leave Emily any earlier than he had to. "I can't believe how the girls kept things going by themselves all this time. They must have worked themselves into the ground."

"They did," Emily said. "People in town pitched in when they could, and your mom kept more than a few families fed in exchange for the help." Emily sighed and stared out through the black windows. "That's the Bellemont I liked when we first moved here. The community that came together to take care of one another. Not biting at each other like they are now."

"It'll blow over," Sam said.

Emily stiffened. "Sure it will, but at what cost to Josette?"

Sam had heard enough talk of this nonsense to last him a lifetime. Susie Brandenburg needed a good spanking, like all children who misbehaved. He also had a feeling that if her parents didn't step up soon to take care of that, Andrew might.

Sam draped his arm over Emily's shoulder and pulled her close, kissing the side of her head. "You remember when you first moved here?" he asked in a low voice, not moving his head from where it rested against hers. He sure did. He'd seen her for the first time in this very diner. She'd come in with some women around his age, girls he'd known when they were all in school together. It had been the perfect opening for him to get introduced to Emily. He'd found a reason to stop and talk to her any time he could after that. Her father had been the new veterinarian in town, and both Emily and her mother had worked in the office. Sam had figured out when Emily usually worked and made sure to be the one to call the office on those days. He'd called about and taken in their animals for so many minor things over the next few months that his father had to put a stop to it and insist that Sam bite the bullet and ask Emily for a date. They couldn't afford Sam's flirting, he'd said.

Her face softened at the memory, and she pulled away enough to gaze at him. "There were some folks here a bit more welcoming than the Brandenburgs are being." Her lips lifted into a nostalgic smile and she sighed.

"And still it took you six months to say yes to a date with me." Sam rubbed at Emily's shoulder, laughing at how persistent he'd always had to be with his future bride.

"You're telling it all wrong. I wanted to go out with you, but you asked at all the wrong times." She leaned further into him, and the smell of her perfume conjured all sorts of memories, some much better than others. Too many of those memories were of him poring over one of her letters, lapping up every word, and unashamedly pressing them to his face and smelling every possible bit of it, day-dreaming of the day they would sit together like this again.

"You kept saying yes to all those other fellows who kept asking you out," he accused.

She laughed. "I did save the best for last, don't you think?" She punctuated this sweet remark with a kiss on his nose, then a quick one for his lips. Sam tightened his arms around her, holding her close to him and savoring the moment. Sometimes being home with her felt like a dream. He couldn't help it that sometimes he woke up in the middle of the night, in the blackness of the living room on that lumpy old mattress, and forgot where he was. It might take a minute or two of mental convincing that he wasn't on a cot or on the ground somewhere in Europe.

He shoved away the memories and took another deep breath of Emily's perfume. "You always did know how to get what you wanted."

She grinned. "A woman has to know that if she wants to get anywhere in this world."

Sam arched an eyebrow at the determination in her words and expression. He had to admit it was quite attractive the way she nodded her head in a short, decisive way and the alluring set of her full lips. "Where else exactly do you plan to get, Emily Holman?" he asked.

She frowned at his question. "Well, someday I'm going to be a Soils Planner at the soils office. Won't that be marvelous?"

Sam tensed but then forced his muscles to relax. He still held Emily in his arms, and he didn't want her to notice the effect her words had on him. He didn't have the strength to argue about their differing opinions tonight. "Mmmm," he said, unable to commit to any other answer.

"You don't agree, of course," she said, turning away from him and staring again out the window. She scooted away, forcing him to drop his hold on her and settle for his arm around her shoulder—stiff as it was.

It was a bad idea to retaliate. The words spilled off his tongue anyway. "I wonder how long that will take, so that perhaps when you've finished with that we can talk about setting a wedding date."

"We ought to set one tonight. There's no reason I can't have both a career and a family." She swiveled back to him. "Perhaps sometime in the spring. April or May would be a lovely month to get married in."

"Next spring?" Sam's surprised half-shout made Emily jump back.

She recovered in true Emily Holman form. "You disagree?" she asked in an unperturbed tone.

"Yes. Of course I do." Spring was several months away and too long for Sam to wait. He'd already been waiting long enough to marry his sweetheart. "I've been looking forward to having a home and starting our family, Emily. A house I expect you to run." Gosh darn it, dreams of that home—with Emily—had carried him through the war, and now it was the only thing that made sleeping on a pullout couch bearable.

She straightened her back and folded her arms. The slick vinyl of the diner booth seats made it too easy for her to put more distance between them. "Oh, that's what you *expect*, do you?"

He ground his teeth together. "I don't see why I should have to put up with any less." It had been over six years since his first date with Emily, and though it had taken him another year to convince her to go steady and the war had interrupted things—in any case, hurrying up their long-planned wedding wasn't too much to ask.

"Oh! Put up with?" Emily scooted out of the booth and stood up, her expression burning. "You are so pigheaded, Sam Larson." She whirled and stomped away, nearly running into Alice bringing their food. Sam flipped open his wallet and threw a few dollars onto the table before hopping up to follow Emily.

"What's going on?" Alice called after him, but Sam rushed on and out the door after Emily, who marched down the block and toward her apartment building. He couldn't let her get too far. Knowing her so long had at least given him a good insight into her temper and how to best diffuse it, if he could at all. She had so much passion in her for whatever she set out to achieve. He admired it, but it worked against him more times than he liked.

In a few strides, he caught up and took her arm. "Listen, I'm sorry, Emily. Let's go back and have dinner."

"I'm not hungry any more. Nothing you say can convince me to return to the diner to have dinner with a stubborn fool like yourself. I'm going home."

This time Sam controlled his comments about a pot calling the kettle black. "At least let me drive you."

She wiggled away from his grasp. "No, thank you."

"Emily, I can't let you walk home by yourself after dark," he protested. Why did she have to insist that she do everything her way? What kind of woman would have time to keep house after working a job all day? He'd never heard anything so nonsensical. She'd work herself to the bone. Why, it took three women at home to keep up with everything—of course, a lot of that had to do with the farm, but there was housework aplenty too.

"You may follow me if it would make you feel better, but I will not allow you to walk me home." She increased her pace, her back straight, ignoring him with a slight lift to her chin. Sam settled into walking beside her the few blocks to her apartment. There'd be no discussing levelheaded things with her tonight. It was too bad. That chicken fried steak he'd left behind at the diner looked awfully good. And by the time he got back from walking Emily home, it would have gone cold.

He ought to get used to it. If he planned on marrying a girl intent on keeping her *career*, it wouldn't be the last time he had to eat a cold dinner.

⹀ CHAPTER EIGHT ⹀

"It looks so marvelous." Josette clapped her hands and admired the way Andrew's mother's long, shining cherrywood table looked in their living room, surrounded by the beautiful chairs that matched the set. How had Katherine kept it in such good condition after raising so many children who had eaten there, after all the food from the farm that had been chopped there, after all the cans of food that had cooled there?

"Perhaps after tonight I'll buy you a new table," he proposed.

Josette clutched the lace tablecloth to her chest with one hand and ran her fingers over the smooth, waxed wood. "It wouldn't be able to tell the stories this one can. It was so kind of your mother to loan it to us for the night. Can you imagine all of us trying to cram around that table in the kitchen?" Josette laughed and unfurled the tablecloth, waving it high into the air before letting it settle on the table.

"She was happy to—so long as Sam and I promised to bring it back in the condition we took it from the kitchen. She rode in the truck down here just to supervise." Andrew chuckled.

"I don't blame her." Josette straightened the tablecloth and then turned to the kitchen for the plates. "Won't you help me? Our guests should be here soon."

Andrew grinned at the excited energy in Josette's stride as he followed. He'd encouraged her to host this dinner party, and the distraction from the feud with Susie had done his wife immense good. Josette had always enjoyed social occasions and had gathered up their friends in London for formal dinners she seemed to conjure out of nowhere. Josette Beauchamp could make a four-course meal out of a little ham or bacon, a scant amount of cheese or butter, some crackers, or anything else that might have been rationed.

He took the plates and forks she stacked in his arms as he scanned the kitchen and took a deep breath of the inviting aroma of her cooking. Tonight she'd had much more to work with, thanks to a bountiful harvest and his sisters bringing several cows, pigs, and chickens successfully through the war. He didn't doubt this dinner party would be as successful as those in London had been. Sam and Emily had agreed to come, along with a couple Emily knew, and Vera had suggested her friend Eleanor and her husband, Alvin.

Allies, he thought to himself and bit back a bitter laugh to himself. He laid out the plates, lining them up with each chair. They worked alongside each other to finish setting the table, Josette ferrying items back and forth and issuing instructions. He met her in the kitchen, setting out the hors d'oeuvres on a tray as tires crunched on the gravel road in front of their house.

He took her in his arms. "Everything looks wonderful. Reminds me of our old parties in London, back when I had to kiss you good night at the door." He reached to cup her cheek in his hand and gazed at her. The feeling that he could never gaze at her enough overwhelmed him. He'd wanted to marry her after knowing her for only a few weeks, though he hadn't expressed it until later. In those days, the uncertainty of what would happen during the war—even in the relative safety of their desk jobs at the OSS office in London—made his hopes for their future dreamlike.

He closed the distance between their lips, kissing her softly, careful not to mess her hair as he slid his hand to the nape of her neck, drawing her closer and closer but not close enough. She melted into him and he used his other hand to press against her back.

A hard rap on the door brought their kiss to a close, and Andrew grinned at the rosy flush to Josette's cheeks and the excited shine in her blue eyes. "Would you like to get that, Mrs. Larson, or should I?"

She leaned toward him and kissed his cheek, and the feathery-soft brush of her lips and cheeks against his face had him wishing they could postpone the party a few moments longer. "That's my favorite term of endearment you have for me. Mrs. Larson," she whispered.

"That's because you don't appreciate my French accent."

With a laugh, she backed away to pick up the tray of appetizers. "Won't you get it while I bring these in?"

"Anything you wish, *Madame* Larson." He made sure to butcher his French as he hurried to the door, and her laugh rang behind him. He opened the door to reveal Alvin and Eleanor Pendley, greeting Alvin with a handshake and giving Eleanor an affectionate hug. She'd been Vera's friend for ages.

"Oh, dear!" Eleanor reached up and took Andrew's cheeks in her hands before letting him go. "You've gotten so tall and grown-up. I feel so old when I think of how Vera and I used to babysit you when you could barely walk." She smiled widely at Josette as she joined them with the tray. "You probably don't remember me from the reception."

"Eleanor, right?" Josette asked, holding out the tray to them.

"Yes—oh . . ." Eleanor drew in a breath at the sight of the tray. Andrew had been impressed as well. And they should be. Josette had been cooking for days. "These look marvelous. What is it?"

"These are Provençal vegetable tarts—" Andrew said.

"Oh, stop, Andrew," Josette cried. "He speaks quite passable French, but this evening he's teasing me." She handed him the tray and gestured to the hors d'oeuvres that resembled small biscuits. "These are cheese *gougères* and these last are *tartes flambées*."

"Oh, I do much prefer your accent to Andrew's," Eleanor said, picking up one of the *tartes flambées*, made with bacon and onions and the lightest, fluffiest pastry Andrew had ever tasted. "You make it all sound so high-class."

They laughed over Eleanor's awe as Josette ushered them farther into the room to have a seat on the couch, which had been pushed up against the wall. Andrew set the tray on the end table just in time for the doorbell to ring and for the remainder of their guests to arrive. Sam introduced Paul and Melody, friends who had driven from the next town over to spend the evening.

"Tell me all about France," Melody said when she settled on a seat of the couch, her husband, Paul, perching on the arm. "Isn't it so romantic to have grown up there?"

The sunshine in Josette's beaming expression filled Andrew's chest. "I hardly grew up there at all," she protested. "My father was an English diplomat, and we spent time all over the world before he and my mother died."

"How exciting," Melody replied the same time Eleanor let loose another gasp of awe. "But Sam did tell us that you lived in France during the war."

"Yes," Josette said. "Being my father's daughter gave me connections, and I went back at the request of the SOE."

"Jo's being modest," Andrew said. "She knows several languages and, thanks to her mother, had many connections in France, especially government ones, that we were very interested in having. And when that got too dangerous, she came and trained others. She was marvelous at it. A natural."

"How dull cleaning house and cooking dinner must seem now." Eleanor took another cheese *gougères*.

"Heavens no," Josette protested. "I much prefer this life to whatever excitement I had in France and England."

Melody and Paul both reached for the hors d'oeuvres tray once more. "You're an excellent cook, so it's no wonder you don't mind being a wife. I can't do a thing with all the vegetables Paul brings home from his father's farm. I think we have stew three times a week!"

"I'd be happy to have you over to talk about some ideas." Josette leaned forward from her seat in the chair.

With every moment the conversation went on, Andrew's worries over how Josette would fare in Bellemont lessened. Here were two women more than willing to befriend his wife. Perhaps Josette was right that the trouble with Susie would blow over. If the women in Bellemont took time to get to know Josette, they couldn't help but like her. She had a genuineness that drew people to her.

Andrew's job at OSS had been dull and uninteresting, in his opinion, but every day Josette had asked in earnest about it—begging him for details of things he found mundane and making it seem like vital work. He'd striven to work harder and do his best at it after only a week or so in her company, thanks to the importance she'd seen in him.

Andrew counted the evening a success from that moment right on through dinner. They all exclaimed over Josette's cooking, but that wasn't what brought contentment to Andrew. Everyone blossomed and lit up in Josette's company, even Josette herself. She was again the girl who delighted in impromptu dinners at her tiny flat, plates on their knees as they sat on the rickety wooden chairs and the floor. The food and accommodations had never been the important things.

He followed her into the kitchen after dinner to help her serve the dessert. She'd made a strawberry pie Susie would have screamed in jealousy over had she seen it. Josette had arranged the halved strawberries—that she'd cut into small hearts—into an intricate spiral pattern and edged it in whipped cream using some cake-decorating tools she'd borrowed from his mother. Andrew had licked some whipped cream from the bowl earlier that day and was hard-pressed to remember Susie's being half as good.

"It's going well, don't you think?" Josette asked, bouncing on her black heels as she came forward and took his hands eagerly in hers.

"Of course. I didn't doubt it would." He used her grip to pull her closer and kiss her. How could he help himself with those pretty, bright-red lips curved up into an excited grin?

"Now look, you've got lipstick all over you." Josette giggled as she reached into his slacks pocket and took his handkerchief out for him, wiping away the traces of her makeup. "It's just like in London, isn't it?" She spun away from him, opening the refrigerator to retrieve her pie. It didn't surprise him that her thoughts on the evening ran along the same line as his. He'd really fallen for Josette during some of those dinners, watching her take care of everyone there, sneaking some of her rations to men that would be dropping into France soon or women whose boyfriends had been injured or worse, always knowing who needed to be lifted.

"Even better," he said, picking up the small plates they'd borrowed from his mother. He leaned in to kiss her cheek. "Tonight I don't have to say goodbye."

She beamed and pushed open the door to the living room, walking through and displaying her pie. Andrew followed, enjoying the *oohs* and *aahs* as the guests caught sight of Josette's artful pie.

Yes, he'd call this night a success in more ways than one.

= ★ =

Josette parked the Larson's Chevy sedan down the road from the Brandenburgs' two-story home, the four columns holding up the front porch, intimidating her. It had an air of possessiveness, like some of the luxurious homes she'd visited in London. The Brandenburgs' home had the reputation of being the grandest building in Bellemont, and it lived up to that claim.

But the Brandenburgs were not the lords of the manor here in Wyoming. Andrew and various other members of his family had threatened for days to give Susie the talking-to she deserved. Sam even mentioned something about taking a switch to her backside. Their loyalty warmed her heart, especially since they'd taken to her so quickly and welcomed her as one of their own, though they hadn't known her a month ago. But if anyone was going to give Susie a talking-to about her behavior, Josette would. She loved Andrew and his willingness to dive headlong into this silly battle. As endearing as it was, it would only serve to push Susie further.

Josette opened the heavy car door, checked her face in the rearview mirror one more time, and got out. She gathered up all her courage as she hurried forward and rang the bell the moment she stepped up to the lovely door, its dark wood and golden door handle polished so they glinted and gleamed in the sunlight. As she waited, she held on to the excitement from her dinner party. Her guests had enjoyed themselves and she'd had a marvelous time. She let her success and happiness buoy her up for the confrontation ahead.

A middle-aged woman in a housekeeper's uniform answered the door. Her eyebrows shot up in surprise. "Yes?" She didn't tag on a name to her greeting, but by her cautious expression, Josette figured the woman must know who she was.

"I'm here to see Miss Brandenburg, please."

The woman opened the door wider, then led Josette through the classically designed entryway with its marbled linoleum with darker inlayed patterns and into a small sitting room near the door. "Wait here, please. Who shall I say is calling?"

"Josette Larson," Josette said and then perched on the edge of a Queen Anne chair, upholstered in a pale-green, flowery print. Had she stepped back into the Victorian era somehow when she entered the Brandenburg home?

The housekeeper nodded and hurried away. Not much later, Susie appeared, an expression of curiosity on her face when she paused in the doorway. She covered it with cool superiority. Josette shot out of the chair, eager to stand on equal footing and not be looked down on.

"Mrs. Larson. What a surprise." Susie didn't move to sit. Perhaps that had been Josette's first mistake when the women had visited her—allowing them to sit and feel welcome.

"I'm sure it is a surprise," Josette began. "I've come because we've had poor first impressions of each other, and I'm hoping we can start over and set things right." If Josette was prepared to forget all that had passed between them so far, maybe Susie could too. After all, Susie had far less to forgive, didn't she?

Susie's eyes widened, and she drew her pretty little mouth down in a small *O* before saying, "I don't know what you're talking about, Mrs. Larson."

Josette clenched her small purse in her hands instead of lunging forward and tightening them around Susie's neck. "Perhaps you didn't realize," Josette began in an even tone, "that your comments about France on your last visit were rather offensive to me." Not to mention her constant snubbing and encouraging others to do so as well.

Susie tensed, but that was the most reaction she showed to Josette's words. "I'm sure you must have misunderstood me."

"Perhaps," Josette ground out. Sam might be onto something with that switch idea. "It must have been a misunderstanding, then, when you and your friends passed over my quiche at the picnic."

If anything, Susie played more innocent than before. "I'm sorry, Mrs. Larson, but I do not particularly like quiche. I can't say why the others chose not to eat it. Perhaps they had heard it wasn't very good."

A good many members of the Larson family had declared it delicious, but Josette was well aware of their bias and that Susie would feel no more guilt than she had for her prejudicial remarks about France.

"That may be true," Josette finally said. She moved out of the sitting room and past Susie back toward the door. "I suppose since everything has been cleared up, I ought to go. Good afternoon."

"It must be in your nature, then," Susie said in a sweet voice as Josette put her hand on the doorknob.

Josette paused and turned halfway, wondering why she bothered to ask, "What must be?"

"Running away." Susie smiled in a satisfied way. "And leaving someone else to come and fight the battle for you."

Josette narrowed her eyes. "You know very little about war, Miss Brandenburg. Much less than I do, which you would do well to remember." She flung open the door and strode out without bothering to close it behind her.

If Josette let Andrew have his way—and right now the anger searing inside of her tempted her to do just that—having someone else take up this fight might be exactly what Susie got. And her and Andrew's reunion wouldn't go off like anything Susie expected.

= ★ =

Andrew perused the letter again, sighing to himself as he sank down into the comfortable, worn chair. Something felt off as he ran his fingers absently over the arms. He scrutinized it and realized Josette had recovered it. He hopped up to study it closer. Well, she had done a fine job of it too. She had spent a good deal of time making this house their home, taking things his mother had found in the attic and making everything wonderful and homey. What would she think of the contents of the letter when he told her about it?

The door flew open, shuddering the small house as Josette marched in. "Jo?" he asked, seeing her tear-stained face. He forgot about the letter, letting it fall into the chair as he turned to face his wife.

She flung herself into his arms. "That . . . girl. That silly . . . silly . . . girl." Her words shuddered with her hiccupping breath.

Andrew tightened his grip, his thoughts returning to the letter. Perhaps, after all, Josette would welcome it. "What has Susie done now?" he asked. He'd hoped their successful evening party had been a sign of more welcome for his wife here in Bellemont, but he'd forgotten that Melody and Paul, the only guests that weren't close to the Larsons in some way, lived five miles away, outside of a neighboring farming community and for the most part out from under the Brandenburgs' grasp. So of course they would treat Josette without the narrowmindedness those in Bellemont did at the Brandenburgs' example.

Josette didn't answer for several minutes as she leaned against him and wept into his shoulder. Finally, she drew herself up and wiped her eyes. "I went over there to see if we could start over and maybe end all this. She acted as though she couldn't possibly have done anything to offend me at all and that I was in the wrong for taking it that way. And then she finished off the visit by saying it must be in my nature to run away and allow others to fight my battles for me." Andrew bristled, and he let go of Josette to walk to the door. This was the final straw. But Josette grabbed his arm and shook her head at him. She took a deep, trembling breath.

"At first I wanted you to go and settle this however you had to, but I've had time during the drive to think it over. I didn't tell you to make you mad, dear. I told you to get it off my chest. She is set on acting this way no matter what we do, and if you march down there, it will only make things worse."

"I see you're suggesting we be the ones to keep the peace," he growled.

She managed to laugh at him through what remained of her tears. "I won't lie, Andrew. It would satisfy me very much to hear you tell her how awful she's behaving—but only for a few minutes. When it's all said and done, I'd rather people didn't think I stooped to her level."

He brushed his thumb over her cheek, catching a stray tear there, and she leaned her head into his hand. What kind of strength did she believe he had? He couldn't stand here and watch Josette cry over Susie's nastiness and not do anything about it. "Then how about we get out of town?" he asked.

"Oh, are you on that again?" Josette said. "You know how important it is for you to stay and help with the farm."

"Sam can hire someone else, Jo, and I think he'd rather we left so he could have the house." Andrew leaned over to pick up the letter. "The truth is, *mon amour*, that Harry Davis has written me and offered me a job in London."

She blinked at him. "Harry Davis?"

"A fellow I worked with from SOE. He's taken over his father's shoe business. They have a few factories in England and Europe, and he says he could use someone to read all the reports and glean the important stuff out for him—like the old days." He winked at Josette and they both laughed.

"You might find reading reports on shoemaking quite boring compared to all the excitement of the intelligence reports at OSS," Josette teased. If anything, Andrew was grateful the letter had taken her mind off Susie's thoughtless words.

"My darling, those intelligence reports were often more boring than anything else."

"You're just trying to be modest."

"There's no point in you thinking I'm anything important now, Jo. You're already married to me. My so-called glamorous life as a spy is exposed." The way Josette's smile crept wider little by little might have Andrew joking like this all day with her. He couldn't stand to see her heart broken. And he didn't care a wink about the farm if taking her to London and getting her away from Bellemont would keep her happy. "Well, how about it?" he asked.

Josette reached for the letter, skimming over it. "It's not a decision we ought to make in a day, and especially not in the heat of another argument with Susie. We might like living in London again, but you missed your family so much when we were there before, and you could hardly wait to be discharged. And your letters from Washington were full of how excited you were to bring me home to Bellemont and the farm."

"Maybe I was just being a romantic. I can't have you unhappy."

She kissed his nose and then folded up the letter. "We'll think about it. And now I must get dinner ready."

He wrapped her in his arms one more time anyway, kissing her soundly before he let her go to the kitchen, her cheeks pink. He settled back in the chair again, listening to Josette work in the kitchen as he mulled over going back to England. Thanks to the OSS's work with SOE, they both had plenty of friends there, and eventually they'd feel just at home there as in Bellemont.

But would he miss the farm the way he had during the war? Very little brought him more joy than to stand at the top of a field, gazing over flourishing beet plants or stalks of corn and being filled with satisfaction knowing he'd had a hand in planting it. He'd miss the accomplishment that came with his work on the farm, the connection he had to the land here. But he would walk away from it all if Josette wanted him to. He loved her too much to confine her to a life of contention and competition with Susie and her chums. He stood and walked to the small bookcase in the corner of the room by the door, tucking the letter into one of the books there. Josette was right that they ought to think on it much more and not make a rash decision, but Andrew wanted that opportunity ready should they choose it.

= CHAPTER NINE =

DOMINICK STUDIED THE NEWSPAPERS AND magazines in the rack next to the checkout at Bellemont General Store. The title, "Former French Resistance Member Gives Exclusive Interview of Harrowing Life During the War" jumped off the page of one of the newspapers. He reached for it and fingered the front page. If he opened the magazine and read the article, how many names would he recognize? How many of them would be people he would never get to see come home? He put it back in the rack and stepped up to the checkout counter.

"Hello there, Dominick." Mr. Curtis, the owner of the store, greeted him and took his basket of items. "You already read that article?" he asked, nodding toward the newspaper.

"No," Dominick said. "But I figure I already know enough about that kind of thing."

When Mr. Curtis's demeanor brightened with interest, Dominick knew he'd said the wrong thing. At least if he wanted to hurry through the grocery store line without giving away his secrets.

"Oh, do you?" Mr. Curtis said, pausing as he rang up the purchases. "Those resistance folks are brave men and women. Some say they turned the tide of the war over there."

Dominick nodded, wishing Mr. Curtis would hurry up. "I'll have to agree with that," he said. As he surveyed the small store, wishing for anything to distract him, he caught sight of Vera Trumbell in the nearby dry goods aisle, staring at a canister of oatmeal. It gave him an idea. He could at least use his mysterious war past to help with the Larson-Brandenburg mess.

"Too many people involved to all make that article," Dominick continued. "Like Josette Larson, for instance. One of those same heroes—right here in town." He cleared his throat, already embarrassed. He sounded too forward.

Hopefully Mrs. Trumbell couldn't hear him making a fool of himself—but he shouldn't care about that.

Mr. Curtis lost his interest. "Ahh, yes. I heard something about that." He moved along with ringing up Dominick's groceries.

"Then you already know about the work she did helping downed pilots get out of France? I heard she hid two in her basement once with two SS officers billeted next door." He nodded solemnly at Mr. Curtis.

"Good of her, I suppose," Mr. Curtis said, but Dominick couldn't tell if his interest had been piqued again or not. "One never knows how to feel about letting women in on work like that. Next they'll want to fight alongside the men."

"I worked with too many brave women to agree, Mr. Curtis, and know of too many women—even right here in Bellemont—who stepped up for their county. Like how the Larson women kept their farm going without Mr. Larson and his boys. And how Mrs. Curtis ran the store for you while you were gone." Dominick unloaded a few more groceries for Mr. Curtis to ring up.

"Now that's different." Mr. Curtis didn't look at Dominick. "Some things like that had to be done. Wasn't any way around it, with most of the men gone."

Dominick chuckled. "Well, that's true enough I suppose. Hard for us to judge with no Nazis here banging on our door and taking away our neighbors." He let that sink in for a moment. "But I can't argue with your opinion. It's that opinion that made having women around a good idea—Nazis never suspected a woman might hide weapons for the Maquis in a baby carriage. Too soft for things like that, eh?" He gave Mr. Curtis a pointed look. It surprised him to hear the words coming out of his mouth. He, of all people, knew what had happened to women who risked their lives to help the Resistance, and soldiers, and the OSS. But for the first time in a while, a sense of accomplishment trickled through him—for standing up for his beliefs again, even in such a small way.

Mr. Curtis turned red. "Are you calling me a Nazi, Dominick?" he blustered.

"No, sir," Dominick said, hoping his amusement didn't show in his face. Mr. Curtis finished the transaction in brooding silence, mumbling his obligatory, "Have a nice day," as Dominick left with his groceries. Dominick kept the smile of success off his face until he got onto the sidewalk and turned in the direction of his house.

"Mr. Whitaker! Mr. Whitaker!" Mrs. Trumbell hurried out the door after him, her daughter bouncing on her hip and no oatmeal in her hands. "Wait, Mr. Whitaker!" She waved. She stopped next to him, breathing a bit hard. Some hair had worked its way free of her rolled hairstyle, falling over her eyes. She tucked it behind an ear, took another breath, and then laughed. "I must look like a madwoman, all out of breath and running after you."

Not at all, with her cheeks rosy and stray hairs still swaying in front of her face in the light breeze. No, madwoman wasn't the term he'd use.

"No," he said. "You don't."

The color in her cheeks deepened as she met his gaze. Not for the first time around Mrs. Trumbell, Dominick felt like he laid all his thoughts bare in a simple sentence. Three words, to be exact.

Her next words tumbled out as she attempted to cover the embarrassing silence. "I heard what you told Mr. Curtis about Josette. That was so kind of you."

"I was only telling the truth."

Mrs. Trumbell stared at the ground, and the stray lock fell forward again. Without looking at him she swept her hand back and shoved it into a pin. Dominick smiled at the way a whole section had now loosened.

"I didn't know you knew Josette before," she said, finally meeting his gaze again. Her hair had now sagged all on one side, threatening to come loose. The idea of her dark hair falling over her shoulder struck him like a bullet, and his breath caught in his throat. He swallowed hard against the desire to pull all the pins out for her and let it tumble over his fingers.

He drew in a deep breath to keep his voice even when he spoke. "I didn't. I knew people who did, who told me about some of the things she did."

Mrs. Trumbell set her little girl down, holding her hand as she walked around and around her mother's feet. "Well, we're all happy to hear at least one person in town speak well of her. Andrew wanted her to like Bellemont so much—and she's trying to fall in love with it, for his sake. It's so hard for her, though, when everyone seems set against her."

He noticed that her expression had lost some of that *c'est la vie* quality he always liked about it. Worry clouded her eyes—for her sister-in-law? Though he'd stumbled through his defense to Mr. Curtis, Dominick was glad he'd done it if it would make Mrs. Trumbell worry less.

He didn't know what to say except for crazy things like, "I'll make sure to tell everyone I see," or inviting her to dinner some time. "You forgot your oatmeal," came out instead, his voice sounding husky with what he kept back.

Mrs. Trumbell's eyebrows furrowed. "Oatmeal?"

He cleared his throat. "You were looking at oatmeal earlier."

"Oh." She smiled at him. "Well, thank you again, Mr. Whitaker."

"Dominick. You should call me Dominick." And why should she do that? So that taking the mother of one of his students to a movie sometime wouldn't be awkward? "It makes me feel old when you call me that, and I'm trying not to feel so old these days." He meant to make a joke, but he'd let out more than he wanted to of himself. The sympathy that passed through her expression before she smiled back said so.

"If you get to be young Dominick, then I absolutely must be young Vera."

Dominick had never enjoyed such an uncomfortable conversation in his life. The desire to get away from her was as intense as the desire to draw her closer. Perhaps he was the mad one. "I suppose so," he said.

Vera's daughter pulled on her mother's hand from one side, and before Vera could switch hands, the little girl's momentum jerked Vera toward Dominick. She reached up to catch herself against him, her hand landing on his chest. And his first instinct was to keep her upright, so his hand caught her waist. For several seconds they stood like that, staring at each other and forgetting that anyone walking down Main Street might see them, looking like they were embracing.

"Are you okay?" Dominick asked, but he didn't let go. He wouldn't have an excuse to stand so close to her again, unless he did it on purpose. He couldn't do it on purpose. She hesitated, and for a moment Dominick wondered how she might have been hurt. He scanned what he could of her, not noting any turned ankles that he could see.

She pushed herself away and said breathlessly, "Yes. Of course. Thank you." She reached down to pick up the little girl and hold her against her hip tightly. "Mr.—Dominick, that's a pitiful supply of food you have there," she said in a rush. "You had better come over for dinner tonight." She nodded decisively at him.

And he almost accepted, but her thoughtful manner reminded him of something else. He couldn't insert himself into her life when she needed far more than him.

"I can't. Sorry." He twisted his lips into a rueful smile before he hurried down the street again, his chest still warm from where Vera had rested her hand against him. No, he'd best not find excuses to pursue a relationship with her, much as it enticed him. But it wouldn't do him any harm to spend his walk back to his house thinking about how comfortable and almost . . . relieved it had made him to hold her. For a few moments, her touch could banish everything troubling from his past, and he could nearly remember the carefree life he'd left in California when he'd gone off to Europe to war. Vera was the best medicine he'd found so far. Too bad he had to limit his dosage so strictly.

☰ ★ ☰

"Vee? What are you doing? We need to leave." Fay stood in the doorway of their room, far more put together than Vera was. She wore flawless victory rolls in her pinned-up, dark-blonde hair and a full, dark-blue dress. Fay's tiny waist, shown off to a tee in the dress, taunted Vera. After four children, she would never command those kind of curves again. Her figure, though still good, could be better described as bumpy. She huffed out an irritated sigh.

"Well, you don't have four children to get bathed and combed and dressed." She ran a hand over the loose curls she'd already taken out of her curlers and hoped they hadn't fallen too much since she'd had to go and break up a fight between Jack Junior and Peter and focus them on getting dressed. At least she had her makeup done. And her long hair drew attention to her neck, still very fine and untouched by the bearing of several children.

"Well, I'll take care of the kids," Fay said. "You finish getting ready." She shoved Vera back toward the bathroom.

"Thank you, Fay." Vera shut the bathroom door behind her and leaned against it. She hadn't been so intent on looking her best for a Fall Festival for many years—back when she was first trying to get Jack's attention. She thought about how after her encounter with Dominick outside Mr. Curtis's the week before, she'd had to hold Audrey against her to hide how her hands shook.

Snapping herself out of her silly daydreams, she unrolled the rest of her curls, but the mindless task didn't take her mind off Dominick. Everywhere she went, people had talked about how Josette was as much a hero as many of the boys coming home. How brave she'd been to stand up to the Germans. From the way Mr. Curtis reacted to Dominick's story, it was unlikely he had spread it. She supposed someone else might have heard what Dominick said to him, but she didn't think so. She suspected it had been Dominick himself. He had stepped out of his carefully constructed shell; he had let out one of his secrets from his past—his involvement with the OSS. She blew out a shaky breath, thinking about why he might have done that.

She parted her curls to the side and ran a brush over them then took a step back from the mirror and tried to see a full-length image of herself. Did she look like the young Vera in her green-striped dress with its full skirt and fitted waist?

"Vee, come *on*," Fay's voice interrupted before she could answer that.

= CHAPTER TEN =

Josette had never seen so many pumpkin pies all in one place. They filled the table before them, and only twenty minutes into Bellemont's Fall Festival, they'd already sold well over a dozen. Everyone stopped by the table to comment on how they had to go home with one of Kathryn Larson's famous pumpkin pies. And to Josette's surprise, they all smiled at her and told her what a pleasure it was to see her and how they hoped to get to know her better now that she lived in Bellemont.

"What is going on?" she asked Vera in a low voice as Kathryn handed over pies to a couple. The woman had just finished telling Josette how lovely her dress was.

"I think Dominick . . . Whitaker may have said a few things about you to some people," Vera said. She took a quarter from a boy a little older than Jack Junior and passed him a pie. She turned to pick up a few more pies from the box behind them to fill the empty spaces on the table.

Josette took note of how Vera had called him by his first name instead of Mr. Whitaker, as she'd referred to him before. She refrained from asking. Teasing about Vera's romantic interest in Mr. Whitaker was Fay's sisterly duty. "What could Mr. Whitaker know about me?" she asked instead.

"He told me he'd heard about you from others. In the OSS," she added in a hushed voice. "It seems he's made you a town hero. As good as any of the boys coming home."

"I'm not . . . it's not like I—"

Vera put a hand on her shoulder and shook her head. "But you did. We all did brave things, even here at home. It was just easier for you to get killed for the brave things you did."

Josette couldn't argue with any of that. She didn't have time to anyway.

"My mother sent me over for two of your wonderful pies, Mrs. Larson," a young lady with honey-colored hair said as she bounced up to the table.

Josette recognized her as one of Susie's closest friends, so she braced herself for the bubbliness to drop away when she caught sight of Josette. Instead, the girl turned right to her. "Oh, Josette—is that all right if I call you that? We've all known Andrew so long, but—" She cut herself off and looked embarrassed. "Well, anyway, let's get sodas sometime. I'm dying to hear about France and how you . . . You see, I think we could be good friends, don't you?" She cast Josette a pleading stare, as though if Josette said no, it might crush her.

"Yes, we should." A real smile jumped to Josette's lips. The excitement that bubbled inside her reminded her of the night of their dinner party. She didn't need the acceptance of the people in town to love Bellemont—Andrew was here, and his family loved her. But having friends would help her feel at home.

The other girl who had come with Susie that day, a tall girl with silver-blue eyes and hair so blonde it looked almost white, hurried over to the first girl. "Did you ask her, Evie?" she asked in a hushed voice.

Evie beamed at Josette. "She said yes."

The second girl leaned against Evie in relief. "Wonderful. What a pretty dress, Josette. Did you bring it from France?"

Josette's joyful smile threatened to break her cheeks. The friendship pouring over her from the town felt far better than the judgment and curious looks from before. She didn't know what had broken Susie's hold over the women of the town, but she was glad for it. And despite the cowardly way they'd acted in her home, Josette was ready to give these women a second chance.

"To tell you the truth, I had only one dress left from France, and by the time I got to England, it was so dirty and torn, I had to patch and scrub it. It's hardly fit to wear anywhere." She meant it as a joke, but the girls' mouths opened in awe.

"That sounds so exciting—escaping with only the clothes on your back!" Evie leaned forward, waiting for Josette to continue. Josette shared a look with Vera, who shrugged and went back to doling out pies.

The girl with white-blonde hair, Ruth, shot out a hand to take Josette's. "I hope you can forgive us for the terrible way we acted when we visited you with Susie—and those awful things she said. I hope you know we didn't agree with any of it—"

"And we should have said something," Evie said. "Shows how much braver you are than us. Why, you've faced down the Germans, and we couldn't even stand up to Susie Brandenburg."

"Oh, now . . ." Josette's face burned from the compliments, and her heart warmed at the friendship they were daring to show her now. It didn't matter now how late it had come. "Sometimes facing down a friend can be harder than dealing with an enemy. We're all brave in our own ways," she said, borrowing Vera's sentiment. Her sister-in-law cast her a quick smile over her shoulder.

"Well, we've sure shown that we Americans aren't as high and mighty as we think we are." Ruth nodded determinedly, as though she believed she deserved her self-depreciation. "Bellemont has certainly proved the last few weeks that we might have sided with the Germans if they'd come marching through here."

"Thank heavens none of you will have to face that possibility." Josette squeezed the hand Ruth still held.

"In any case, will you forgive us?" Evie asked.

"Of course," Josette answered without hesitation.

"What are you doing, Evie and Ruth?" a sickly sweet voice said, and Josette and the other two girls turned to see Susie striding up to the table. Though Susie had plastered a composed smile on her face, Josette drew back at the anger alight in her expression.

Ruth put a hand on her hip and shook her head at Susie. "Buying pies from the Larsons."

"What did I tell you about that this year?" Susie demanded in a strained whisper.

Evie rolled her eyes. "You are being such a child, Susie. My mother specifically asked me to buy these pies."

"Not. This. Year." Susie pressed her lips together and gave Evie a meaningful look.

"No, Susie. Everyone buys pies from the Larsons, and you're the only one who won't this year. Haven't you seen the booth? Busy as ever. Maybe even busier." Ruth threw her arm out to gesture to the steady stream of people buying pies despite Susie's supposed edict. "Josette is a nice girl, and I want to be her friend." Ruth took a firm stance in front of the table, challenging Susie to contradict her.

Susie threw her arms to her side and clenched her fists. "That dirty French girl stole Andrew from me!" Susie cried.

Josette's jaw dropped and the anger that had swelled the day she tried to set things right with Susie rose so that it rang in her ears. She stepped forward to give Susie a proper put-down, but before she could open her mouth, Kathryn turned away from the customer that had plopped a handful of quarters onto the table.

"Susie Brandenburg!" She gasped.

"Oh, Susie!" Evie cried. "Stop it. You Dear John'd Andrew for Jimmy Bidwell ages ago. Everybody knows that."

Susie screamed in frustration, attracting attention from all the surrounding booths. "Shut up, Evelyn!" She grabbed up a pie from the table and shoved it, cream topping and all, right into Evie's face. The action shocked everyone, perhaps Susie herself considering the way her hand flew to her mouth.

"Now, girls—" Kathryn tried again. Vera and Josette scrambled around the table, both ready to separate Evie and Susie, but they moved too late.

"How dare you!" Evie screeched and flung a pie at Susie, who ducked in time for the pie to tumble over her shoulder and splatter on the front of Vera's dress as she moved to grab Susie.

"Oh!" she cried in surprise, and her momentary lapse gave Susie the opening to grab another pie.

"Stop it! Oh, stop it, we spent hours on—" Josette begged, but Susie let fly her second pie and it landed on top of Josette's head, whipped cream and pumpkin draining down through her hair and dropping onto her shoulders. She swallowed a giggle as she wiped the pie from her cheeks. Evie had come to her defense! An all-out fight broke out between the girls as Ruth, Susie, and Evie grabbed pie after pie to throw at each other and the Larson women tried to stop it.

"What's going on over here?" a male voice shouted over the din, one Josette recognized as Sam's.

"Oh, stop that girl," Emily said, pointing at Susie and rushing into the fray. "All the pies!" For her effort, she received a stray pie to the face. Josette felt helpless and slipped over the pumpkin-splattered ground to get to Susie, watching as pies disappeared from the table and ended up on the ground around them.

"Susan Brandenburg, what in heaven's name have you done?"

This time all action froze. Susie, with pumpkin and whipped cream dripping from her hair and smeared on her clothes, stopped in the act of lifting another pie from the table. She slowly turned to face the foreboding figure of her mother.

"What happened?" Andrew whispered, coming up behind Josette.

But Josette's laughter bubbled up and it nearly choked her trying to keep it down. The scene was so ridiculous, whipped cream and pumpkin splattered all over her, Vera, Susie, Evie, and the ground around them.

She could only get out, "Well . . . pie."

≡ ★ ≡

Some pies had survived the battle. Only a dozen or so of the dozens they'd made had been casualties. Laughter still threatened to overtake Josette every time she thought of the way Susie's eyes had widened and her mouth dropped in horror when she'd heard her mother's voice. Josette and Vera had found some extra rags amidst the supplies Kathryn had brought and wiped themselves up enough to finish selling the remaining pies. After all the commotion, they sold out in the next hour, which Kathryn said, in awe, had never happened before.

"Usually we bring home at least half a dozen," she'd said while shaking her head.

That evening, after Josette had enjoyed cider, dancing, and carnival games with Andrew, they came home and fell onto the couch for Josette to explain in detail what had happened at the pie booth. She snuggled up next to him. Away from the scene itself, she found it sillier than it had been in the first place. She spent half the story laughing at one thing or another—how Vera had tried to grab at Susie once, only to have her hands slide from Susie's arms because of the whipped cream covering them both. How Emily had slipped in a pile of pumpkin and come up with pie filling streaked down her backside.

But her smile widened the most when she thought about Evie and Ruth asking her to go with them for a soda sometime. Something about winning them over filled her with a sense of triumph, though it hadn't been her at all. Her family—yes, she could surely call the Larsons that—had done so much, and even Mr. Whitaker.

Andrew pulled her closer then so that her head rested against his arms, and he gazed right down into her face, stroking her hair that now fell around her shoulders. They giggled together again when he pulled away with a few stray crumbs. She couldn't do much for the mess until she got a proper bath, and right now, next to Andrew, it wasn't that important.

"Mr. Whitaker may have been the one to tell everyone about you, and he may have been the one the town finally listened to, but you're the girl who did all those things, *ma chère*."

"Oh, Andrew," she whispered, reaching up to cup his cheeks in her hands. "That was such pretty French."

"Oh, was it now, *madame*?" He smirked, and then let loose a full oratory in French that nearly had Josette swooning. Perhaps it was because he was her husband, or perhaps it was the fact that she hadn't been in France or heard a proper Frenchman speak for a long time—but it sounded like poetry, the way he made the words dance off his tongue.

"You are a tease, *monsieur*." She pulled his face down to hers, kissing him with enthusiasm. Despite the ridiculousness of the evening, she found the moment as perfect as the early days of their romance had been—even better, for now she had him forever.

As he drew her onto his lap, the story of the pie fiasco forgotten, they were interrupted by a knock at the door. They turned to peer out the window, catching a glimpse of two women standing on their small wooden porch—it was hardly more than two steps and a small space at the top with just room enough for their visitors.

"It's Susie and her mother," Andrew said in a low voice. "Shall we pretend we haven't returned home yet?"

Josette laughed and rested her face against the hollow of his neck. He smelled of his aftershave and cinnamon. "They've probably seen us already. We'd better answer." With reluctance, she swung her legs off Andrew's and stood, waiting as he crossed the room and answered the door.

The second he swung it open, and before he could get a word of greeting out, Mrs. Brandenburg marched in with Susie in her wake. Susie's wet hair had been pulled into a simple ponytail at the nape of her neck, and this time, *her* gaze never strayed from the floor as she entered.

"Good evening, Andrew. Mrs. Larson," Mrs. Brandenburg said.

"Good evening," both Andrew and Josette murmured back, Josette as surprised as any to hear Mrs. Brandenburg address her with so much respect. Andrew returned to stand next to Josette, taking her hand in a supportive way.

Mrs. Brandenburg got right to the point. "It has come to my attention that I was misled as to your character, Mrs. Larson." She cast a look at her daughter. "Which I shamefully used as an excuse to participate in excluding you from the community. I wish you to know, Mrs. Larson, that I will not attempt to justify any of it, and I hope you will accept my apologies for my actions and for those I encouraged to act likewise."

It took Josette several moments to answer. Not out of an inability to forgive, but out of sheer shock at hearing the so-called Queen of Bellemont society apologizing to her—and sounding like she meant it. It was quite one thing to have Susie's two friends offer apologies, but Susie's own mother? It astounded Josette, to say the least.

"Thank you, Mrs. Brandenburg."

"We have already been by the farmhouse and repaid your mother for the pies," the matron went on. "Of course, she'll be turning it over to the Women's Club, as we all do with our proceeds from the Fall Festival, but I felt that we needed to make the gesture."

"Of course," Josette murmured at Mrs. Brandenburg's pretentious statement, and Andrew offered a bewildered, "Thank you."

"Susie, do you have something to say?" Mrs. Brandenburg prodded, her voice losing any warmth it might have held while speaking to Josette and Andrew. The coldness in it made even Josette shiver.

Susie stepped forward, lifting her gaze for the first time. "I'm sorry," she said in a clipped tone, and from the rigid lines in her face, Josette knew she didn't mean a word of it.

Mrs. Brandenburg pressed her lips together and huffed out a frustrated sigh. "In any case, Mrs. Larson, forgive me for my tardiness in saying welcome to Bellemont. Good evening." She marched right back to the door, with Susie in tow, and they left as suddenly as they'd come.

Andrew and Josette stared at each other for several long moments before they both dissolved into laughter. He swept her up into his arms, twirling her around before setting her down and kissing her. She wrapped her arms around his neck, twisting her fingers through his hair.

"Well, Mrs. Larson," he said. "The question remains about that job in London."

Josette smiled adoringly up at him. "Didn't you hear Mrs. Brandenburg?" she asked. "We are welcome in Bellemont."

And thank heaven, because despite Susie Brandenburg's best efforts, it had grown on Josette.

★

PART II
G. I. BRIDE

⚏ CHAPTER ELEVEN ⚏

Bellemont, Wyoming—December 1946

EMILY HOLMAN FLIPPED THROUGH THE soil survey paperwork for the Stengers' farm and smiled to herself. She had helped Mr. Burns do the survey and, though she lacked the college education the Soil Conservation Service asked for in its technicians, Mr. Burns said it wouldn't surprise him to see her out doing surveys on her own one day. What would Sam Larson think of that?

The thought ruined her personal moment of triumph. Sam would think it was silly and not fit for his future wife. Why hadn't all he'd seen during the war broadened his perspective some? His own sister-in-law had done things once considered fit for only soldiers. Not to mention the countless women who served as nurses and ambulance drivers and who knew what else. Emily had read about some women fighting, *fighting*, with local resistance groups. For heaven's sake, it wasn't as though she'd asked to sign up to fight in the army.

She slipped the paperwork into its folder, readying it for Mr. Burns to review. He was quite young—perhaps around Sam's age—to supervise an office, but he ran a tight ship nonetheless, much as she supposed he had while serving as a lieutenant commander in the navy.

She ought to forgive Sam his attitude, she supposed. After all, he hadn't been around Bellemont and witnessed how the war had forced the women in town to step up to keep everything going. His own farm was a case in point. Mrs. Larson and Sam's sisters, Vera and Fay, had kept the place going. Even when Mr. Larson had come home because he lost his arm, he couldn't help much—still couldn't because of his poor health. Life had changed during the war, especially for women, but Sam expected everything to go back to just the way it was before he left.

On the surface, too much at the farm had gone back to Sam's idea of "normal". The women had gladly turned over the farmwork to Sam and his brother Andrew when they'd returned. And oh, poor Russell, God rest his soul. They *would* miss his help. Fay would have to continue working when spring came because they wouldn't have Russell. Darn her, everyone knew she resented every second of it. Emily huffed to herself and opened up another folder with another batch of papers.

"Is something wrong, miss?" an unfamiliar voice asked.

Emily looked up from her desk in the front of the office and met the deep-blue eyes of a handsome man. She checked herself. She was engaged, after all.

"Wrong?" she asked.

He strode toward her desk, stopping right at the front so she had to tilt her head at an uncomfortable angle to meet his gaze. His smile widened with each moment she watched him.

"Your eyebrows are together in an awful mess, and that sigh you just let out sounded displeased," he said.

Emily didn't need another male in Bellemont looking down on her, so she stood up. "Excuse me, sir. May I help you?" The fact that he might need some technical assistance from the SCS was the only thing that kept her tone civil when she considered how forward this stranger had acted.

"You might show me to my office," he said, perching on the edge of her desk so that they stood at eye level now. "I'm John Mason, the new soil conservationist."

"Oh." Emily gripped her hands together. It had slipped her mind completely that the new conservationist would start today. With the farms and ranches in the area getting up and going again now, their work had increased, making it necessary for the Bellemont office to acquire another employee. "It's this way, Mr. Mason. And pleased to meet you, sir." She stepped around the desk to lead him to the vacant room next to Mr. Burns's office. He hadn't come in yet for the day—chances were he'd gone out to the Bidwells' right off to see how the new well was coming along.

"I'd like to say the pleasure is all mine, but you haven't given me your name yet," Mr. Mason said.

Emily hesitated and spun around, only to have him nearly run into her. "Excuse me, Mr. Mason. I'm so sorry." She stepped back. "I'm Emily Holman."

"Good to meet you, Miss Holman." He took off his hat and nodded to her.

"Thank you." Cheeks burning, Emily turned again and marched into the office, determined not to continue her current flustered act. "Here you are," she said.

He walked into the room and set his briefcase onto the empty desk. Emily's heart did a little hop, but only because she had imagined too many times that one day this desk might be hers.

Well, not if Sam had anything to say about it, and that made her heart hop again, this time downward. She *wanted* to marry Sam. She loved him. It may have taken him months to get her to go on a date with him after she first moved to Bellemont with her parents seven years before, and years, really, to convince her to marry him, but along the way she had become quite attached to him. He had shared everything with her in his letters while he was away fighting—his fears and his triumphs. She had done the same. She knew him inside out.

So why didn't he know her as well? And why couldn't he understand what she wanted wasn't that bad?

"Miss Holman?" Mr. Mason snapped his fingers from where he sat behind his desk.

"Oh, I'm so sorry, sir." Without another word, she fled his office, and to her further mortification, she heard him chuckle.

She dropped down onto her chair. Perhaps if she and Sam set a wedding date, maybe nearer than next spring—although the way Mrs. Larson's lilacs bloomed in the spring and the sweet smell they would cast would make a lovely backdrop for a wedding—it would keep her from losing her mind at work over their situation. January? Or February? Perhaps Valentine's Day. She'd talk to Sam about it this evening. She'd promised Mrs. Larson and the girls to go and help make butter.

Butter. She frowned again to herself. One of the many things Sam expected her to do once she was his wife. Why couldn't they buy it from his mother? Or from the Bellemont General Store? Plenty of women bought all their groceries there—and even ready-made food. Why did Sam expect her to be the same excellent housewife, making everything from scratch, that his mother was?

A gust of cold air announced another visitor to the office, this one behind a bunch of daisies.

"Too busy for a quick visit?" Sam asked, presenting the flowers to her.

"Of course not." Emily reached for a vase behind her desk and set the flowers inside. She'd have to get water later. She'd kept the vase handy these last few weeks since Sam had been bringing flowers regularly after their ruined date two months before. "What's the occasion?" she asked.

"Slow day." He shrugged. "How about you?"

"Already?" she asked, squinting at the clock on the wall. Only nine-thirty.

"That's winter on a farm for you. With both me and Andrew working, the to-do list is getting shorter and shorter by the day. If Vera would let me, I'd start doing Jack's and Peter's chores."

Emily lowered her voice and nodded toward the office Mr. Mason had taken over. "The new conservationist got here today."

Sam's eyes brightened, but he didn't broach the topic of her leaving as he had the first time Emily had mentioned a new employee coming to the office. He'd kept his peace remarkably well when she'd told him they had gotten a new conservationist because they needed *more* employees in the local office, not fewer. If only she could count on his silence meaning his acceptance of her desire to continue working after their marriage.

"And how is he settling in?" he asked.

"Quite nicely," Mr. Mason said, stepping out of the office. "Excuse me for eavesdropping." He held out his hand to Sam. "I'm John Mason."

"Sam Larson."

Mr. Mason nodded at him before turning back to Emily. "When I spoke with Oliver yesterday, he mentioned he had some files for me to get started on. Have you got those?"

Sam cast her a rueful smile. "That's my cue, I suppose." He waved to them both and turned to the door, but not before Emily caught the tension in his face. His thoughts seemed to shout at her: another of their moments ruined by her job.

She didn't waste time watching him leave or letting guilt creep inside of her. They'd had plenty of dates ruined by escaped cows or flooding irrigation. But Sam's pigheadedness wouldn't allow her the same courtesy. And it hadn't even been a date. *He'd* dropped in on her during work hours. Good heavens.

She opened the drawer of her desk and pulled out the stack of papers Mr. Burns had asked her to ready for Mr. Mason. "Right here." She handed them over, though she wanted to keep them for herself. She knew as much as Mr. Mason, she bet. At least enough to take over these files.

Mr. Mason perused through them quickly before looking back at her. "Oliver wasn't exaggerating about your efficiency. Thank you." He started back to his office and stopped. "He said you were getting married. I hate to lose someone so efficient so soon after I've arrived."

"Don't worry, sir," Emily said, heat rising in her cheeks again at his praise. "I won't be leaving anytime soon." She wondered if he caught her lack of confirmation about not getting married soon.

He didn't indicate it if he had. He flashed a charming smile. "Good to know you're staying on," he said and disappeared into his office.

Well, at least one man thought so.

⹀ CHAPTER TWELVE ⹀

ELEANOR PENDLEY MOVED THE IRON back and forth in even strokes, listening to her best friend, Vera Trumbell, express her gratitude that harvest season was over and that next spring she wouldn't have to worry a bit about planting.

"And Sam is complaining that he wants to let the boys off the hook so he can milk the cow in the evenings and have something to do." Vera shook her head and laughed. "But I brought my boys to the farm to work."

"I'm sure they wouldn't mind it once in a while," Eleanor said, happy to have Vera for company as they both ironed. Now that Eleanor had quit her job at the bank and taken up her job as housewife full time, she missed the conversation she used to have with all the customers. Though keeping house kept her busy, it was often lonely in her small home. She'd lived with her parents while her husband, Alvin, had been away fighting. It hadn't made sense for her and Alvin to have a home of their own at the time, not when they didn't know when they would live in it together. She'd had her parents' company every evening. She wouldn't trade that company for Alvin being home, but it was an adjustment.

"No, the boys wouldn't mind," Vera agreed, her attention on the clothes she pressed for Eleanor. That was how they planned their visits—Vera would bring her iron over to Eleanor's and they'd chat while completing the chores. Or Eleanor would bring her mending to Vera's and they'd sit and talk while they worked. Eleanor hadn't dreamed that keeping house for more than herself would require so much work, but the laundry alone! And the starching and the ironing on top of it. It took a girl three days—and what would she do when they had little ones?

Eleanor's hand went to her stomach—well, no movement. She had only missed one cycle, and the constant nausea gave it away more than anything. She glanced up at Vera to see if her friend had noticed and then went back to ironing, murmuring, "Mmm," at something Vera had said about, "A day here and there."

"How does Alvin like his job at the sugar beet factory?" Vera asked.

"Oh, he likes it just fine. He always comes home with a big smile and a big appetite." She laughed at the comment, but in truth, she often worried about their budget and the cost of feeding them both on Alvin's salary. "We ought to have a garden next year." The words burst out of her. She knew from watching her mother and the Larsons that growing one's own food was an arduous task, but if it kept her from really pinching pennies, she'd take the extra work.

"Yes, I don't know how we'd feed everyone if we hadn't planted such a large one. Of course, I wasn't saying that all those days I had to put away can after can of beans." Vera let out another laugh.

Feeding everyone. Why, Eleanor hadn't considered how they'd have to add another person to feed into their budget. What would Alvin say about that? He lamented enough as it was about his low wage and what they ought to do. All those nights she'd dreamed of having him home and the comfort of sleeping next to him, of having dinner together every night, of holding his hand while they listened to a radio program together. She hadn't considered it would come with more worries. She'd thought the worrying would end when he came home safe and sound.

Vera's tinkling laughter stopped, and Eleanor peered up to find Vera watching her. "Is everything all right, El? You look upset."

Eleanor would've liked nothing better than to spill her news to Vera and let her friend reassure her. Vera had had four kids—all before Eleanor managed to get one. She'd had her first one young, too, and all the way out in California with nobody to help out. It must have been terrifying. She would reassure Eleanor that everything would work out, and Vera had a way of making Eleanor believe it too. But she shouldn't go spouting off news like that before she'd figured out how to tell her own husband. Besides, she wanted to be certain— absolutely certain— that she was pregnant before she told anyone, including Alvin. Although, it wouldn't hurt to mention her suspicions to him. They ought to share the same things she did with Vera. Well, not the womanly things, the nonsense that a man wouldn't care about, but the things best friends shared with each other. Alvin was her best friend now. It had been hard to imagine that with him away and gone almost right after they'd gotten hitched—

"El?" Vera prodded.

"Oh." Eleanor forced a carefree laugh of her own. "All this laundry! And you've always got three times as much as me, of course. How do you do it all?"

Vera hesitated in answering, studying Eleanor before letting her concern go. "Fay helps me. Quite cheerfully, in fact. Says it's right and proper women's work. Ha!" There was that carefree laugh again. Vera had always been easygoing and cheerful, but Eleanor couldn't remember her laughing this much. Vera hadn't mentioned anything to Eleanor about it, but maybe the gossip about her and Dominick Whitaker had some truth to it. "I wish she'd said that in front of Emily," Vera went on. "Would've been a rousing discussion, and I would have liked to see Sam try and pick sides."

"Is she still working at the conservation office?" A part of Eleanor envied Emily that she was still working. She wouldn't mind leaving chores behind for the office every now and again.

"Much to Sam's chagrin, and still wanting to wait a few more months to get married. Poor fellow. No wonder he's trying to find more things to do."

Eleanor chuckled to herself at the mischievous little smile that snuck back up on Vera's face. She couldn't help broaching the subject. "I heard Mrs. Curtis and Mrs. Hogarth whispering to themselves at the store about when Dominick Whitaker was going to ask you for a date. Have you got an opinion?"

The smile disappeared in a flash, replaced by a deep red hue to Vera's cheeks. "Oh, El." She gasped. Then she laughed. "Of course I do, but I'm not so sure it's proper. He's Jack Junior's teacher after all, and Sam keeps ominously saying how dangerous he is—as if that helps."

They giggled together, and the comfort of their school days warmed Eleanor. She recalled the way Vera had whispered to her about Jack Trumbell.

Vera set down her iron and studied Eleanor seriously. "You know what though, El? I do want to get married again. I miss having someone to listen to me when the boys have gotten rowdy and all they do is pick at each other. Or when Audrey is especially needy and there's someone else to hold her and cuddle her. I mean, sure, I have my family for all that, but it's different. Being on your own. And kissing. It may shock you, El, but I could really go for a thorough kiss." She blushed again, but despite the gravity of her speech, her last statement sent them into another fit of girlish laughter. Oh, Vera must like Mr. Whitaker to be so happy even while just ironing clothes.

"It is awful nice," Eleanor admitted, and then Vera raised her eyebrows, setting Eleanor's cheeks ablaze. "Having someone to talk to, I mean. Having a husband." It was. Sure, sometimes she despaired over picking up after Alvin all the time, doing all the housework, even for just the two of them, and worrying over dinner and their finances. But life without him had been plain lonely.

Eleanor had once known exactly how lonely Vera felt. She made sure Vera was focused on her ironing again and then gave her tummy a quick pat. She was happy to have Alvin back by her side.

"And kiss," Vera insisted with a wave of the iron in Eleanor's direction.

"Oh, Vee." Eleanor ducked her face closer to the shirt she ironed, her face flaming. "Stop it."

Vera sighed, but it held no weight. When Eleanor finally peeked up, Vera still grinned at her. "I suppose twenty-seven is too old to giggle over good-looking men, isn't it?"

"Do you like him?" Eleanor asked. She picked up the shirt and took care in draping it on a hanger and then hanging it on the rack near them.

"I do—too much for my own good. I can't help wanting to take care of him." Vera pressed her lips together, maybe embarrassed by it.

"He does seem like he needs someone to take care of him." Everyone in Bellemont was accustomed to Mr. Whitaker's solemn attitude. "Perhaps that should be you."

Vera nodded and hummed as she went back to the shirt she was ironing, a small smile working its way back onto her lips. It took Eleanor back—not only to the days she watched her friend talk about Jack and him asking her for dates and then burst over him asking her to marry him—it also took Eleanor back to her whirlwind courtship with Alvin and the smile she'd gone to bed with on her lips every night.

All her friends had been married by then, all of them with at least one or two children of their own. Eleanor had given up hope, especially with all the men in town off fighting. Then Alvin Pendley had come home on leave. It had been love at first sight for Eleanor. He'd come into a church social looking so smart in a pair of navy-blue slacks and a crisp white shirt, topped off with a coordinating navy-blue tie. She'd caught her breath at his tall form and stopped breathing altogether when he met her gaze and crossed the room to ask her to dance.

Despite the time Eleanor had spent swallowing jealousy over Vera's early marriage and children, she didn't begrudge her friend the opportunity to have that again—especially since her happiness had been cut short. Perhaps Dominick Whitaker needed someone to take care of him like Eleanor had needed Alvin to take care of her.

Perhaps Vera needed someone to take care of her too.

⹀ CHAPTER THIRTEEN ⹀

NOW THAT SHE WAS HERE, Vera Larson Trumbell had to admit that volunteering for the Frances E. Warren Elementary School Christmas Fair had been a good idea—even if the school secretary, Mrs. Hogarth, had browbeaten her into it.

"Now, Mrs. Trumbell, you haven't volunteered for anything since you moved here," Mrs. Hogarth had said.

"Well, I know," Vera had responded, the guilt piling in her stomach despite her good reasons for not volunteering. "It's been awfully busy out here at the farm, and I have small children—"

Mrs. Hogarth wouldn't hear any of it. "Oh, come now. You've got Fay and your mother, not to mention Andrew's wife. They could watch the children for you."

It hadn't been any use arguing. And now that Vera had entered the gym adorned with a large Christmas tree in one corner and red, green, and white streamers hung from every direction, she liked the idea of helping without worrying what Tom and Audrey were getting into or if Jack Junior and Peter were fighting again. She hadn't anything to worry about. Mom and Fay would bring the children to town to see the fair and then take them home to get them all to bed on time. Vera sighed to herself. Her nights off had come few and far between the last few years. Getting to have them more often was one adjustment from the war days she didn't mind making.

"There you are, Mrs. Trumbell," Mrs. Hogarth called from a table on the opposite side of the gym. The thin but tough older woman skirted around it and strode toward her. It always put Vera a bit off her footing for the school secretary to call her Mrs. anything. Mrs. Hogarth had worked at the school when Vera went there as a child.

"Yes, here I am, just as promised, Mrs. Hogarth." Vera shrugged out of her coat, gloves, and knitted hat. The temperature had dropped near enough to zero in the last week or so to warrant something so unfashionable as that—knitted by her own two hands the winter before.

"I'll take those." Mrs. Hogarth held out her hands for the items, tucking them under her arm before starting across the gym again. "You'll forgive me for not putting you in charge of the pie booth." She glanced over her shoulder to wink at Vera, and Vera laughed at the reference.

"Of course. I'd rather not scrub pie out of another dress," she said easily.

"I thought since young Jack Junior is in Mr. Whitaker's class, you two would get on well running the ring toss."

Vera tripped and righted herself quickly. All night at Dominick's side. "Mr. Whitaker?" she said, her voice trilling upward and putting on display that every nerve in her had started buzzing.

Mrs. Hogarth paused and turned to face Vera. Vera in turn saw right through the faux concern on the older woman's face. Why, Mrs. Hogarth had planned this. Seemed she was taking the idea of getting Dominick and Vera together into her own hands.

"Yes, is that a problem?" she asked.

"Of course not," Vera said. She had no intention of passing up the opportunity to spend time with him, even if she worried that she couldn't function the entire evening without silly daydreams occupying her thoughts at every turn. They too often focused on Dominick *without* him standing next to her.

Mrs. Hogarth brightened, and she led the rest of the way across the wooden floor toward a table filled with milk bottles. Dominick stood behind it, dapper in a pair of gray trousers and a black sweater with a festive green tie peeking out the top. His gaze held Vera's as she approached with Mrs. Hogarth, and, though impassive, it unnerved her even more to have him study her so closely. Those eyes, those eyes—full of a story Vera longed for him to tell her.

"Hello, Dominick," she said, injecting as much cheer as she could into the greeting to cover the way the butterflies in her stomach had flown into a frenzy.

"Hello, Vera," he replied.

"Mrs. Hogarth says I'm here to help you out with the ring toss." She waited on the other side of the table for his approval.

He gave it with a shrug. "Sounds fine."

Mrs. Hogarth beamed. "I'll leave you two to get things organized." She disappeared with Vera's coat, leaving them alone.

"Shall I take tickets while you take care of the game?" Vera suggested.

"Sure," Dominick said with another shrug. Did she imagine that he clenched his jaw as he worked on arranging the milk bottles? He'd probably guessed Mrs.

Hogarth's tactic as well as Vera had. The secretary's scheming had been written all over her face. It would take a fool not to notice, and Dominick Whitaker was no fool.

Vera shifted some of the bottles on her side of the table into offsetting rows, careful not to move too close to him. Still, the electricity jumped off him and into her, and without much effort she found herself pondering the blissful idea of him wrapping his arms around her and holding her against him the way he almost had two months ago in front of Curtis's store.

"So . . . has Josette . . ." Dominick cleared his throat and avoided her gaze. "Does she like Bellemont now?"

"Some of the fervor of her newfound popularity has died down, but that hasn't disillusioned her yet," Vera answered, quirking a smile in his direction. It had been mostly Dominick's doing, leading people in town to finding out some of Josette's bravery in France during the war.

"Perhaps a winter here will?" Dominick suggested with the beginning of one of his own smiles. It happened so rarely, Vera had to force herself not to stare at how it transformed his already-handsome face into something breathtaking and almost approachable.

"Well, yes. It does take a great deal of effort to persuade her to leave her spot in front of the fire at her house." Vera pushed a few more bottles into place. "And how about you? Our winters haven't run you off yet? My son told me that you come from California."

A shadow passed over his face. "I had a few winters sleeping under the stars during the war to make it seem like a paradise to have a proper coat and gloves."

His tone was so heavy with ache that guilt stung Vera for voicing the question, though she couldn't have known how he would turn the conversation.

"Then I suppose you could teach us proud Wyomingites a thing or two about winter survival." Funny how her desire to have him wrap his arms around her had turned into the urge to wrap hers around him, to brush her fingers along his jawline and plant a kiss there with a promise that someday the terrible memories there would fade. She mentally shook herself from that daydream. If she could understand one thing, it was how the war could rob a man of his happiness. She'd witnessed its absence in Jack the first time he came home on leave. Felt it in the way he'd held her those precious few nights. In the daytime, with the children, he could fake his usual charming smile. At night, he'd allowed her to hold him through the worst of his fears—especially those of returning. But it couldn't hold back his love for his country and his need to rejoin his brothers. She had become fiercely proud of him for that, and she would have liked to see what kind of man it would have made him into. Different from the carefree young man she'd married.

When she emerged from her thoughts, she found Dominick watching her. She forced a nervous titter. "Jack told me about some of those bitter nights— only he spent most of his time in the Pacific somewhere, so it can't have gotten cold, really."

"Sometimes it's not the temperature that gets you," Dominick murmured— to himself. She recognized that and pretended as though she hadn't heard. The way he grimaced told her enough about how he felt about unlocking memories. Dreadfully painful ones—she could tell because the hurt emanated off him. How she'd like to bear some of that for him. How she'd like for him to trust her with it, the way Jack had. Or was that something she missed about marriage and not something she needed from Dominick?

"Is it difficult for you to think of him?" he asked.

When Vera turned to study him again, she found him rolling a milk bottle between his hands and avoiding her gaze. "No," she said. It kept her sane sometimes. Reminded her that he hadn't been a dream.

"Of course not," Dominick said gruffly, but the way he stared absently across the room made her suspect he hadn't meant it toward her. He held the milk bottle tighter. "You don't have any reason not to want to think of him."

Those words said so much about him and the things he locked up. She wished she could decipher it, but he would have to let her in first so she could try.

She agreed with him instead. "No. He wasn't a perfect man by any means, and there were certainly times I could have given him a knock upside the head—but those times remind me how much we loved each other too."

Dominick nodded. He remained quiet as he searched the gym. The fair had opened its doors. Before long, they had their first customers, and though they only trickled in and were spaced far enough to allow for conversation, neither he nor Vera forced it.

Their hands brushed as they both moved to readjust the milk bottles after the first few children's rings had knocked them this way and that. Their gazes met, possibly to find an explanation for how something so simple affected them so greatly. Vera wished she could explain the way her heart thumped after he'd stepped away.

More kids came, and then more, and then so many that she had time only to glance at him now and then. If Mrs. Hogarth had really wanted to push them together, she might have put them in charge of a less-popular game.

"Mom! Mom!" Familiar voices pulled Vera's concentration away from taking tickets as she realized she had reached out for them from Jack Junior and Peter without recognizing the two.

"Look how many I have already, Mom," Peter said, holding out a pile of winning tickets. He hadn't noticed Vera's inattention. "Bet I can win more than you here, Jack," he boasted. "How many does it cost to play this one, Mom? It doesn't matter, since I have plenty."

"Remember your manners, Peter," Vera said. "Five tickets, son." Both Jack and Peter handed over their five, and Dominick handed them the rings. Vera got so caught up in watching them throw and cheer each other on despite Peter's boastings that it took a nudge from Dominick to remind her that other children stood waiting. But he smiled again as she reached to take the tickets from the two girls next in line. Again it struck her in a heart-stopping way, and she wished he would wear that expression more than his usual melancholy one. Although her heart probably couldn't take that.

"Look at how many rings I got, Mom," Jack Junior interrupted the moment, pointing. "How many tickets do I win, Mr. Whitaker? Peter, I bet we have enough for that sled." He pointed to the prize table—gifts donated from businesses and people of Bellemont. Vera hoped it wouldn't disappoint them too much to discover the sled cost far more tickets than they had collected thus far. She didn't doubt her boys could succeed in getting it, though, especially working together.

"That's twenty tickets," she said before Dominick could count and answer. "Well done." She handed over the winnings and surprised Jack Junior by scooping an arm around his neck to hug him and plant a kiss on his forehead.

"Aw, Mom." He wiggled away, and once Peter had collected his tickets—and deftly avoided any attempts from Vera to hug and kiss him too—they rushed back into the crowd.

"He's a good boy," Dominick said, gathering the rings to hand to the little girls. "He's doing well in school. He and Bobby Brandenburg seem to have made up." He chuckled, and it took all of Vera's focus to count out the tickets that another child handed her.

"Thank you. I've always thought he was rather exceptional." She counted the tickets a second time to make sure—and to keep her attention on something besides Dominick. "Of course, I'm his mother."

"The most important person to think so, in my opinion."

She dared a peek at his face, wishing for another glimpse into the soul of a man she found wonderfully difficult to read. A small, reflective smile. *He had a good mother*, she thought.

She smiled too. "Thank you again."

⯎ CHAPTER FOURTEEN ⯎

ELEANOR HADN'T KNOWN ALVIN WAS a reader. In truth, she'd known precious little about Alvin when she'd married him two years before. He'd been three years older in school and their romance before he left for the war had been a whirlwind. His proposal had come after only two months away, and they'd married at the first opportunity. Then it hadn't seemed important to know the small details. Wouldn't they have fifty years to ponder those things? She knew he loved her.

Every so often, she would peer at him sideways from where they sat together on the sofa with the music from *Highways in Melody* on the radio in the background while he read and she crocheted. His expressions varied by the page. How did one get such a range of emotions from a beat-up Western novel he must have read a dozen times before, considering the worn pages, many of them bent this way and that? It was the best entertainment she could think of at the moment: observing him and discovering another small detail about him.

She turned back to the pile of yarn in her lap. Had Alvin guessed at the purpose for the bright-green blanket she'd started? He hadn't said anything. She'd run over the many ways to have the conversation all day long. Of course, it was only a suspicion so far. She meant to tell him that. It seemed wise to start out with some simple statement about having a family and confess to him when the moment came up. She couldn't wait to share this with him, for their first real moment of partnership. A baby. Her a mother, him a father. The idea made excitement burst inside her.

I want to have ten children or so, don't you? he'd once written her. *I loved my big family, and I think it would cheat the children out of something if we were selfish and had only one or two.* She had read that letter so many times it had started to tear at the folds. She'd read it quite a few times just today.

Alvin turned a page and she looked up, meeting his eye. He grinned and leaned over to kiss her cheek before going back to his book. She crocheted a few more stitches and considered what to say. *Remember how we used to talk about having ten children? What do you think about that?* It sounded well enough. A good introduction. She absently held up the blanket and rearranged it on her lap.

"What are you making there, dear? It looks like a baby blanket," Alvin said.

Eleanor beamed. That was a better introduction to the topic than she could have hoped for. "Well, we'll need one sooner or later, don't you think?" she teased.

He chuckled, but she noticed his jaw tightening. "Yes, perhaps."

Eleanor froze. "Perhaps?" That was an unexpected turn in the conversation.

Alvin set his book aside and put his arm around her shoulder, pulling her close to him and laying a kiss on her lips. When he pulled back, he stroked the side of her cheek, staring at her for a long time without speaking. He'd done that often and said sometimes he still couldn't believe he got to be home now, with her. And would he wake up sometime and find out it was a dream? That sort of talk—and his gaze—always set her insides on fire.

"I feel as though we have some catching up to do before we add a baby to the mix, don't you?" he asked softly, still stroking the side of her cheek. A wisp of sadness that she couldn't place touched his expression. Perhaps memories of the times when it seemed hopeless that he'd see her again—those emotions were familiar to her too. Sometimes she still woke up at night, gasping from the fragments of a dream in which Alvin was still fighting somewhere, dying somewhere, and wasn't coming home. The anguish would well up inside her and she'd have to reach her arm across the bed, touch him, lie next to him, remind herself he was home and safe.

The fact, however, remained that they only had about seven or eight months before they added a baby to the mix, as far as Eleanor could tell. It seemed like enough. "Maybe we do," she said back, her stomach twirling and her chest tightening, and she couldn't decide if it was from disappointment at Alvin's words or remnants from his kiss moments earlier.

"I want to figure you all out. Once the babies come, it'll be a long time before we have much time to ourselves again. Don't you want to enjoy this for a little while?"

He ought to have thought about *that* sooner rather than later. Her cheeks blazed. If he'd wanted to prevent having a baby, he ought to have done something about that. To hide her embarrassment, she laid her head on his chest, letting her crochet project fall into her lap. They *had* been separated for the better part of two years, but those months had been months of getting to know him in the lines of his letters. She had poured over them so much, drunk in every detail, savored every syllable. He had written to her often and in great detail of his childhood—riding horses with his grandfather over his ranch for days on end when Alvin was a kid, the house on Quebec Street that he'd grown up on and the room that he'd finally got to himself when his older siblings had grown up and moved away. Had he not soaked up her letters the same way? Yes, time with him was precious, but she already knew every detail.

She bit back a sigh, frustrated with how to proceed. Should she reveal the secret now and risk his disappointment? She hated keeping something like this bottled up. She wanted Alvin to share her joy . . . and wouldn't he? Or should she spend some time warming him up to the idea?

"I'll always enjoy being with you, dear," she said. She had to choke back the words, *but we don't have much more time in any case . . .*

He ran his fingers through her hair and then kissed the top of her head. It confused Eleanor's emotions even more. He had a way of making her feel so loved, protected, desired—the way Eleanor had always wanted to feel. The way she'd watched her friends and their husbands, as each of them married one by one and left her alone. Alvin had been a godsend when she'd needed him the most.

"Won't you read to me?" she said. "Maybe it'll help me understand why you love this book so much." She reached up and fingered the dog-eared pages of the paperback.

"I don't know that I love it so much. It's familiar. The only book I had with me over there. It reminded me of my grandfather—it was more of a comfort when I read it than anything else."

She nodded into his chest. "I see."

"That old cowboy could stand anything. When I read this book, I remembered that I came from tough stock. Helped me weather some rough spots."

Eleanor wrapped her arm around his waist. Some of his letters had always done the same for her. Like the one that told her about the first time he really noticed her, sitting next to her friend Gwen at the drug store. *You smiled and the whole room lit up with the glow of it.* When she had been passed over by so many men, those lines meant the world to her—sustained her through the times they were apart.

Another day would do to tell him about the baby. If Alvin wanted more moments like this with her, she'd let him have them. She'd give that man anything. He'd been through so much—seen so much more than a man should have to. She had plenty of time to tell him.

"Yes," she said, "I know what you mean. Won't you tell me more? About your grandfather's ranch?"

He closed the book, keeping his place with his thumb. "Once, he told me you could ride for days and not come to the end of it. Of course, that was back in the old days, when the cattlemen all claimed the land." He laughed to himself. Eleanor adored his laugh. She had missed the sound of it in the time he was gone and had almost forgotten what it sounded like. "Grandpa always promised grandma he'd build her a big, fancy house like the ones she saw pictures of in England—old-looking country houses. And he did."

"The Brandenburgs' home." Eleanor knew this part of the story.

"Yeah," Alvin said wistfully and stared out the window a moment. "I can remember it if I try really hard. The halls seemed so big to me, but I was real small. Bet if I went there today, it'd be a lot different."

Eleanor rubbed his hand gently where he'd rested it on her arm. Grandma Pendley had gotten sick. So sick that Grandpa Pendley had sold everything and took her out east to get well. They'd both died out there before Alvin turned fourteen. He had said once, that from the letters from Grandpa before he died, Alvin always suspected he'd died of a broken heart. *That woman was his life. She stood by him and came out west with him to make a fortune. He would have walked through fire for her.* Alvin had written Eleanor often about the example of marriage his grandparents' had been. It had shown her that Alvin would walk through fire for her too.

By the time she turned away from her thoughts and back to him, he had his nose back in the book, his eyebrows furrowed at whatever action raced across the page for him. With a smile, she readjusted herself and went back to her crocheting. It wouldn't hurt to wait another day or two.

≡ CHAPTER FIFTEEN ≡

SAM PULLED THE CHEVY IN front of the Soil Conservation Service's office and put it in park, leaning over to put his arm around Emily.

"Thank you for taking me to lunch. It was lovely. You sure are spoiling me lately," she said. She did enjoy these small moments with him, even if it was just an hour for lunch in the middle of the day.

He chuckled and squeezed her closer. "That's what it's like to be the girl of a farmer. Spoiled in the winter, neglected in the summer."

"And here I thought it was because we agreed to a wedding date."

"That too," Sam said. They both shivered. The old Chevy couldn't keep up with the cold weather December had brought. "You ought to get inside where it's warm."

She tilted her head back to admire him. They'd gotten on so well the last few weeks—a far cry from the constant spats they'd seemed to have over the wedding date and whether or not Emily would work once they got married.

"I'm always warm with you, Sam," she murmured, hoping for a few more moments to keep her warm the rest of the day.

"Any more talk like that and I might have to kiss you," he said and did just that.

His thoughtfulness that day made her want to please him. "I'm going to Mrs. Starry's shop to pick out a dress today," she said. "I'm going to get that one with all the lace and the full skirt. You know, the one I showed you a picture of?"

Sam pulled her close again, tightening his grip around her, and the pleasure of succeeding in making him happy spread through her.

"I think you did that because you *don't* remember, Sam," she teased, and shivered again.

"Of course I do. I wouldn't forget a thing like that." But they both laughed, because of course he had.

"Warm me up a bit more before I have to go," she said, and he did by holding her tight for a few more minutes. His warm breath washed over her cheek as he sighed with contentment—and happiness swirled over her with it. He had held her like this the night he asked her to marry him . . . well, the time he'd asked her that she had finally agreed. She wanted a life with Sam. The distance of him being in Europe, the time they'd spent apart, all of it drove home to Emily how empty the rest of her life would be without him.

But she knew what becoming a wife would mean. She knew what saying yes to Sam would bring, as much as she loved him. Now her time at the Soil Conservation Service office had only solidified further her dreams of a career.

Perhaps he'd never realized what it meant to her to say yes, she would marry him. His relief and happiness at finally receiving the affirmative after asking so many times had been palpable that night.

"I love you, Sam. With all my heart." She held him tighter, meaning it so much. She had never wavered in her love for him. Sometimes it felt as though her dreams tore her apart, but they never stole her affection.

"I love you more," he said softly.

She went inside the office perfectly toasty from head to toe. When she took out her compact to fix her lipstick, she noticed the warmth showed in the rosy hue of her cheeks.

"Have a nice lunch?" Mr. Mason asked from the door of his office. The smirk on his face embarrassed Emily as she hurried around to take her seat at her own desk. "I see that Sam Larson dropped you off."

"I had a very nice lunch. Thank you for asking, Mr. Mason." Emily busied herself with opening a file full of paperwork for a soil erosion survey.

Either he didn't get her hint or he ignored it, coming into the room. He took up a post next to her chair, leaning against the sturdy oak desk she worked at. It didn't matter if he wanted to chat, since there was no one else in the office and no one expected either. But his proximity made Emily uncomfortable, and she never could decide if it was on account of his darn good looks or because he insisted on flirting with her when he knew she was engaged. Mr. Burns was young and attractive as well, but it had never flustered Emily. Perhaps because he treated her as a colleague and didn't try to flirt.

"Oliver says you and Sam have settled on a wedding date." Mr. Mason folded his arms, looking comfortable in his perch and as though he didn't mean to go back to his office any time soon.

Emily swallowed nervously and scanned the first page of the survey she held without taking in any of it. "Yes. We thought February fourteenth would be quite romantic."

"Mmmm." Mr. Mason frowned, his thick dark brows drawing down over his blue eyes. "And when can we expect your notice? It will take quite a hunt to find someone to replace you. To find someone half as good as you."

Emily sucked in a breath and she met Mr. Mason's calculated gaze. "What do you mean by that?" she asked. She suspected Mr. Mason had baited her on purpose, considering his frown looked rather forced. Perhaps he had seen Emily's reluctance to quit when she got married. She shouldn't fall into a trap of letting him make her angry with Sam over the issue when she needn't be right now. Once they married, Sam would see that her working wouldn't prevent her from keeping their house up to his strict standards.

"Well, I assume that once you marry, you'll leave the job here, of course." Fingers tapping on his elbows, he let his expression relax into something hopeful.

"There is no 'of course' about it, Mr. Mason," she said coolly. "Not that it's any of your business, but Sam and I are still discussing what I shall do once we're married."

This brought out a laugh from Mr. Mason. "And Sam says that once you're married, he wants you home, where you belong. Am I right?"

He was. And that made Emily angrier at Mr. Mason. "That may be how Sam feels, but that does not mean I intend to quit."

Mr. Mason unfolded his arms and reached out to take one of her hands in his. It was soft, so unlike Sam's—roughened by hard work. "Nor should you, Miss Holman," he said genuinely, stroking the top of her hand with his thumb and gripping it in his. Her heart bounced around in her chest and she couldn't think straight about what to do. Mr. Mason went on, "It wouldn't surprise me if Mr. Burns promoted you soon—that is, if we can count on you sticking around. I would be so awfully disappointed to see you go."

"How kind of you to say," she said in a strangled voice and then had the sense to pull her hand away. What *would* it be like to be held by a man who supported her ambitions? To kiss a man who accepted her dreams? "I'll certainly stick around," she said in a clearer voice.

Mr. Mason stood and put his hands in his pockets as he backed away from the desk. From the heat in her cheeks, Emily suspected her face was blazing, but she squared her shoulders anyway.

"Excellent news. I knew I could count on you, Miss Holman." He said her name as though it were coated in honey.

"Yes, sir." Emily stared after him, still stunned by his manner and his pronouncement about her being ready for promotion. Promoted? Her? Well, she'd always dreamed of it, especially during the war when things had seemed to drag on and it felt like Sam would never come home.

Mr. Mason smiled and disappeared into his office. Emily turned her attention back to the file. She wanted to marry Sam—but when it came down to it, would he stand in the way of her achieving her goals?

Emily knew the answer to that but, darn it, she'd have to make him see sense.

☰ CHAPTER SIXTEEN ☰

"OH, DRAT," ELEANOR MUTTERED UNDER her breath. She put her finger to her mouth automatically, sucking at the prick in her finger. She leaned over to inspect the pair of Alvin's pants she was mending for any blood and then inspected her finger again. None there either, although it stung.

She sat up straighter on the sofa, trying to keep her mind on the task at hand. She couldn't keep her mind on things, no matter how hard she tried. The last week had felt so lonely. Nothing to distract her from day to day except a never-ending round of housework. And though Eleanor had broached the subject of babies from time to time with Alvin, nothing had changed on that front.

The night before, she had asked over dinner, "You talked about having a family so many times in your letters, I always figured you'd want to get started right away."

His returning comment had bordered on hostile. His eyes had darkened and he'd repeated what he'd said before, only his tone was shorter. "We've got years and years for that, Eleanor. What's made you so impatient?"

Years and years. She'd thought about it all evening. She hadn't slept well last night either as his words rolled around in her head. She wasn't young anymore. Already twenty-six! What did he mean years and years? And him going on like they could plan when to have a baby. The idea of her having to face Mr. Ridges at the drug store to buy something to prevent getting pregnant—well, embarrassment at the mere thought burned through her. She wouldn't have had the slightest idea what to buy, and asking someone for advice on that was out of the question. She couldn't imagine going to Vera for help. Besides, Alvin hadn't broached the topic with her and yet he had this foolish notion that they could wait to have a baby.

The fact was that she was sick of waiting. She'd waited long enough. To be honest, she'd had plenty of time to herself lately. For instance, she'd had all morning alone to brood over this while she did housework. Having a baby around might keep her company a bit better.

Her hand rested on her stomach again. Another missed cycle this week, and her so sick that Alvin had noticed and suggested she take it easy. She needed to tell him, but what if he didn't want this baby? He went on so much about waiting, Eleanor couldn't help fearing the worst. And if he didn't? How would she bear it?

A knock startled her. She threw the mending down on the sofa, not even taking care to stick the needle somewhere safe, and ran for the door. It was probably the postman, but a few words with someone else seemed to mean the difference in her sanity today.

Vera stood at the door, a loaf of bread wrapped in a dishtowel in her hands and sending off aromas that Eleanor's sensitive stomach gurgled over. "Hello there, El."

Eleanor threw her arms around her friend. "Thank heavens you've come."

Vera patted her back and then pushed her away, peering at Eleanor with narrowed eyes. "You're pale as a sheet—maybe a bit green. Are you feeling okay?"

Emotion welled up in Eleanor's chest. She shook her head. "Oh, I'm a mess, Vee," she blubbered.

Keeping an arm around Eleanor, Vera maneuvered her way into the house and shut the door. Eleanor hadn't noticed how much cold air her friend had brought in with her until it disappeared and left her shivering. Vera sat Eleanor on the sofa, opposite the pile of mending, and disappeared into the kitchen to put the bread away. When she returned, she laid a hand on Eleanor's head.

"You're clammy too. You ought to be in bed. Is it the flu?" she asked. "It's been going around. All four of mine have had it. Jack Junior was out of school for nearly a week."

"I don't think so," Eleanor said weakly. With Vera babying her, she realized she did feel awfully bad. That gurgle in her stomach might not have been hunger for the bread. She swallowed back some bile.

Vera's lips quirked. "Weren't you too sick last Tuesday to come out and help us bake doughnuts?" she asked. Eleanor nodded. "Are you certain of it?"

"As near as I can be, I suppose," Eleanor said.

Vera's expression slid into a frown at the dejection in Eleanor's tone. "You sound devastated, El. I thought you'd been waiting around forever to have a baby."

"I haaaaaave," Eleanor wailed. "But Alvin doesn't want one."

Vera patted Eleanor's hand and reached for a throw from the back of the couch, tucking it around Eleanor's shoulders. "That's silly. Why not?"

"Every time I bring it up to tell him, he goes on and on about us waiting to have a family and spending some time to get to know each other first." She sniffled, and Vera handed her a handkerchief.

"I'm sure it's a misunderstanding, dear. Once you tell him the news, he'll be over the moon."

"Maybe," Eleanor mumbled. She wiped a hand over her forehead. Vera still had her coat on. "Aren't you staying?" she asked. Her chin trembled, and she hated it. Eleanor had always been a bit high-strung, but this was taking it to another level. "I sound so pitiful," she said.

Vera hesitated and then shrugged out of her coat, tossing it onto a nearby chair. "That's your condition, El. Jack once caught me bawling over a bowl of soup because I'd made it just like my mother and it made me miss her so much I burst into tears."

Eleanor chuckled and reached for her friend's hand. "Thanks, Vee." She squeezed it. Even when Vera had lived in California, her letters had reminded Eleanor to keep her chin up and brave the loneliness that sometimes threatened to overwhelm her.

"We'll have a good chat, and you'll see. Tonight when Alvin comes home, you'll tell him, and everything will be perfectly all right." She leaned over to hug Eleanor, making her feel better already. Vera had a way of doing that.

≡ ★ ≡

Alvin Pendley walked into his house, looking forward to a quiet evening with Eleanor by his side. The smell of bread lingered faintly, and Alvin wondered if his wife had made some. She'd looked awfully tired when he left the house this morning for the sugar beet factory, and maybe a touch sick. He hoped she hadn't already started dinner. He wasn't much of a cook, but he hoped to lighten her load a bit tonight by scrounging something up for them. Eleanor took such good care of him.

"El?" he called, poking his head in the kitchen and finding her standing next to the stove, one hand braced on the counter and the other stirring something in a pot on the stove.

"Oh, you're home." She smiled at him and then swallowed hard before turning back to the pot.

He strode across the kitchen to put his arms around her. "El? You okay? You don't look so well."

"I'm . . ." She stared up at him and opened her mouth again. "I'm . . . okay," she said, ducking her gaze to the front of his shirt. "I just heated up some soup, and Vera brought bread over earlier. I hope you don't mind that it's not much."

"Of course not." He kissed the side of her mouth. "Let me finish that, and you go take a seat at the table. You ought to lie down and not worry about my dinner." He led her over to their tiny kitchen table and steadied her while she sat on one of the rickety wooden chairs. The whole set had come with the house. Hopefully sometime soon Alvin would get promoted to supervisor and he could buy Eleanor some nice things. A pretty wooden dining room table like the one they'd seen in the Sears catalog. They couldn't fit anything too big in this kitchen—or afford it, for that matter—but they didn't need much.

"Oh, it was nothing," Eleanor said, resting her elbow on the table and then leaning her head into her hand. "Just a can of tomato soup. Anyone could have done it."

"Including me," Alvin said pointedly, and Eleanor laughed.

"I suppose so." Her gaze went down again, and when she looked back up, her countenance seemed troubled. And exhausted. He made a mental note to get some soup into her and then put her to bed.

"Alvin, there's something . . ." Her voice trailed off and she took a deep breath and sat up. "We need to talk about starting a family." She nodded to herself, as though she'd made a decision.

Alvin sighed. "Oh, honey, let's not discuss it tonight. You're not feeling well, and I don't want to upset you."

Her face fell, and Alvin couldn't see why it would. He wasn't used to having to interpret her expressions and the tone of her words. So much of their courtship had taken place over letters. He thought he understood everything about her, but then the time came to live with her every day, and life had been more confusing than he'd been prepared for.

"Why would it upset me?" she asked, and the tremble in her voice sounded like she might cry at any moment. Had she really been so set on having kids right away? She'd never pushed the subject before in her letters or when he'd first come home.

He took a deep breath to keep his voice as calm as possible. He'd been excited to start a family too, but those dreams had since faded. He couldn't explain why to Eleanor. At least not yet. It was too humiliating. Besides, she was so tired and not thinking straight. Couching his situation in terms of postponing their family plans bought him time before he had to admit the truth. He needed time. He had no idea how to explain to a woman—even if she was his wife—what had happened to him.

"Honey, you know how I feel about us waiting," he said. "There's plenty of time to talk about a family—"

"There is not plenty of time, Alvin Pendley!" Eleanor stood up and her voice pitched shrilly. "I'm nearly thirty years old, in case you've forgotten."

Alvin stumbled back at her outburst. Could her insistence on starting now have something to do with her age? Guilt stuck in his throat for not having admitted to her right away about the dim possibility of them having children. That was something he ought to have told his bride. But he couldn't have written it, allowed her to find out when she was holding a sheet of paper and not him.

He clenched his jaw. This marriage business was more complicated than he'd ever given it credit. He'd never heard his mother take that kind of tone with his father . . . why, she wouldn't have dared. Yes, Eleanor had been unwell, and he would bet that contributed to her fragile temper, but really, how was he to know? He'd only lived with her a few months. He would have to tread ground carefully, he supposed.

"Oh, El, honey. You're only twenty-five. That's not even close to thirty."

"Twenty-six," she corrected with a bark.

Well, that had been the wrong move, but he'd never had his ear bitten off before by a woman for forgetting her age and saying younger. He turned off the stove so he wouldn't burn the soup and eased forward to reach out to Eleanor. He had to keep a level head, for the both of them. That's how his father had approached things, and though Alvin and Eleanor had been married nigh on two years, his parents' marriage was still more familiar to Alvin than his own.

"I want to spend some time getting to know you," he said evenly. "Now let's discuss it more later, when you're feeling—"

"I thought I already knew you." She covered her face with her hands and cried into them, her next words difficult to distinguish. "You talked in your letters all about us having ten or so kids and what a wonderful family we'd be, and all you've talked about since getting home is waiting and I'm tired of it." Her legs trembled under her and tears slipped down her cheeks.

Nerves tightened around Alvin's chest. At least her temper had allowed her to speak freely with him. He'd gotten her hopes up, but when he'd sent those letters, he believed they would have a large family, just like they'd both dreamed about. His embarrassing injury changed everything. And, for the life of him, he didn't know how to tell her, this woman he sometimes felt so foreign with, though hundreds of letters between them had held every tiny detail.

He closed his eyes. "Sweetheart, I'm sorry, but we just can't have children."

Eleanor gasped and then her hand flew to her chest. "Oh, Alvin—how could you say such a thing?"

"I'm sorry, El. It's the truth." Defeat wound its way through him at her sorrow. He had surely broken her heart, taking the idea of children away from her. Would she have married him if she'd known this would happen?

She moved her hand to her mouth and then turned and fled the room.

"El—" He hurried after her, but she had already scampered to the top of the stairs. He hesitated to follow her farther. She was already so upset; how could they have a calm conversation now? He would let her rest and explain everything later. He stepped back to the stove and tested the soup, heated enough for him to have a bowl, so he sliced a piece of bread and served himself some. Just as he sat down, the sound of something banging down the stairs interrupted him. He hopped up from his chair and rushed into the living room, prepared to find Eleanor at the bottom of the stairs.

He did find her at the bottom of the stairs, but not in the crumpled heap as the banging sounds had made him fear. She stood with her suitcase in hand and her coat, hat, and gloves on. "El?"

"I'm going to my mother's." She lifted her chin, though it trembled.

"Now, Eleanor. Let me explain before you make a rash decision." He rushed toward her, arms extended, but she backed away and held a hand up. A crumpled white handkerchief mocked him as her hand shook at him.

"I've realized that we are too different. I've come to see that the man I wrote for two years is entirely different than you. I *want* the children you promised me—" Her voice broke, and her hand went to her stomach. Pain sliced through Alvin as they both shared for a moment the bitter disappointment that she would never bear his children. He reached for her again. Through the humiliation, Eleanor's letters had been comforting and understanding, urging him to keep his chin up, with words of how she wished she could nurse him back to health. But now she rebuffed him once more. Perhaps he too had not really known the woman he married.

"I think it would be best if we went our separate ways." She sniffled again and stared at the floor.

Her words struck right at Alvin's heart. He wanted kids more than ever, but he couldn't grant that wish for Eleanor. And if she couldn't have children, she was right. He wasn't the man for her anymore.

"You can't walk to your mother's in the dark. It's freezing out there, and you're sick," he protested feebly. It was unfair, but he couldn't stand the notion of life without her.

"I don't care," she said, disappointment in his answer written in her expression.

"At least let me drive you." He walked past her to get his coat, but he didn't miss the shudder in her breath. He ignored it. Eleanor would make a great mother. He couldn't rob her of that. His grandfather had done everything he could to make sure his wife had whatever she needed. Eleanor's need for children had been evident from the moment they'd first talked about a family. The longing bled through every sentence she wrote about her friends' children and their accomplishments and shone in every word about her own hopes for the future. What kind of selfish man would take that away because he loved a woman? No. The best man he had ever known had taught him that love meant making sacrifices.

They rode the three blocks to the Holbrook house in silence except for Eleanor's quiet sniffles. He didn't move to comfort her. It would make the separation worse. When he stopped at the curb, he stared out the windshield at the dark street so she wouldn't see how difficult it was for him to leave her here.

"Goodbye, Alvin," she said quietly before she opened the door.

"Goodbye."

She sniffled again and got out of the car. When he was sure she couldn't see him, he dared to watch and make sure she got safely into the house. What more could he have said—what more *should* he have said? It seemed so wrong to beg her to stay when he was asking her to sacrifice so much by doing so. She wanted a family. He couldn't provide one.

He'd convinced himself that the instant connection he'd made with Eleanor was the real deal—true love. The kind of love that could weather anything. He hadn't misunderstood her devotion, at least he didn't believe that, but perhaps he'd misunderstood his ability to be the kind of husband she deserved.

He drove away from the home before Mrs. Holbrook could come out and give him a scolding for mistreating her daughter so. With a heavy heart, he returned to his own home. He didn't look forward to an empty house and an empty bed tonight.

≡ ★ ≡

"What do you mean you're at your mother's?" Vera cried into the phone. "Why in the world are you there?" Eleanor blubbered some response that Vera couldn't make out. "Dear, you're going to have to calm down if you want me to understand any of this."

"I tried to tell him again last night, and he wouldn't have it. He said he just couldn't have children—as though there was no changing his mind." Her voice pitched high and wobbled, but at least Vera understood her this time.

"He couldn't mean that," Vera said.

"He must have!" Eleanor's words pitched even higher, but she took a breath and went on. "I told him that if we wanted such different things, perhaps we shouldn't have married. And he drove me to my mother's." She wailed again as soon as she'd gotten the rest of the story out.

"He drove you?" Vera leaned back against the wall next to their old telephone, surprised.

"Yes! So he must not want a baby after all."

"Oh, El. There must be some misunderstanding. You ought to tell him. Perhaps that would change his mind. Plenty of men are scared to have families—the expense and all. I bet if he knew, he'd think differently."

"I practically did, Vee!" Eleanor cried, her words boarding on unintelligible again. "I said how I wanted our children, and I was thinking of our little baby and how his father doesn't love him—or her, but I can't help thinking—oh, but anyway, it was so obvious and he let me go. If he doesn't want a baby, he won't want me *and* a baby. He was so cold last night. He hardly looked at me when he dropped me off. I suppose he's happy to be done with me."

Vera rubbed her hand over her forehead. "Don't talk like that. You know no such thing. Now you spend the day resting, and let your mother take care of you, and I'm sure Alvin will come by to pick you up this evening. You can bet on that."

"I sure hope so," Eleanor mumbled and hung up. It had to be the pregnancy talking. Alvin and Eleanor had been head over heels for each other. Still ruminating to herself, Vera headed back to the living room, where Sam and Emily sat in front of the fire. Emily had a copy of *The Bride's Magazine* in her lap, pointing out things to Sam every so often.

"Who was that?" She looked up when Vera came in and plopped into a chair near the fire. The old farmhouse didn't keep heat as well as it should when the temperature got so low—especially with wind that dropped the temperature below zero and pushed cold air through all the nooks and crannies in the house.

"Eleanor. She's gone home to her mother's."

Emily raised her eyebrows, but instead of looking sympathetic, she glanced at Sam. "I suppose a woman stuck at home with nothing but housework to occupy her time is bound to go crazy one way or another."

Vera bit back a laugh. Sam grunted and kept his attention on the magazine. "If you two can keep a secret, I'll let you in on something," Vera said.

They both perked up now. "What is it?" Emily asked, leaning forward.

"The truth is, Eleanor is pregnant, and Alvin is acting as though he doesn't want children. I have half a mind to march down and give him a talking to and see this whole thing straightened out."

Sam whistled. "She might be right though, Vee. Plenty of fellows changed their mind about families when they saw all the orphaned children from the war. Those kinds of things change a man."

Vera let out a sigh. "I suppose so. Seems rather unfair of him to give up."

Emily sighed and flipped a page in the magazine. "Men can be foolish sometimes when they have an idea that the world works a certain way."

"Oh, come on now, Emily," Sam said. "We're having such a lovely evening."

"You are, I suppose, because I'm sitting here obediently looking at wedding things instead of arguing with you about how I plan to keep on working after we're married." She snapped the magazine shut and glared at Sam.

Vera should leave the two to their argument, but she couldn't bring herself to give up her cozy seat in front of the fire. The kids were playing quietly in their bedroom—she should check on them—and the smell of dinner wafted in from the kitchen. Even Mom had gone up to her room for a quick rest before the meal. No, Vera would stay right here and enjoy the show. She sat back into the soft, well-worn cushions of the recliner, trying to make herself less visible.

"I don't understand why it's so important to you. Don't you want to marry me?"

"Of course I do, Sam. Why does wanting to marry you have to go hand in hand with quitting my job? Mr. Mason says Mr. Burns might promote me sometime soon. Imagine that! Me, a real live soil technician." Her face beamed with the possibilities. Vera smiled to herself. Marrying and being a mother had been fine for her, but what kind of dreams would she have pursued if it hadn't been? She didn't even know.

"Mr. Mason says this, Mr. Mason says that. That's all I hear these days is what Mr. Mason said about something." Sam stood and threw his hands up in the air. "Maybe you ought to talk less to Mr. Mason and more to your fiancé."

Emily rose to face him, hands on her hips. "Oh, I see now you'd like to control who I associate with. That shouldn't surprise me coming from a stubborn old mule like you. Would it be all right if I got my coat and went home, Master?"

Sam clenched his jaw and dropped back onto the sofa. "I'm not going anywhere," he insisted, proving Emily's point almost to a tee.

Now Vera reluctantly stood from her seat. "If you'd really like to go, I'll drive you," she said, scowling at her brother. Emily glared at Sam, but if she was waiting for an apology, she should know by now that it would never come from him.

"Thank you, Vera," Emily snapped.

"You know better," Vera whispered to her brother as she followed Emily and passed him on the couch. He glared at the fire, not responding. "Keep an eye on the children, please," she added. This time he at least grunted a response that she took to mean he would.

Once Emily and Vera sat in the ice-cold Chevy, Emily rubbed her hands and turned to Vera. "Sorry you had to come out in this. Seems as though foolishness is contagious in Bellemont right now. At least among the men. You'd better be careful, or Mr. Whitaker might catch it as well."

Though she blushed that Emily had paired her with Dominick without so much as a thought, she laughed the comment off. "Why should I care if he's foolish—unless he starts teaching Jack Junior the wrong multiplication facts?"

"I see." Emily smiled and rubbed her arms. The car would take the whole trip and back to warm up. Vera pushed a blanket toward her, and Emily draped it over her legs. "If you ask me, he's being pretty foolish already by not asking you for a date."

Vera waved her hand and shrugged. She thought him rather foolish about it too, but she didn't know what was happening in that mind of his. He had his reasons—his brooding expressions always said so. She wondered what those reasons were. Her four children? Quite possibly. Anyone would be foolish not to be concerned about that.

"A promotion?" Vera said, changing the subject. "Exciting, even if Sam doesn't say so."

"Yes. I've dreamed about it since starting work there. Mr. Burns let me go with him quite a few times last summer to do surveys on the farms." Emily bounced a little, and Vera didn't know if it was from trying to keep warm or from her excitement.

"And you want to work there after you've married . . . and have children?" Vera couldn't wrap her mind around the kind of workload that would entail. For heaven's sakes, the woman would have to stay up until midnight every night doing laundry. And in the summers, when Sam spent every daylight hour on the farm? It would be a nightmare.

"We'll see," Emily said, watching the road ahead of them. "Perhaps I'll change my mind then, but shouldn't I get the chance to find out?"

"Have you told Sam that?"

"Oh, him. He can't get past hearing me say I want to keep on working instead of being a dutiful little wife like you and your mother."

Vera laughed. "I'm sorry about that."

Emily sighed. "I'm not. Who else would I get my butter from?"

"I suppose you could hire a housekeeper too. Would Sam go for that?"

Emily shook her head and continued staring. "I doubt it. Don't you? He's awfully old-fashioned. It's a wonder I love him."

Truthfully, since Sam had gotten home, Vera had wondered at the same thing. Did Emily see something in her bullheaded brother that Vera couldn't? "Isn't love grand?" she mused instead. Emily sighed her agreement.

⹀ CHAPTER SEVENTEEN ⹀

ALVIN USUALLY GOT A RIDE home from someone at work since he was eager to get home to his wife. With no Eleanor to come home to, he decided on walking home that evening instead. Besides, he could take a route that would lead by the Holbrook house and maybe catch a glimpse of her. It was unfair to her, but a man couldn't drop his wife off at her mother's and not be expected to want a peek of her.

His parents lived a few streets over from the Holbrooks, and back when Alvin had first courted Eleanor, he'd gotten into the habit of taking evening walks. He smiled wistfully to himself over those summer nights. His leave time had been short, and he hadn't wanted to waste time. He wanted her with him every moment. He would walk by the Holbrook house, which had a big picture window in the front, hoping she might notice him and come out. Every night that she had seen him from the front room, where she sat after dinner with her parents, she would come out and walk with him. Some nights it had taken Alvin several trips around the block to get seen, but it had led to many precious moments together.

After a week of courting, he had asked her to marry him. With only their parents and the few friends they could gather last minute, they married the next afternoon in order to take full advantage of the remaining four days of his leave. Having Eleanor, having a future so full of love, had made returning to Europe easier and harder all at the same time.

Alvin shivered and pulled his fur-lined hat down more over his ears. He had wooed Eleanor during the summer—his evening strolls had been much more enjoyable than this one. He moved quicker, nearing the Holbrook's street. He could see the modest sky-blue house up ahead and the bay window where Eleanor used to sit and sew, crochet, or read as she waited for him to walk by— that much she admitted after marrying him. She wouldn't be waiting for him tonight, so perhaps he could catch more than a quick glimpse of her before she noticed him. He kept to the opposite side of the street, just in case.

He didn't mean to stop when he saw her sitting in the window seat, her head bent over something she was crocheting. He caught a flicker of bright green—the baby blanket she'd been working on before. Guilt crushed through him. It had been stupid to walk this way, stupid that a part of him wanted her to see him—maybe come out to talk to him and come home with him. That blanket reminded him why he couldn't walk up to the door in the first place.

He turned to hurry on, but out of the corner of his eye, he saw Eleanor's head snap up. She turned to the street, leaning forward so the green blanket fell off her lap and putting a hand on the glass as she peered out. Behind her, a lamp shone across her hair, making the dark brown shine. He took a step across the sidewalk, but before he stepped again into the street and crossed it, he remembered himself. If he begged Eleanor to reconsider, to come home, she might, but he would still be taking something from her. As much as he hated living without her, he couldn't ask that of her. *I had given up hope,* she wrote him once, *that my longing to be a mother would ever be fulfilled. When I was younger, it had seemed such a simple thing. Of course I would marry and have a family, but year after year passed with me alone. You are my fairy godmother, or my knight in shining armor, making my fondest wishes come true.* He couldn't grant those wishes anymore. He no longer had any right to the title of her knight in shining armor.

He turned on his heel and hurried down the street.

☰ ★ ☰

Bellemont, Wyoming, left too much time for a man like Dominick alone with his own thoughts. Thoughts that, despite every effort he made, kept rounding back on Vera Trumbell. The way she'd said that her memories of Jack, even the bad ones, reminded her of how much they'd loved each other. Her expression had held such earnestness for him to believe the same way. Heaven help him, he'd tried to see it her way. Tried to smile when memories of Ondine flitted through his mind. He hadn't loved her, but they'd shared a deep friendship, one that perhaps might have led to something more. Yes, it would have. There'd been the excitement at meeting and the warmth that would spread through him when she'd throw her arms around him for one of those impetuous, celebratory hugs of hers. Another rail-line sabotaged. Another pilot rescued. Another German outsmarted. She, Laurent, and Dominick had made a good team.

But Vera's tactic never worked for long. The truth remained that if Ondine and Laurent hadn't known Dominick, they would probably be alive.

He looked up from the papers he'd stayed at the school to grade. The darkness outside the window surprised him, but of course, it was December, and darkness came around five now. A glance at the clock on the wall of his classroom told him he'd sat ruminating for far longer than that. It was nearly six.

He sat back in the chair, stretching his arms over his head. He'd floated above the threatening depression for a while now, but the cold, bleak winter stretching before him didn't help. Neither did Vera—but then again, she did. The idea of finding a way to become whole again for her, to become a man she deserved, had tempted him for weeks now. It had forced him to dig back into his soul. But the fact that he never came to a satisfying conclusion made the pain of it sharper each time.

Yet he needed the calm that her voice, her words, her existence trickled on him. Sometimes, for a moment, talking to her healed those unseen wounds. She couldn't undo his past, but she could soothe it. It made him a selfish man indeed.

He leaned forward and gathered up the papers, preparing to head home or maybe to the diner down the street for some dinner. His stomach growled in agreement with that idea. It'd be nice to call up Vera, though a bite to eat might be too much of a date. He could arrange a meeting about Jack Junior. Unfortunately, the boy was such a good student that it wouldn't make any sense. Why couldn't he get into trouble, for Dominick's sake? Dominick might call on Vera to tell her how well Jack Junior was doing. She might appreciate that.

He scowled to himself. That would be too obvious. A simple note would suffice to tell her. A phone call, if he stretched it.

Why not go out to the farm for a chat? The company would do Dominick good, and spending time around the Larsons didn't constitute any kind of date. They might all cheer him up. Anyone in Bellemont might need company on a cold winter night, not just a man looking for an excuse to spend time with a woman.

He stood and grabbed his coat from the coatrack behind his desk. Yes, he'd put off dinner to do that. With any luck, Mrs. Larson might have something left over to offer him.

As he drove the few miles out to the farm, he missed the summer days he used to walk these roads. Too cold now, though he couldn't deny the beauty— fields covered in white, spreading out before him with lines of trees here and there to break it up. He was almost smiling as he pulled into the Larson drive. The notion of an hour or so in Vera's company perked him up. He parked his two-door Ford sedan and hurried up the steps, knocking on the door.

Sam Larson answered, his scowl deepening when he saw Dominick. "Yes?" Sam asked in a clipped tone.

He glared in such a downright foreboding way, Dominick found himself using his teacher voice. "Is Ve—Mrs. Trumbell here?"

"No," Sam snapped. "She's gone into town with Emily." He took a breath and said in a calmer tone. "Is there something you'd like me to tell her about Jack Junior?" he asked, his jaw still working.

"Well . . . no. I suppose I'll just call again. Good night, Sam."

"I don't think you ought to 'just call' again, Mr. Whitaker," he responded coolly before Dominick could turn. Then he slammed the door in Dominick's face.

The action scattered every piece of good mood that Dominick had managed to scrape together since leaving the school, mostly because Sam had it right. Dominick was no good for Vera. He stomped down the steps and back toward his car, pausing at the back bumper when the Larsons' Chevy pulled in, flashing the lights over him.

A moment later Vera poked her head out the window. "Dominick? Is that you?" And then she opened the car door and hurried toward him. Against his will, he felt like a warm breeze had started blowing in the middle of December. "Is anything wrong?" she asked.

Dominick clenched his fists inside the pockets of his heavy coat. "I came to see you," he muttered. He hated—and loved—the way Vera always read between every line of everything he said. "But Sam said you weren't home," he finished.

Vera pressed her lips together. "What else did he say?" she asked. Dominick didn't dare answer that. "Don't mind him," she said when it was clear he wouldn't answer. "He's in a bad mood. You ought to come in anyway." She smiled hopefully at him.

Dominick turned back to the house, wondering how well the hour might go in the company of a cranky Sam who didn't like Dominick in the first place. Irrationality took over. "Would you like to go to the diner for some pie or something?"

Vera's face lit up. "That sounds wonderful." She glanced over at his Ford. "Come on, get in my car. It's already all warm." She watched him walk around to the passenger side. "I hope you don't mind, but I'd better go in and make sure Mom knows I'll be gone for a bit and that someone is watching my children. I left Sam in charge when I took Emily into town, but—for heaven's sakes, I'm going on, aren't I, and it's cold out here—" She interrupted herself again, with a nervous titter this time, and it lightened Dominick's mood despite himself. He was already concerned about asking Vera for a date, but he nodded at her and got into the car while she hurried into the house.

The ride back into town was silent, but not in an uncomfortable way. The fact that Vera didn't always expect conversation and seemed content with his company comforted him. He itched to put his arm around her, lean closer, kiss her cheek. They should have taken his car. He could have used the cold as an excuse to scoot nearer to her. *Are you cold, darling?* he might ask. Unfortunately, the heater in the Larsons' sedan blasted scorching heat at them since Vera had already taken it into town and back.

The usual dinner rush crowded the street in front of Alice's diner with cars, and since it was miserably cold out, everyone had tried to park as near as they could. Vera parked in a spot about a block away, and as they hurried from the car to the diner, Dominick realized it was the perfect opportunity to hold her close to him.

They came upon a patch of ice, and his hand darted from the deep pocket of his coat without his permission and took her elbow to steady her. She flashed him a grateful, and hopeful, look—her cheeks rosy and eyes bright from the cold, her dainty lips turned up—a sharp blast of bitter-cold wind brought him back to his senses. He'd come out with Vera for the company, for the pleasure of an evening together, though he couldn't deny kissing her would be an immense pleasure. He dropped her elbow and followed her the rest of the way down the sidewalk, trying not to think about how nice and warm they would have been if he'd wrapped his arm around her and held her close as they walked down the street.

☰ ★ ☰

Vera stood inside the door next to Dominick, searching through the crowd of young people and older diners alike for a table or booth, excitement making her heart pound and her fingers tingle. She could chalk that up to the cold outside and their hasty walk from the car to the diner, but that wasn't it. Every time she was near Dominick Whitaker, she felt like a schoolgirl again. He pointed out an empty booth but didn't say anything until they'd sat down and Alice had come to take their orders of apple pie and hot chocolate.

"Thank you. Tonight might have been lonely," he said.

"I know what you mean." Vera laughed to herself. "That must sound crazy coming from someone living in a house with so many people and my brothers around all the time now, but . . . you know what I mean." She pulled off her gloves and pressed her chilled fingers against her cheeks, embarrassed by the way she kept talking and repeating herself.

"Yes, I think I do." He fiddled with the ketchup bottle and didn't look at her.

She had to come up with something to say, if only to keep him from turning in on himself on a night when he'd admitted he needed the company. For a man like him to confess that must mean he desperately needed cheering up.

"Jack Junior is excited about the Christmas pageant you're planning for the class," she said.

"He's perfect for the part of Joseph," Dominick said with one of his half-smiles, and triumph rose through Vera, which was silly. But winning one of those with such a simple statement? It made her heart sing far more than it should.

"He's been practicing, and he's very somber about his important responsibility." She laughed. "He got angry at Audrey when she wouldn't stay in the box he'd made for her to play baby Jesus. And let me tell you, Tom was not pleased at all that Jack Junior asked him to act out Mary."

Laughter burst from Dominick as though it had been caught somewhere inside him for too long. Vera couldn't help beaming at the sound. A laugh! She'd made him laugh—a real one, too, not some half-hearted chuckle.

"I wish I could have seen that." He relaxed into his seat. "You would have liked to see the gentle way he handles Louisa Nikels, who's playing Mary. He's very dutiful."

Vera shook her head, full of pride and ache at the same time. "He learned fast to be the man of the house," she said.

"He must have had a good example."

She nodded, but she didn't want to talk about her husband tonight. Not when Dominick had finally asked her on a date. Alice arrived with their pie, steam rising off both it and the hot chocolate she set before them.

"Can I ask about what you did for the OSS? I mean, I guessed you worked with them because of what you knew about Josette—am I wrong?" She reached for her cup and gripped it. She didn't want to upset him, but she also wanted to give him the opportunity to open up to her.

He swirled the spoon around in his own hot chocolate before answering. "No, you're not wrong." His expression pinched and it took him several moments to answer. "I trained French men and women for missions inside France and sometimes accompanied them."

"I'm sorry. We don't have to talk about it. Only . . . it sounds so exciting." She didn't mean to push him, but the words came anyway.

"It was at times." He took a slow sip of the chocolate and then cut off a bite of the pie with heavy movements.

"And dangerous," she guessed. She had pushed enough for one night, especially for their first time out together alone. "Andrew has told us some stories—of course, he read reports and such. He didn't do any fieldwork. And thanks to you, Josette has told us a few stories too." She racked her brain for something to discuss besides the war and school. "Do you still have family in California?" she asked.

He nodded and his features eased. "My parents and a little sister. I can't convince any of them to come visit me."

"Well, especially not in the winter. But it is quite beautiful in the summer, don't you think?"

His half-smile came back. "Yes."

"What made you decide to come to Bellemont?" she asked.

He finished his bite and even appeared at ease when he answered. "I heard Andrew say something about it once. I didn't really know him. Saw him reading a letter at lunch one day and he looked so happy I asked if it was good news. I could've used some then." He cleared his throat in a way that Vera knew he had said more than he wanted. "He laughed and told me no. That his little sister was complaining about all the work it took to plant a field, and he couldn't wait to get home and do that himself, as simple as it sounded." He took another bite of pie and let silence settle between them for several seconds before he said, "Simple was what I wanted."

She watched him, unsure of how to react to his quiet demeanor. It excited her in an odd way, wondering what she might say next and if he might smile. So different from Jack. His smiles came easily. Still, she reveled in every victory of gaining one from Dominick. It reminded her of a poem her mother had once told her about kisses being like pennies, and how the more pennies one had, the less they were worth. Dominick's smiles were like rare pennies—worth that much more. And then when she realized how she'd thought about kisses, her mind trailed to kissing Dominick and her cheeks burned. She took several bites of pie, scalding her mouth by doing so.

"Are you all right?" Dominick asked, watching her struggle to cool it down—especially since all she had was hot chocolate to drink.

"Fine," she said, tittering and nearly slapping her forehead over her silly behavior. "I didn't realize how hot it still was."

Her idiocy won her another smile, and she realized no matter how many he gave, she might treasure each and every one anyway. "Would you like some water?" He held up his hand to call Alice back to their table.

"Thank you." A few minutes later Vera drank gratefully from the tall glass Alice had brought her. She opened her mouth to continue the conversation about California by saying how she and Jack had lived there, but then she closed it. She took another careful bite of pie instead and wondered if Dominick would say something. He didn't, but it didn't seem uncomfortable for him. On the contrary, he sat with his arm on top of the booth, eating his pie and drinking his hot chocolate with apparent pleasure.

She did the same, deciding that she liked his quiet company as well as she liked making him smile. After they had finished their food, they drove back to the farm for Dominick's car in mostly silence, interspersed by comments about how many stars they could see in the clear sky and then expressing surprise when a deer hopped across the road. Vera had been driving slowly anyway. She pulled into the drive reluctantly. Now Dominick would go home, and even in his silence, she craved his company. The warmth of him next to her filled a spot inside her that needed filling over and over.

"Thank you for the pie," she said, wishing he would ask her for another date.

"Thank you for the company," he said, not exactly smiling, but his expression had calmed in the time they'd spent together. To her surprise, he put his hand on the top of the seat, inching toward her. "Darling . . . ," he said in a low voice, and then he cleared his throat again. Vera recognized it as something he did when he felt he'd said something wrong—but oh, he hadn't. He'd said something so right.

She leaned toward him. "Yes?"

He dropped his arm to her shoulders, pulling her toward him and then laying his cheek against the top of her head. "Thank you," he said again.

She tilted her head back, reaching up to graze his chin with her fingers and softly run one finger over the faint scar. "You're welcome."

He bent and kissed her. Vera had thought that each time she got him to smile was a victory. Now she understood how the soldiers' hearts must have soared on D-day.

"Good night, darling," he said in a husky voice when he pulled away.

Darling. Oh, merciful heavens, she could listen to him say that to her all night. "Good night."

And then he kissed her again and summer might have come early considering how it felt like the inside of the car had erupted in flames. When he pulled away again, he grinned at her—a full, real grin!—and scooted out of the car.

Vera had to sit in the car by herself long after his Ford rumbled out of the drive and down the road. She was quite sure that anyone who looked at her would know that Dominick Whitaker had thrown her helter-skelter with his kisses, and she wanted to keep this to herself for right now.

☰ CHAPTER EIGHTEEN ☰

VERA OPENED THE DOOR TO the farmhouse almost as soon as Eleanor knocked, ushering her inside and out of the icy air. Though the sun shone, making the snow sparkle, it did little to warm the air, as though it was too far away to do anything.

"Come in, come in," Vera said, shutting the door behind her.

Usually, the cozy sight of the Larson front room comforted Eleanor, and truthfully, she had hoped for that this morning. She'd eagerly accepted Vera's invitation to help bake the weekly bread batch for the large Larson clan. She unwound her thick, knitted scarf and took off her hat to hand to Vera. The heaviness of her newfound burdens hadn't eased even for just a minute in this place that had been her second home. She still hoped that spending time with Vera, Kathryn, Fay, and Josette would distract her at least from mulling over her situation every minute.

She blinked and found Vera studying her with compassion. It was an expression so natural to her friend that Eleanor hadn't picked up on it right away.

"Have you heard from Alvin?" Vera asked in a low voice.

Eleanor shook her head and swallowed back a lump that grew in her throat. She had been upset and silly when she stalked out of the house to go stay at her mother's, but she had hoped that the shock of it would jar Alvin enough to decide he couldn't live without her, even if she was pregnant. But it had been two days, and he hadn't called to see how she was doing. He had walked by the house the night before. She didn't know how long he'd been standing on the sidewalk opposite the house when she saw him. Maybe that meant something.

Vera reached out and hugged her. "Have faith, Eleanor," she whispered into her friend's ear. Eleanor had to choke back more emotion. "Things will work out," Vera said.

Eleanor didn't see how they could. She was blessed to have the support of her parents—but even they talked of Alvin coming to his senses sooner or later. Would they feel the same if he didn't? If he continued to disregard his child? Eleanor would be a single mother and divorced. She hated bringing that stigma upon her parents. She hated the thought of her child having to grow up under that cloud. What had she done?

She wanted to have faith, but every hour that passed and Alvin didn't come to get her stretched that faith thinner and thinner. How would she manage motherhood by herself? Vera seemed okay, but people accepted her because her husband had died. They wouldn't treat Eleanor with the same kindness.

She shook the thoughts from her head and stepped out of Vera's embrace. She'd come to bake bread to escape her troubles for a morning. "I heard you were out with Mr. Whitaker last night at Alice's diner," Eleanor said, forcing a smile.

Vera bit her lips together and then let loose a laugh. Though the concern for Eleanor lingered in her eyes, Eleanor could see her friend had a hard time keeping her excitement back.

"Yes, he asked me to come have pie and hot chocolate with him, and it was absolutely marvelous." She clapped her hands together, her face lighting up.

"You're holding something back," Eleanor accused lightheartedly as she linked her arm through Vera's and followed her toward the kitchen. The other women's cheerful voices floated out to them.

"Perhaps." Vera shrugged. She hesitated as they crossed the living room and then stopped and turned to face Eleanor. "I haven't told a soul." She dropped her voice to a bare whisper. "He *kissed* me and called me 'darling' and it was divine." She sighed the last word.

Too many emotions for Eleanor to handle bubbled up inside her. Giddiness, nostalgia, and . . . jealousy. The scene was awfully familiar. The way Vera used to gush about Jack Trumbell and how Eleanor had ached for the same happiness. She'd thought she had it finally.

Vera caught the change. "But you can't breathe a word," she said, disappointment gathering in her expression—her excitement fell away, her expression growing troubled.

Eleanor plastered another smile on. "Of course not." This time she moved toward the kitchen. "Have you already started the bread?" she asked.

Vera chewed on the inside of her cheek before following. "Of course," she said, her voice falsely glad now. "But we have loaves and loaves to bake."

Feeling bad for her terrible reaction to Vera's good news, Eleanor reached back to squeeze her friend's hand. Vera had been through her share of trials too, and she deserved happiness to find her again.

"Perhaps if you didn't give so many away, you wouldn't have to bake so many," Eleanor teased.

"Oh, you know my mother." Vera beamed. "That wouldn't be possible for her."

Eleanor leaned her head against Vera for a moment as they stepped into the bright kitchen. "And that's what I like about you Larsons."

⸗ ★ ⸗

When Eleanor drove home that afternoon, she went by her and Alvin's home and stopped out front. He wasn't there. He'd be at work for another hour or two. She stared at the house and dreamed of how she had pictured their family growing there. Should she go inside, start Alvin's dinner, and then—then when he came home insist that he had to keep her? Alvin was an honorable man. If she told him of the baby and forced the responsibility on him, he would take it.

But he wouldn't want it.

The emotion she'd struggled to contain while at the Larsons' spilled over and tears dripped down her cheeks. Her life—her child's life—would be easier if she begged Alvin to take her back. The baby would have a father, she would keep her husband, and no one would look down upon them. But how would Alvin treat a child he didn't want? Would the child realize it? Would that really be better? Alvin's and her love for each other would fade every day they lived with such a huge difference of opinion between them, especially when she wanted more children.

A tap on the window startled Eleanor and she looked to up to see Mr. Geist, the mailman, standing there. "Is everything all right, Mrs. Pendley?" he asked through the window. "Can I help you with anything?"

She ignored the awful state her face must be in thanks to the tears and forced a big smile. "Oh, I'm just fine, Mr. Geist," she said in a loud enough voice for him to hear. She didn't want to roll down the window in this weather. "Thank you for asking. I was just . . ." She faltered and turned to glance at the house again. "I was heading over to my mother's."

Mr. Geist wrinkled his brow in confusion but nodded and stepped away from the car. She waved as she pulled away, her eyes darting back and forth between the road and the rearview mirror. But she wasn't looking back at Mr. Geist. A huge part of her heart said she should turn around and go home, even if Alvin didn't love her anymore. She loved him, and living without him shattered her heart one little piece at a time.

But she had the baby to think of now. She couldn't go back unless Alvin accepted them both. *Have faith*, Vera had said. Eleanor nodded her head resolutely to no one. "I'll have faith," she said aloud, but she didn't sound convincing at all.

☰ ★ ☰

Sam knocked on the door of Emily's apartment and then stepped back, his hands in his pockets, waiting for her to answer. Her roommate, Florence, answered the door.

"Oh, hello, Sam." Her surprise put Sam on guard. It was as he'd feared. Though he and Emily hadn't spoken in two days, he'd hoped he could spend their usual Friday night date mending the fences—again.

"Hello, Florence. Is Emily here?"

Before Florence could answer, Emily came to the door, her hair damp and hanging against her face. She hadn't expected him if she'd spent the evening so far washing her hair. "Yes, Sam?" she asked.

"I know we haven't spoken—"

"You haven't called me," she snapped, folding her arms and stepping back into the apartment.

"Yes, but I still hoped we might enjoy our usual date." He straightened his back. Truth was, he didn't much like the idea of spending another month or so playing nice about Emily's job to keep the peace. But if he could just get this girl to the altar, she'd see his side of things about staying home. If she tried it for a week or so, she might come to like it. He'd spent too many nights imagining coming home to his sweet girl to give up on it now.

"Then I suppose you haven't heard." If anything, her tone became more imperious.

Sam jammed his teeth together before he jumped the gun and said something awful, though a load of things he might not have heard swam around his brain—her throwing him over for John Mason came to mind.

"Haven't heard what?" He kept his tone even.

"That I've received a promotion to be a soil technician at the office. I don't expect you to be happy about that, though I wish you would."

Sam peered over her shoulder at Florence, who sat in their small kitchen, one ear turned toward the door. He took a deep breath, wishing they could have this conversation in private somewhere. He reached out and took Emily's hand, pulling her into the hallway.

"What are you doing? I'm going to catch a cold with my hair wet and the chill out here," Emily protested and disentangled her hand from his the moment she could. Sam ignored her and shut the door.

"So you've decided to push our wedding back further?" he said, accusation dripping from his voice.

"I've told you over and over that I don't see why that must be so in your eyes." She folded her arms tightly against her again and leaned back into the doorway. She pressed her lips together.

"You have a serious misunderstanding of the duties of a housewife if you think you can work at the soil office and keep up at home." He pointed a stern finger at her.

Emily harrumphed, pushing his finger aside, anger making two bright-red spots stand out on her cheeks. Her voice shook when she spoke. "I am not your mother, Sam Larson, and I don't ever plan to be. I don't relish the idea of making my own butter, and I intend to have an electric washing machine and drying cupboard so I don't have to spend every day washing your blasted socks. If you can't get that idea through your thick head, then we might as well call this wedding off." She ended her shrill speech with a shove at his chest before she turned and fled into her apartment.

He pounded on the door. He couldn't allow her to act so irrationally in a fit of anger at him. "Emily, you can't mean that."

She opened the door once more. Tears had gathered in her eyes, but that didn't stop her from snapping, "I mean it very much. We are through."

And she slammed the door in his face again.

⚌ CHAPTER NINETEEN ⚌

THE LAST FEW DAYS HAD been the longest of Alvin Pendley's life. He didn't care if Eleanor wanted a dozen babies and he couldn't provide her with a one of them. It was selfish, but he wanted his wife back. He couldn't allow people to talk about her the way they would if they divorced. He had to save her from that. But more than anything, he needed Eleanor. When he'd been away during the war, the ache to hold her, to sit beside her, to gaze into her eyes had been acute, but at least he'd known he would see her again. Believing that their marriage had ended was far worse. There had to be something he could do to make up for not being able to give her the family she'd dreamed of. He would promise her any option he could. Love meant sacrificing, but it also meant fighting for something and hoping for everything.

When he got off work that night, he took a long bath and shaved, splashing on some cologne. He stared into the mirror, practicing his speech a few times. Perhaps they could adopt children. Eleanor might be happy with that sort of family. He would explain everything. How the doctor said the bomb fragments had injured him and caused an infection that damaged the area too much. As if the injury hadn't been humiliating enough by itself, the pity in the doctor's expression when he told Alvin how unlikely it was that he would have children had crushed him.

After hearing the whole sad story, would Eleanor accept adoption? He sure hoped so.

The drive to the Holbrooks' took only a few minutes, of course, even on the slick, snow-packed roads. He marched up to the door and rang the bell resolutely, hoping Eleanor would answer.

Bless her heart, she did. "Alvin," she said, surprised and—dare he hope—pleased as well.

"Ellie, I can't stand it another day. I've come to bring you home." He stomped his feet, waiting for her to ask him inside.

Her face brightened and then fell. "Well, I can't see how I should come home when we're at this standstill over starting our family." Her bottom lip trembled, and that broke his heart all over again.

His hopes began to fall a bit at the sadness in her expression. "May I come in so we can discuss it?" he asked.

"Oh!" She jumped back and opened the door wider. "I'm so sorry, Alvin. I didn't mean to make you stand out there in the cold." She ushered him inside and led him into the warm living room, where both Mr. and Mrs. Holbrook sat. Mrs. Holbrook smiled to herself and then bent back over the quilt she'd been working on. Mr. Holbrook raised his newspaper, and Alvin thought he might have chuckled.

"Hello, son," he said a moment later, lowering the paper and revealing a barely sober expression. Alvin straightened when his father-in-law greeted him. At least they hadn't written him off after the poor way he'd treated their daughter.

"Hello, sir," he said, swallowing.

"Mother, Father, Alvin and I have something to discuss in private," Eleanor said.

Mrs. Holbrook set down her quilt. "Of course, dear. We'll go to the kitchen and get some cobbler ready. I'm sure you'd both like a piece when you're done." She stood up. "Come, Norman." Mr. Holbrook got up and followed, keeping his newspaper tucked beneath his arm and winking at Alvin as he walked out behind his wife.

Alvin took a breath. Mr. Holbrook's attitude buoyed him up. "Thank you," he said, though both of them had already disappeared down the hallway. "Let's sit down." He took Eleanor's hand, comforted by the warmth there and the relief that coursed through him to hold her this way. It reminded him of holding her for the first time when he got back from the war. He'd stood there at the train station, his arms wrapped around her, with no desire to move for anything. He could've stood there all night like that with her. So many nights during the war, he'd stared up at the top of a tent or a barracks or into the sky and wondered if it would be his last—wondered if he'd hold his wife again. That same desperation had plagued him the last two nights, and it nearly broke him.

Eleanor left her hand in his when they sat on the loveseat, and he drew courage from that to admit to her why they couldn't start a family. "I know why you left, dear," he said in a quiet voice.

She started then said in a trembling voice, "I thought I was obvious enough, though Vera doubted me."

His eyebrows furrowed. Vera doubted her? What could that mean? He would have to ask later. This conversation was difficult enough. "I'm sorry that I can't change this for us. I would do anything."

She yanked her hand back, and with it went most of Alvin's hope. "How can you say you would do anything?" she cried. "I realize things must have been hard on you in the war and all, but I don't understand, Alvin."

There she went with her lip trembling again and her eyes filling with tears. He reached for her hand again, gripping it firmly so she couldn't pull away. If she didn't understand how this couldn't be fixed, now was the time to be specific. "Please listen to me, El," he begged. "This is difficult to say."

She stopped struggling and this time she regarded him with confusion written into her expression. "What do you mean? You've been saying the same thing for weeks."

"Let me explain why," he said. "You see . . ." He cleared his throat. Difficult, not to mention embarrassing, to discuss this sort of thing with a woman, even his wife. "There was—I had an injury. And . . ." He took his hand away this time, leaning over his knees and covering his face. "And it's impossible for me—for us—to have kids now, El. I mean that there was too much damage, and the army doc said I couldn't. I'm sorry. So sorry. I know how badly you want to have a family, and I'd do anything to give you a hundred kids." The words came rushing out of him now—it was a relief to get them out, to have her know and to hope for comfort from her. "I tried to tell myself I could let you go so you could have what you want, but the truth is, I can't live without you. We could adopt—and that would be okay, wouldn't it, El?" he pleaded. "I would do anything to keep you with me."

Shock had been written on her face, but after a moment she blinked and started laughing.

Laughing!

Full-bellied, holding her stomach and falling back into the sofa. Alvin jumped to his feet, anger building in the pit of his stomach. He had opened his heart about one of the worst experiences of the war for him and she was laughing? He smashed his hat back onto his head.

"I see that I was wrong in my opinion of the situation," he snapped.

"Oh, Alvin . . . ," she said between gasps of laughter, reaching for him again. She struggled to her feet, tears now rolling down her cheeks, which confused Alvin further. "Wait, Alvin, please. I'm sorry, but I can't stop laughing—or crying!" Her shoulders shook more, and he didn't know what to do: stalk out on her or take her in his arms to comfort her.

"Alvin . . ." She took a deep breath and wiped her eyes. "I don't know why that doctor told you that you couldn't have children, but he was wrong. So very wrong."

He stared at her. "How can you know that . . ." But his words trailed off as she laid his hand over her stomach and stared at him. He felt as though someone had punched him in the gut. "Eleanor . . . ?"

"I thought you meant you didn't *want* kids," she whispered, gripping his hand on her stomach fiercely. Her laughter had drained away now. "I was so afraid you wouldn't want this one."

His own emotion surprised him. After months of believing he'd robbed Eleanor of her—their!—dreams. "I've never wanted anything so badly . . . I don't know how, sweetheart!" He wrapped his arms around her, lifting her off her feet as he hugged her and they laughed together. Alvin kissed her hard, all his joy spilling out of him. He couldn't keep from smiling. Him! A father!

"It's a miracle," he shouted. He threw his head back, laughing. Brought by the noise, no doubt, Mr. and Mrs. Holbrook came rushing into the room. "I'm going to be a father." Still holding Eleanor's hand, he ran to meet them, pumping Mr. Holbrook's hand.

"Yes, Alvin, we heard." Mrs. Holbrook laughed and threw her arms around both Eleanor and Alvin.

"Congratulations, son." Mr. Holbrook gripped his hand back.

Alvin turned to Eleanor, taken aback by the way her face glowed. He held her to him. "Why didn't you tell me?" he asked.

"Tell you? I thought I made it so obvious when I told you I wanted our children, and I held my stomach—how could you not see? And dear, why didn't *you* tell me? You played down your injury so much, as though you'd hardly been hurt. And, honestly, you made it sound as though not having children was your choice, not a matter of believing it impossible." Her voice had turned stern, and she placed one hand on her hip.

Alvin grinned, unbothered by her scolding, and smothered her with another kiss. Like the day at the train station, he could stand here and hold his wife forever, even with her parents looking on. It was the moment of a lifetime. A true miracle. He had thought the day she married him that she had made him a happy man. It was nothing to the joy of her making him a father—of making him a father against the odds.

"Shall we go home now, El?" He leaned back enough to gaze into her eyes.

"Yes. Let's do that. As soon as we've had some cobbler."

Alvin grinned—so wide he wasn't sure it would ever go away. "That's a great idea, my dear."

★

PART III
ISN'T IT ROMANTIC!

⚌ CHAPTER TWENTY ⚌

Bellemont, Wyoming—April 1947

FAY LARSON PARKED THE TRACTOR and sat back in the seat, removing her work gloves and glaring at her hands. She ran one finger along the palm of the other hand, angry at the calluses there. She used to have pretty, soft, nonfarming hands. Boys like Joey Gibson didn't want to hold hands with girls with calluses. They wanted to talk about how amazing it was that a few girls could keep a farm going for five years and how good old Fay was just like one of the boys.

She hopped down off the tractor. When she was younger, getting to drive the tractor was a treat. She had looked forward to the excitement and responsibility. Being one of the younger ones of the Larson brood, she hadn't gotten a lot of opportunities. The war had sure made up for that.

A car driving down the road toward the field caught her attention as she started back toward the farmhouse, especially when it pulled off to the side of the road in front of the field and a man got out. She paused and moved toward him as he ducked back into the car and retrieved a clipboard. He wore nice slacks and a shirt and tie, attire that stood out on the farm, even if he had loosened his tie at some point during his day, undone the top button of his shirt, and rolled up his sleeves. His hat sat askew on his head, giving him a roguish look that made her heart skip a beat or two. My, he was handsome, too. Tall, slender, and vaguely familiar, though she couldn't place him.

"Hello," she called, walking faster.

"Good afternoon . . . Miss Larson, right?" He lifted his hat at her. "How do you do?"

"Fine," she said, confused at why he was parked near their field with his official-looking clipboard. "May I help you, sir?"

"Oliver Burns," he introduced himself and smiled. He had the slightest dimple just above the right corner of his lip. Fay had a weakness for dimples.

"I spoke with Mr. Larson—Sam, I mean—about coming out to do a soil survey."

For a long time, Fay had anticipated Sam and Andrew coming back to take over—but they might have at least mentioned something to her. She stamped down the resentment that bubbled up. She still worked with them a lot more than she liked. She would until they sold more crops this fall, but they were the ones in charge now. As she had dreamed about since they went to fight the war. The last few years, she, Mom, and Vera had only planted enough to feed them and some hay for extra cash, leaving the other fields fallow. Now that they'd planned to plant more fields, the profit they'd earn from the extra crops would help to hire a new hand for next year. Then she could wash her hands of this farming business.

"I see," she said, nodding and hoping she looked knowledgeable. "Is there anything you need?" Fay didn't know a thing about soil surveys, though Sam and Andrew had talked about taking advantage of some of the programs the Soil Conservation Service had to help them get going again.

Mr. Burns started to smile—as though he might have seen through her attempts—and then stopped. "No, I don't think so."

"All right." Fay nodded at him again, something wiggling around in her stomach at the kind way Mr. Burns had watched out for her feelings. Joey Gibson had never said anything to make her stomach flutter in an exciting way. He didn't have a dimple, either.

"Good day, then." She stretched out to shake his hand, more conscious than ever of how rough they were.

Mr. Burns gripped hers, no disgust in his expression about how manly her hands must feel—but maybe, like Joey, he thought of her as one of the boys. Disappointment twisted in her chest, but Mr. Burns's grin deepened and she thought maybe he held her hand longer than he needed before letting go.

"Good day, Miss Larson."

Oh, but didn't that sound charming to be called Miss Larson. A smile fluttered across her lips as she turned away and headed back toward the house. She rubbed her hands on the front of her stiff pants as if she could rub the calluses right off.

≡ ★ ≡

Vera took a long, deep breath of the country air and then scrunched her nose in disgust and giggled. Too much cow smell and not enough new spring smell.

"What is it?" Dominick asked from beside her. He used the hand he held hers with to gently pull her closer to him as they walked down the road between the Larson farmhouse and town.

"Cows," she said and took another deep breath. "Ruining my spring walk."

He chuckled, and she enjoyed the peace and contentment brought by an easy, relaxed sound like that coming from him. She had sensed a change in him the last few months as they saw more and more of each other, and joy and accomplishment filled her that she could take care of him that way. They walked on in companionable silence. Dominick never needed to fill quiet moments with conversation, and with him, Vera was learning the comfort of simple togetherness too. Instead of forcing him to talk, she reveled in walking by his side, the pleasure of her hand in his, and the delight in seeing blossoms on the willow trees and shoots of green in the fields around them. The day had been warmer than usual for this time of year, though with the sun setting, a slight chill slipped into the air around them.

"Do you know what I like about spring in Wyoming?" she asked.

"Hmm?"

Vera grinned at Dominick's lack of words. "It comes after a long winter, so we welcome it as soon as it comes. We're so eager for it."

"It's a renewal of your spirit," he said quietly and smiled.

"Mmm-hmm." She didn't need to add any words to his description.

After another few minutes in silence, it surprised Vera that Dominick broke the quiet. "How does Audrey like her new responsibilities in the chicken coop?" he asked.

Her heart warmed that he'd remembered her mentioning that during one of their phone conversations the week before. His belief that he wouldn't be a good father for her children often held him back in their relationship, but she knew otherwise. He showed interest and concern for them often.

"She hasn't begun complaining yet," Vera said, leaning into him as they walked. They had nearly reached town and would need to turn around soon. "Jack Junior and Peter are good about helping her, and she feels so grown-up having a chore like everyone else."

"With so many helpers on that farm, it's a wonder Fay needs to do any work at all." Dominick winked at her and Vera laughed.

"Everyone but me—and possibly Mom—thinks Jack Junior is ready to drive the tractor for her." Vera chewed on her lip. "He's so young, but he's about the same age Sam was when Dad let him." She sighed.

"He's probably even more mature than Sam was," Dominick mulled. It reassured her to hear of his trust in Jack Junior. She might give in to Jack Junior's pleadings, but she couldn't help wanting to keep him her little boy for a few years longer. He'd already had to grow up so much.

She laughed. "He's likely more mature than Sam is now." Dominick laughed with her. They paused as they reached the intersection the road from the Larson farm made with the main highway, standing together and looking toward town before they both turned to make the walk back to the farmhouse, their pace slower than before, neither of them eager to end their evening walk together.

The sun dipped behind the mountains and the cool air became more pronounced. Vera pulled her sweater tighter with one hand and made sure to stay close to Dominick for warmth.

"You're cold. Should we hurry?" he asked, letting go of her hand to encircle his arm about her waist and hold her next to him.

"Not at all." She tilted her head back against his arm to stare at him.

"At least take my jacket, darling."

No matter how many times he called her "darling," she would never tire of it. Warmth enveloped her long before he draped his jacket over her shoulders. She sighed with contentment. Dominick answered by placing a kiss on her temple that conveyed his agreement far better than any words. She loved that about him—his ability to express his affection for her without speaking at all.

As the farmhouse came into view, she found herself hoping, and not for the first time, that her time with him wouldn't be fleeting. She had grown to love this man and hoped with every bit of her soul that he loved her as much.

⹀ ★ ⹀

Fay sat in a booth at the diner, her chin in her hands, not paying any attention to the people around her. She and her friends had all sort of tried to pick up where they'd left off after the war, before all their lives had changed. Before the boys had shipped off for far-off places and seen dreadful things. Before the girls had made the best of life in Bellemont. Before Fay had put her heart and soul into running the family farm and keeping herself, Mom, Vera, and the kids alive.

"Want something to drink, Fay?" Joey asked, leaning over from the booth behind them.

"No, thanks." What was the use in sharing a soda with a fellow who could only go on and on about how neat it was that she could drive a tractor? None. She could take all that hard work and toss it. She wanted hats and pretty dresses and lacy handkerchiefs again. She wanted back the years she had lost to the war. The fun she had missed out on. But in the eyes of men like Joey or any other fellow in town, she had changed and she couldn't go back.

"You sure?" He tipped an eyebrow at her.

She waved him off. Someday Joey would take over his father's farm west of town. Fay didn't intend to be a farmer's wife. She loved her family, sure thing, but once the boys could handle things without her, she intended to go to college or something. Find a fellow who could keep her *off* a farm.

"Okay." Joey frowned, disappointment showing in his expression before he turned to Annie Miller.

"Well, hello there, Miss Larson."

The familiar voice made Fay's head snap up to meet the handsome, dimpled gaze of Mr. Burns. She wished the heat didn't rise to her face so quickly. My, he had such a nice smile. Straight white teeth and nice lips.

"Hello, Mr. Burns," she said. She stood and stepped away from the table to greet him. "How nice to see you." She didn't know a lot about the man who ran the office Emily had thrown Sam over for, but he didn't seem so bad. Of course, Sam only had horrible things to say about Mr. Mason, whom they'd seen out with Emily a time or two since she and Sam had broken off their engagement.

Mr. Burns wasn't a farmer though, which counted for something with her. She continued the conversation. "How did your survey go?" she asked. Anything that could help the farm was fine with Fay. Any extra money to get her out of grubby trousers and off that darn tractor. Especially if that someone to help was as handsome as Mr. Burns.

"Pretty well." He gestured toward the table. "Have you got anything to drink?" he asked.

"I just arrived a few moments ago." Her heart lifted with excitement that *he* might ask to buy her something.

"May I buy you a soda, Miss Larson?" His smile spread and that dimple deepened. Gosh, what a handsome face he had.

Half of her wanted to correct him and let him call her Fay, but another part of her liked the sweet way he called her Miss. Not just Fay. Not one of the boys. Miss Larson. It rolled of his tongue awfully well, too. "How kind of you. Yes, please."

"I came here for one of those delicious chocolate malts. What would you like?" He ran his fingers around the brim of his hat in his hands

"Oh, a Coke would be fine."

Mr. Burns scanned the group she'd come with. Casting a glance over her shoulder, Fay noticed Annie and a couple of the other girls trying not to watch them. "It's a little crowded over here, isn't it?" Mr. Burns said. "Shall we sit at that table?" He nodded across the diner to an empty booth. He didn't wait for Fay to nod before he laid a hand lightly on her back and guided the way. Warmth and tingles ran up her spine.

He waited until she'd scooted into one side of the booth before heading to the counter to order their drinks. When he came back, he placed his hat on the far side of the table and took his seat across from her.

"I suppose you have probably had enough talk about farming lately, haven't you?" he asked.

She started. "How would you know something like that?"

He chuckled. "Oh, your brother Sam mentioned you were eager for him and Andrew to take things over."

Foolishness at her reaction dampened the tingles that had started earlier. "That's the truth. And don't tell me it's quite an accomplishment what us girls did, keeping things going out at the farm. I'm well aware of that." She forced a laugh when she realized she'd let her mouth get away from her, and in front of Mr. Burns, no less.

"All right." He chuckled again. "Though I think exactly that, I'll refrain from praising you about it. Shall I critique your farming techniques instead? Would that make you feel better?"

"Oh, no! You'd better not. Anyone will tell you I'm the most hotheaded Larson there is." She flashed one of those flirty smiles Vera used with Dominick, and Mr. Burns grinned back.

Alice brought their drinks, and Mr. Burns poked about in his with the straw for a moment. "I have heard about your temper," he said.

Probably from Emily, Fay guessed. She'd had a thing or two to say to her brother's former fiancée when she found out Emily had gone to the show with Mr. Mason. Fay swirled her own straw and avoided looking up at Mr. Burns. She wondered what Emily had said about her.

"I hope nothing too bad." Fay forced another laugh and took a drink of her soda.

"Don't worry. It wasn't." He watched her as he leaned over to drink from his malt.

Fay needed to turn the subject of the conversation away from herself. "How is the Soil Conservation Service, Mr. Burns? I'll bet you're doing all sorts of good work with it here in Bellemont."

Again she had the idea that he knew what she was doing and again he didn't laugh at her. "We are very busy. Bellemont is a good place for a man who wants to revolutionize farming."

"Revolutionize?" Fay leaned forward, intrigued.

"Change the way people think. The world is different now, and so is farming and what we need it for." His demeanor lit up as he spoke, drawing Fay closer.

"How interesting," she said in a breathless sort of voice, which felt funny when one was talking about farming. But Mr. Burns made it sound as exciting as the idea of college and dances, and not a yawner like tilling fields or picking beans. "And how do you plan on revolutionizing farming?" she asked.

Mr. Burns hesitated. "People here aren't so keen on the idea of the government getting involved in their affairs, even if it would mean a higher yield." He avoided her gaze and went back to drinking his malt for a moment.

"When the day comes that we turn it all over to machines—that'll be the day I celebrate," Fay said, hoping to lure out his ideas.

His smile—and that darn dimple—returned. "I suppose all that work you did that I'm not supposed to commend you on hasn't made you more proud of the farm, then? Just eager to be rid of it?"

"I suppose I'm not as bad as all that. It would have broken my brothers' hearts—at least Sam's, not to mention Dad's—if they'd lost it, the way so many people did back before the war and all. But come now, tell me all about your plans for upending Bellemont."

Though his amused expression remained, he clenched his malt glass a bit harder than he had been. "Farming is no longer a nostalgic way of life—the hardy pioneer, surviving off the land. It's a business, and if folks around here want to keep their farms, they need to start thinking of it that way. A business for profit, not one that just makes ends meet."

With every word, the pace of Fay's nod picked up. She couldn't have said it better herself. She was tired of working until past dark and getting up at dawn, simply to break even! To put food on the table for the winter and to sell a few gallons of milk or some hay or some of Mom's homemade jams and such for some extra money here and there.

"Oh, exactly, Mr. Burns. And you can help us do that?" She could kiss him if he said yes. Honestly, she could kiss him whatever he said next.

"I hope so, Miss Larson." He drained the last of his malt, and though caution sat heavy in his expression, her heart lifted at the thought of wearing lacy gloves again and not getting them caught on her stupid farm hands. Of taking an afternoon—think of it! Smack in the middle of the day!—stroll with Mr. Burns and wearing a darling hat and one of those lacy, fluffy Parisienne-style dresses that seemed to be on every page of the magazines.

"I sure hope so too." She sighed.

≡ CHAPTER TWENTY-ONE ≡

VERA LEANED AGAINST THE KITCHEN doorway, watching Jack Junior and Peter chop vegetables with their grandmother. "You're sure, Mom?" she asked. "I shouldn't leave so much—"

Kathryn laughed her off, still keeping an eye on the boys beside her. "Stop that. Nobody wants to be around you tonight if you have to cancel your date with Dominick. Go on. We'll be fine."

Vera had to laugh. "I'm not that bad," she said.

"You two don't go out nearly as often as you should anyway. When Jack was courting you, I could hardly keep you home long enough to do a chore or two. Now you're lucky to get in a night a week—you ought to take that. And no more of this 'are you sure' business. You afraid I can't feed some children and put them to bed every once in a while? I raised five of my own, didn't I? And never—" Kathryn bit her lip, cutting off the last of one of her old favorite sayings. *And never killed a one.*

Vera hurried across the kitchen to hug her mother. "Oh, of course I trust you, Mom," she said in a rush. "I feel guilty is all, with Fay out tonight too."

"Between your father, Sam, and I, we ought to be able to handle things." Kathryn winked then dabbed at her eyes with the corner of her apron. "Now go get your coat. Dominick will be here any minute, and you don't want Sam catching him again."

That put a bee in Vera's bonnet. She left a kiss on her mother's cheek—and took a moment to inhale that powdery gardenia scent lingering on her— before hurrying up the stairs. Since that first night Dominick had kissed her last December, she hadn't let Sam "catch" him at all. His horrible mood had sort of leveled out after a while, but one never knew if hearing that Emily had gone on another date with Mr. Mason would set him off again.

Sam stood at the bottom of the stairs when she got there, frowning at her. She buttoned up her light jacket and walked past him, pinning her hat in place. "Now Sam, I don't need a lecture from you tonight, thank you very much. With four kids of my own now, I'm well able to take care of myself."

"It's those kids I'm thinking of, Vee." He followed her into the living room. "I wrote a fellow who could tell us more than Andrew knows about Dominick."

"You ought to stick with Mr. Whitaker. I'm not sure you two are on friendly enough terms for first names yet," she said dryly, watching through the front windows for any sign of Dominick.

"Vee, you know he's a dangerous man. You've said yourself that he won't talk about the war at all. And Phil said so too. Now I don't blame a guy for having to get his hands dirty—we all had to a time or two—but Phil says there was some talk of Dominick getting a couple of kids killed." Sam reached and took hold of Vera's shoulders, turning her to face him.

She stepped out of his grip. "That's enough, Sam. I've told you before that I don't want to hear about what your friends who knew someone who knew someone in OSS have to say about Dominick. I can make up my mind for myself." Headlights flashed in the window, and Vera hurried away and out the door, trying to push Sam's words out. Whatever had happened to Dominick during the war, he didn't want to talk about it. And she could understand if he, or anyone else, thought he'd been responsible for innocent people dying. She shook it away. A lot of men had been responsible for things like that. Jack had lamented to her in his letters more than once about coming upon bombed-out villages full of the bodies of civilians.

Dominick met her in the yard. "Sam in one of his moods again?" he asked with a quirked eyebrow.

Vera waved him off and threw on a smile. "Another letter full of rumors."

Dominick's expression darkened, and he put his hands in his pockets instead of reaching for her hand. "And how do you know they're rumors?" he asked, slowing his step beside hers as they made their way back to his car.

She stopped and turned to face him, looping her arms around his waist. "Until you're ready to tell me otherwise, I choose not to judge you by what others say about you."

"I'm not a good man, Vee. I've done things—"

"Shhh." She reached up to cover his mouth with her finger. "Don't start on that again tonight. Not when I haven't seen you for a full week. You'll have to save this for a time when we are fortunate to have back-to-back nights out, which won't be until the summer, you know."

He didn't laugh at her, though she hadn't exactly expected him to if he'd decided to head down this moody path. "Darling, be serious. If you knew about . . . if you knew the truth, you'd never want to see me again."

"If you would tell me, then I could decide that for myself, Dominick," she said in her stern voice, the one usually reserved for her sons.

His expression softened, and he pulled his hands from his pockets to wrap his arms around her back and pull her closer. "I'm too afraid you might actually not want to see me again, and I can't help putting it off."

She melted against him, her heart humming as he kissed her. "But you will someday," she said softly.

"I suppose so." He ended the conversation by holding her tighter and kissing her more, which she never opposed. Dominick Whitaker was a good, gentle man. Whatever people said about the things he'd done, she didn't care. He was a hero like her brothers. Like Jack had been.

And though it was silly, she loved him all the more for hoping to keep her innocent a while longer.

= ★ =

Fay turned down the corner of her magazine, marking the spot of the black Dior evening dress and hummed to herself. Maybe someday—someday soon even!— she'd have use for a dress like this. She'd have to make it herself, of course. Even if she got some lovely job in a city somewhere, she'd never be able to afford a Dior. But it was so feminine. Exactly what Fay could wish for: a deep V-neck, a formfitting waistline, and a skirt that belled out in such a pretty way. Why, the simple black pumps made Fay green with envy over the whole ensemble.

She could picture herself on the arm of some handsome gentleman in a tux at a fancy party. She smiled as she imagined it could be Oliver Burns. He didn't fit with her big-city plans, of course, but a girl could dream any way she wanted to. Maybe going with a businessman—even a farming businessman— would lead to sophisticated things like dinner parties or plays. The women's club in town had once put on a play.

The phone rang, and since Fay was the only one nearby, she hopped up to answer it, expecting it to be Dominick for Vera. "Hello?" Fay kept half her attention on the next page of her magazine.

"Hello." The cheerful voice was familiar, but it wasn't Dominick's. "This is Oliver Burns. I'm calling to speak with Miss Larson—Fay, that is."

"Oh!" Fay giggled a bit to herself. "This is she. And I do happen to be the only Miss Larson in residence." She couldn't help but tease him.

"That's right." He chuckled. "I've called to ask if you would like to have dinner with me."

Fay fingered the picture of the Dior dress. If only she had it right this minute, although it was too fancy for Alice's. Fay didn't care. "I'd love to, Mr. Burns."

"Would six o'clock be too early?"

"Six o'clock would be perfect." Fay grinned. "I'll be ready."

They said their goodbyes, and Fay rushed up the stairs to prepare. Why, she only had a few hours, and she had to get curlers in her hair right away.

≡ ★ ≡

Fay stood impatiently at the top of the stairs, wondering if it was six o'clock yet. She had been ready for a full twenty minutes, dressed in her favorite dress and her hair in soft waves she figured Ingrid Bergman would be jealous of. She held her hands out to admire her gloves. She felt sophisticated indeed. She had overdressed for the diner, but she didn't care. For one night, she would live her dreams, even if that meant standing out among all the kids who'd be hanging out at the diner this time of night.

The doorbell rang, and Fay leaned over to peek at Vera jumping up from her spot on the couch to answer. Fay grinned to think of their old dating protocol reversed. One sister waiting at the top of the stairs and the other set to answer the door. They had both decided long ago that descending the stairs—as rickety as the farmhouse stairs were—was the most romantic way to begin a date.

"Come in, Mr. Burns," Vera said as she opened the door. That was Fay's cue to start down. She took the stairs carefully in the blue pumps she'd borrowed from Vera. She'd bought them in California, and they were the fanciest thing either of them had ever owned.

"Good evening, Miss Larson." Mr. Burns stood just inside the door, his hat in his hand and looking so striking in his black double-breasted suit. Would it be forward if she mentioned he was making all her dreams come true?

"Good evening, Mr. Burns." She quickened her step across the floor, eager to get to him. He held out a hand in greeting, and she reached out to take it, butterflies swinging into action in her stomach at his touch. "Shall we?"

He nodded, turning to open the door and keeping her hand in his before he tucked it under his arm to escort her out to his car. He drove a plain, old Ford sedan, but Fay hadn't expected anything very fancy in Bellemont, Wyoming. He opened the door for her and held her hand while she got in, like gentlemen did in the movies. Good gracious, her knees were wobbly by the time she settled herself inside.

Mr. Burns rounded the car from behind and then got in on the driver's side, starting the car up right away and rolling out of the driveway. He glanced at her as he pulled onto the dirt road that led from the farmhouse into town, giving her a nervous smile.

"How was your day today?" he asked after a few moments had passed in silence—not a bad kind, but sort of anxious for Fay. She wanted this date to go well. Mr. Burns talked so sweet, bought her sodas like a gentleman, and believed her the lady she kept wishing to be. She shouldn't count all her eggs yet and plan too far into the future, but he seemed like the sort of fellow who could give her the life she had dreamed about. A small, nice house, a husband coming home at a reasonable hour every day (winter *or* summer), and someone who didn't mind socializing a bit here and there.

"Oh," she said softly when she realized that Mr. Burns's expression had turned more anxious than her own at all the moments she'd sat in silence, woolgathering. "It was fine."

"Not too much farmwork for you then?" He winked at her.

She had to chuckle. Sam and Andrew had needed her to help plant one of the fields, and she'd spent all morning on a tractor pulling a grain driller. She'd forgotten all about it in the wake of Mr. Burns asking her out. That was something!

"I did some planting today, but I suppose it wasn't too bad." She refrained from mentioning that his invitation had made her day better. "How was your day?"

He gave her a half-smile. "Are you sure you want to know? It would be more talk about farming."

"I don't hate it *that* much. At least not talking about it. It's the doing that gets me." She rubbed her thumb against some calluses on her palm. Hopefully Mr. Burns wouldn't notice them beneath her gloves.

"I convinced a few folks to let the SCS help them out, so that's a few more families who'll be successful this year, and a few more families with a little extra spending money. I call that a good day's work."

His proud smile made those butterflies in her stomach flap around some more, and she nearly sighed at how handsome he was.

"You must like your job a great deal," she said.

"I do. Even when things are frustrating. It's satisfying to help people, especially farmers. They've been the backbone of this country for a long time, and I'd hate for us to forget too many of them because machines are taking over or big corporations are buying so many small farms and combining them."

She sighed, pleased with his energy. "It would sure be nice to have a job I cared about that much."

"What kind of job would you care about that much?" he asked, studying her before he looked both ways and pulled onto the main highway that went through town. They passed the diner, and Fay watched it go by with confusion. Where else would Mr. Burns take her for dinner?

"Oh, anything but farming, of course," she said in a distracted way as she considered the options.

Mr. Burns surprised her by pulling up in front of The Twilight Café, an upscale restaurant inside Bellemont's fanciest hotel. She drew in a breath of surprise. What a dream come true! The Twilight even had dancing. Once Mr. Burns got out to come around and get her door, she let out a quiet squeal of delight. Oh, what would Vera say to this? Dominick had taken her to The Twilight to dance one night, but they hadn't had dinner. Vera had said the prices were astonishing and she wouldn't let Dominick pay for something like that.

Fay would certainly let Mr. Burns buy her dinner here. None of the fellows she'd gone out with before had ever thought of taking a girl to The Twilight Café. Mr. Burns opened her door and held a hand out for her as the valet came out from the entrance.

"Good evening, Mr. Burns," the valet said, taking the keys, and Fay's heart leapt in pleasure. It should bother her more that this wasn't an extra-special occasion to Mr. Burns, to take Fay out on a date, but the idea that he frequented such a place nearly had *her* proposing to *him*. And on the first date!

She held on to his arm as they stepped inside, and a coat check girl—a girl a few years younger than Fay in school—took their things and then led them inside the restaurant. The tables were in a big circle around the edge, and a small band played "Isn't It Romantic?" with a few couples swaying to the gentle, lilting rhythm. She hummed under her breath.

"Would you like to dance?" Mr. Burns asked.

"Oh, yes." It was all Fay could do not to sigh again. Soon she was foxtrotting with him, swirling around the floor with his arm around her waist and his gorgeous dimple beaming down at her. "I haven't danced in so long," she admitted.

"Neither have I," Mr. Burns said.

She raised an eyebrow at him. "The valet seemed to know you rather well."

He offered her a mockingly serious smile. "Miss Larson, the steak here is better than at any place I've been."

"You come here for the steak?" She had to giggle at that.

"The music isn't so bad."

Did she imagine that he inched her a bit closer? "It's wonderful," she said. Not just the music either—she, Fay Larson, was dancing at The Twilight Café with the handsomest man in town, her hand gripped by his, her forehead inches away from resting comfortably on his shoulder.

The song drew to a close. She clapped with Mr. Burns, and he turned to her. "Would you like to dance some more or eat?" She chewed on her bottom lip. Some of the entrées coming from the kitchen looked and smelled divine, and that was saying something for Fay. Her mother was the best cook around.

Mr. Burns had held on to her hand, probably in anticipation of leading her away or maybe dancing some more, but he hadn't let go and tingles danced over her skin. She had the urge to ditch her gloves, and she had never before wished for a man to notice her calluses. But she'd like to tangle her fingers through his and revel in the warmth of his touch.

"Once we eat, we can dance all night if you wish," he said, his expression full of amusement at her silly, wide-eyed wonder.

"All night?" she teased.

He threaded her hand through his arm as he led the way to their table, keeping his other hand on top of it. He tilted his head down to speak to her so that his breath ruffled some of her hair and his lips nearly brushed her temple.

"If you wish."

The band had begun to play "Cheek to Cheek", and she found herself singing quietly along, "I'm in heaven," to herself, but a soft chuckle from Mr. Burns said he'd heard as well. She smiled and continued humming along, despite her audience, and swaying as they walked. "I'm in heaven," she repeated, not caring if Mr. Burns knew how he'd lifted her and made her forget about all that pesky farm stuff.

≡ ★ ≡

Oliver half-stood out of his chair, peering through his open door when the front door to the office opened. Then he caught himself and sat down. It wasn't likely Fay Larson would accompany her brothers to their meeting this morning. He shouldn't allow one date to put him on pins and needles. But though he knew from her own account and from his conversations with her brother Sam that she wanted to wash her hands of their family farm as soon as she could, they had spent a wonderful evening together a few nights back. He hoped she'd enjoyed the few hours they'd spent dancing as much as he had, and that she anticipated seeing him as well.

Voices rose in the front office, and more than curiosity about Fay made Oliver rise out of his chair again. Though Emily had been promoted, she still sat at the front desk and filled many of the other duties she'd had before, including greeting visitors to the office.

As he suspected, Sam and Andrew Larson had entered. He was pleased to see that Fay *had* accompanied them. The voices sounded cool but polite.

Through his open office door, he watched Emily approach his office, tap on the door, and then step aside for the siblings to enter. He circled his desk to shake their hands, noting the stiff way Sam greeted him. He hoped that had more to do with encountering Emily than any possible resentment toward the Soil Conservation Service. When he came to Fay, Oliver held on to her hand a moment longer than he had her brothers'.

"It's good to see you—" He had to cut himself off from calling her Fay. Though he'd thought of her in friendly terms in his head, she seemed to enjoy when he called her Miss. She would beam and those bright-brown eyes would shine with pleasure. "Miss Larson." He nodded at the men, noting their smiles and forcing back embarrassment. He was a grown man interested in a woman. No need to be ashamed of that.

"Please, take a seat," he said, holding one of the chairs for Fay. "I'll go out and get another. I hadn't realized Miss Larson would be coming."

The men chuckled and Fay scowled at them. "Well, we ran that farm pretty well without you, so I don't know what you find so funny about me taking an interest in Mr. Burns's plans to help us." Her cheeks turned a rosy shade, which of course Oliver found quite charming. He hoped she took a lot more interest—and not just in farm business. Perhaps he'd ask her out again after their meeting. He hoped for another evening in her company. In fact, he'd been invited to a dinner party that weekend. He bet Fay would get a kick out of doing something like that. She'd seemed on cloud nine the night he'd taken her to The Twilight Café. She had told him of her plans of going to a bigger city and getting a job or perhaps going to college, and she'd filled the conversation with how her time would be packed with more social activities than Bellemont typically had to offer. Being stuck on a farm while the boys had seen far-off places had made her all the more set to fly the coop.

Her brothers hid their smiles and nodded, neither one mentioning what Oliver guessed they were thinking about Fay's "interest" in plans for the farm. Oliver left the office to fetch another chair, a contented smile on his face. He couldn't wait to tell her the ideas he had that would help her take a less-active part in running the farm.

"You don't mind if I borrow this?" he asked Emily, reaching for one of the chairs in front of her desk.

"Not at all." Emily struck the keys of her typewriter with definite annoyance. More than once since scheduling this meeting he'd worried about the possibility of fireworks when he put Sam and Emily under the same roof. He trusted that Emily could behave as a professional. He wouldn't have recommended to the state office that they promote her if he didn't.

"Would you like to look in?" Oliver teased. Emily *had* requested to sit in on many of these meetings to get a feel for them.

She raised her gaze long enough to tilt a skeptical eyebrow at him before resuming her typing. Oliver chuckled softly and scooted the chair into the office.

"Thank you," Sam said, taking it from Oliver and setting it behind Fay and Andrew. "What have you got for us?" he asked.

Oliver took his own seat back behind his desk and gathered up some papers. "Well, we should start with your west hay fields. Our surveys classify them as highly erodible."

Fay leaned forward in her chair, her expression full of the same doe-eyed interest she'd shown at the diner. "Highly erodible. What does that mean?"

"It means that planting constantly, in combination with the wind, has already removed much of the soil, and continuing to plant on those fields will exacerbate the condition."

Fay's face registered confusion at his assessment. Sam spoke up. "It sounds as though you want us to quit planting those fields, Mr. Burns."

Out of the corner of his eye, Oliver noticed Fay tensing and sitting back. It hadn't taken much time to gather that Fay had stored up more than her share of bitterness where the farm was concerned. He'd have to tread carefully so that she and her brothers understood that what he proposed was best for the farm in the long run—even if he wanted nothing more than to help Fay step off the tractor and turn things over to the men in her family.

"Well, yes. But of course we have programs that will reimburse you for letting the fields lay fallow. The important thing to remember is that we are looking out for the future of the farm. And of course, you will have many options—"

"We've heard enough." Fay stood up, shoving her hands back into her gloves. "*Not* planting fields is of no help to us, Mr. Burns." She spat his name out in a way that caused Oliver's stomach to plummet.

"Fay, hold on a minute," Andrew said, standing and holding out a hand to her. "Let Mr. Burns finish."

She shook her head impatiently. "I believe this is the part where Mr. Burns convinces us that farming is a business, and that we must start thinking that way if we want our farm to succeed, though he thinks differently of business than I do. I suppose if he were to advise Mr. Curtis on his grocery store, he might tell him to close off the dairy aisle to avoid competition with the area farms." She huffed and glared at her brothers, who had both now risen.

"Really, Fay," a voice said from the doorway, surprising everyone in the room when Emily appeared there. "You might as well listen. Mr. Burns has some good ideas for improving things for your family."

Now Sam had stiffened as well. Oliver shared a glance with Andrew, noticing exasperation crossing his expression.

"Perhaps Fay is right," Sam said, his jaw working as he surveyed Emily with hostility. "Mr. Burns approached us with promises of government programs that would help us get the farm back on its feet. I'm not sure how continuing to leave a once-prospering field fallow will help anything. He must have misunderstood our situation. Let's go, Andrew." He strode from the room.

Oliver pressed his lips together as he watched Fay march out after Sam.

"Andrew," Mr. Burns held out his hand to try and explain to someone, and the younger brother seemed his best bet. "You're risking losing those fields forever if you don't do something to stop the soil erosion."

Andrew sighed to himself and nodded. "I see what you're saying, Mr. Burns. Perhaps in a year or so, we'll be in a position to do something about it. To get back on our feet, perhaps we need to take the risk . . ." He let his sentence trail off before he followed the others out.

Oliver muttered his exasperation at the situation under his breath. It wasn't the first time a farmer had ignored his advice. He shouldn't take the situation with the Larsons so personally. That thought didn't help him, and neither did wondering why Emily had interrupted. He'd only been teasing when he'd asked her about sitting in on the meeting with the Larsons. She was the last person he would ask in the room when approaching Sam about shutting down a field. He knew from experience the folks around here hesitated a great deal when it came to leaving much-needed fields empty.

"There's compensation, Sam," Emily said as the others traipsed through the office. "Don't be stubborn."

The red in Sam's face made it obvious that his former fiancée had said the wrong thing. "We may not be as rich as some people in town, Miss Holman, but we have not gone so far as having to accept government charity." He tipped his hat roughly and left. Fay gave a tight nod of her own before following.

Oliver slumped back onto his desk chair. Fay had been so excited about his ideas before, but he should have seen this coming. If the farm succeeded and made a big enough profit to hire another hand, she could tell hard farmwork good riddance. But they hadn't stayed long enough for him to explain some of the options. He ran a hand over his chin and stared at the papers in front of him before glancing out at Emily. She had resumed her seat at the desk, her typing more furious than ever. She dared a look in his direction, but he didn't trust himself right now. She of all people should have known better than to present things to Sam the way she did. Oliver barely knew the man and he still recognized the pride that drove him, like it did too many of the men of Bellemont. He got up and shut his office door before going back to his desk again. He had to come up with a way to help the Larsons and still get across the importance of leaving those fields be and letting them recover.

The question was, did he want a solution for the betterment of the land? Or did he want it to please Fay Larson?

⹀ CHAPTER TWENTY-TWO ⹀

FAY ARCED THE AX HIGH and brought it down hard on the log, accomplishment spreading through her as sure as the large crack split through the log. She shoved the two pieces aside and set up another piece on the stump they used to split. They wouldn't need firewood for a while, now that spring was in full swing and summer on its way—of course, in Wyoming, you never knew. An April shower could turn just as easily into an April blizzard. But wood always needed to be split and set aside to dry for the following winter. Splitting wood helped Fay express her frustration. It was the one farm chore she didn't mind that much, even when it left her shoulders sore and her hands raw.

She swung again, picturing Oliver's enthusiastic expression as he explained all that nonsense about farming for profit. He'd been so eager, talking on and on about how to help people. How to revolutionize farming and make it all profitable again. She'd leaned across that table and lapped it all up, letting his words spark hope and excitement inside her. Why, if they followed his bright ideas, she'd be working on this farm until she turned eighty.

Crack! Another log splintered in two and fell to the sides. Wiping some sweat away from her forehead, she lifted another log onto the stump, but instead of swinging right away, she leaned against the ax, catching her breath.

Oh, she hated Oliver Burns and his silly dimple. And the fact that tears stung in her eyes. They'd had such a wonderful evening. She'd really thought things could *go* somewhere. But he didn't understand her or her family at all.

"Hey, Fay!" Sam's voice called, and she looked up to see him jogging into the yard from the barn. He paused, frowning when he saw the pile of wood she'd split. "Thought Vee wanted the boys to do that after school."

Fay glared at him. Sam held his hands up in surrender and backed away a step or two. "Well, maybe you can make it up to her by taking the boys to go deliver milk," he said.

Fay sighed and laid down the ax. "Sure." She might as well get used to all this rotten stuff. At the rate they were going, she'd be farming all her life. Forget about having any fun or moving to a city or dancing all night at The Twilight Café. She pulled off her work gloves and headed for the truck to load up the milk they often sold to some of their neighbors. When Jack Junior and Peter came, delivering milk wasn't so bad. All she had to do was drive up and down the road. They got in and out of the truck and took the milk to the doors.

By the time she had the jugs loaded, Jack Junior and Peter were home from school. She hollered at them to get changed into their work clothes as they tumbled off the bus.

"Was that the boys I saw coming home?" Vera said, coming around the corner of the house.

"Yeah, I need them to help me deliver milk." Fay leaned against the truck door while she waited for them to return.

"Oh, I was going to tell them to get busy on the wood." As Vera said it, her gaze trailed to the pile sitting around the splitting stump. "Hmmm." She arched her eyebrows at Fay and added, "I suppose they could stack it when they get back."

Fay colored, half-embarrassed for her tantrum and for getting her hopes up about a man because he wanted to help the farm. Of all the silly reasons to fall for a man. Mr. Burns had been doing his job. It was downright ridiculous of her to get all worked up when he—but really it was the SCS—had let her down.

"I had some time today," she said sullenly.

Vera chewed on her lip and then leaned up against the truck with Fay. "Sam told me what Mr. Burns said about the fields and how SCS can't help like we thought they could."

Fay nodded, the disappointment still swirling around her, although she couldn't figure out if it was because she'd likely have to work at least another year with her brothers or because it would never work out between her and Oliver Burns.

"Sam thinks the profits from those fields will have to go back into the farm instead of hiring somebody new. Without extra money from somewhere, it's going to take a lot longer than we thought to expand the farm again." Saying it out loud brought a lump of emotion to her throat. She had hoped too much. All through the war she'd told herself she could get through the backbreaking labor and the stress of farming with Mom and Vera and the occasional teenage boy if it meant her brothers would come home and take it all over. In the back of her mind she'd known she'd have to help for a bit. But the possibilities of being free from it had stretched before her, waiting for her to snatch them. Now that time stretched out before her too.

"Seeing as how you've already done enough work for today, why don't you take the rest of the evening off? I'll drive the boys around to deliver milk." Vera patted Fay on the shoulder and moved her away from the truck.

"That's okay. It's just driving. It's not hard."

"I almost forgot. Joey Gibson called. That's what I came out to tell you. He wants to know if you'll go to that church social with him tonight." Vera didn't move from her new position in front of the door. The boys came out of the back door of the farmhouse and hopped into the back of the truck with the milk.

Fay scowled at the thought of going to the church social with Joey. Next to Oliver Burns, he seemed like a boy. And still a farmer. "I'd rather not."

Vera bit back a smile. "Go anyway. You might have some fun, Fay, and you're sorely in need of it." Without waiting for any more protests, she climbed into the truck and started it up with a rumble. She waved as she pulled out and onto the road, the boys shouting goodbye to Fay too.

Fay watched the truck disappear behind the dust it kicked up before turning to the house. Well, the church social was an excuse to put on a pretty dress and do her hair. She might as well take advantage of it.

≡ ★ ≡

"Wash up for dinner, please," Vera told Jack Junior and Peter as they came in after finishing the milk deliveries.

"Yes, ma'am," Peter said with a salute and disappeared down the hallway to the bathroom.

Vera took a long breath of the beef-stew-scented air of the kitchen. "Smells good, Mom," she said, moving to the sink to wash her own hands. "Would you like me to set the table?"

A knock at the door interrupted. "I'll set the table; you get the door. Your father's still out with Sam and Andrew." Her mother reached for the plates.

To Vera's delight, Dominick stood on the top step when she opened the door. "Well, good evening, Dominick Whitaker," she said, reaching for his hand and pulling him inside. "What a pleasure to see you."

Dominick drew Vera into his arms and kissed her soundly. "Good evening to you too," he said.

His kiss for a greeting meant a good mood. Vera's heart lifted. He'd greeted her like that more and more and with less and less of the old memories hanging over his eyes.

"I thought we might take the kids down to the social and get them some pie. Ruby Baldwin said her grandpa was making root beer," he said, his hands lingering around Vera's waist.

Vera hesitated. She and Dominick rarely went out alone more than once a week, and since he'd taken her to dinner already this week, she worried about leaving the kids with her parents again. But her and Dominick taking the kids was a lot like . . . a real family again. She could picture him teaching her boys how to fish or carrying Audrey on his shoulders, but she didn't dare get her hopes up too high, and she didn't dare let her children expect it. They liked Dominick, but so far Vera had kept the interactions in the social sense to a minimum, and while she had explained to Jack Junior and Peter that she and Dominick were good friends, she hadn't ventured telling them more than that.

"What is it?" he asked when her hesitation slipped into several more moments of silence. He dropped his hands and stepped back to take a better look at her.

Vera glanced toward the kitchen, where her mother directed the boys in finishing to set the table. "Do you mind if we take a quick walk?" she asked. Dominick furrowed his brows at her but shook his head. "Mom?" Vera called. When Kathryn's figure came into the doorway between the two rooms, a smile broke out on her face. "We're going for a walk. We'll be back soon," Vera said.

"Go ahead. I'll save some stew for you both." She disappeared back through the doorway without another word.

Vera grabbed a coat from the rack beside the door, and Dominick opened the door for her, following her down the steps into the cool spring-evening air. "What is it?" he asked again, once they made their way across the lawn and toward the road.

Vera angled herself toward him as they walked, the words rolling over in her mind. She began by taking his hand and saying fervently, "I love you, Dominick."

He nodded. It wasn't too momentous. They had said it before. "I love you too, darling."

"I know. And you know that I need a husband. I'd like that man to be you. But I also know that you're not sure you're up for that, which I understand. Until you are, I can't let my children see you as more than my friend—and going to the social together would be more. Especially with everyone in town speculating and adding their opinions."

Dominick stared up the road for too long. So long that Vera's insides started to flutter around, and she wondered if she'd said it all wrong. "Of course," he said. "I didn't think of it that way." He let out a long sigh. "I wish . . . I'd like to be a husband and father, but—"

Vera stopped and turned to face him. "You're a good man," she said with feeling, clutching the front of his coat. "You are."

Dominick reached up to take her wrists, and he closed his eyes and shook his head. "Don't, Vera. You don't know . . . you don't know what I've done."

Her chest burned at how he thought so little of himself. He was never anything but gentle with her, and Jack Junior talked of him in the best terms as a teacher. He respected Dominick and so did Vera. She pulled herself toward him.

"Every man in this country has 'done' something. It was a war." She gulped. She didn't like to talk about Jack with Dominick, but in this case she made an exception. "You won't spoil my opinion of you. Jack told me things too. Of how he'd had to shoot men when he'd stood so close he could see the fear in their eyes, and how they were just scared kids. He—" She choked off. Remembering how Jack had sobbed because of it made her stomach turn. It had broken down the man she thought could never stop smiling.

Dominick wrapped his arms around her. "It's not the same," he mumbled into her shoulder.

She pulled back to look up at him. "How can I know? You won't trust me to. You won't tell me."

He sighed, heavy with regret. He broke away and turned toward the house. "Would it be all right if I had dinner with you?"

Vera put her hand into his. "Dominick . . ." She pulled him to a stop. They couldn't go on seeing each other if he didn't believe himself good enough to marry her—if he never would. The words stuck in her throat, but she forced them out. For her children. For her. For Dominick too. "If you can't tell me—if you can't trust me, then perhaps we'd better stop—"

"Not tonight, Vee." He shook his head at her and put an arm around her shoulder. "Not tonight . . . but what about dinner?"

She rested her head against his chest and gripped his shirt in her fingers. No. Not tonight. It would have been best, but she couldn't force it. "Of course. That's different. Dinner is fine."

They walked back slowly, leaning on each other. Heaviness weighed her down, as though she had walked to the end of the happy days she'd spent with Dominick. She'd helped to bring a smile to his face more often than not. He'd seemed so much lighter, and he'd lifted her as well. She sighed, and he kissed the top of her head. He whispered, "I know," as though he'd read her mind and agreed with the heavy thoughts there.

By the time they reached the house, they had straightened and entered with smiles that neither of them felt.

≡ ★ ≡

Dominick didn't mind the quiet moment he had to himself here on the top step in front of the Larson's house while Vera put the children to bed. Since beginning to spend more time with Vera last winter, he'd found comfort in this house. Sam usually avoided him if he was around, so despite the high number of occupants for such a small place, he'd never felt more at peace than when he spent time there. With the warmer weather, Mrs. Larson had opened a window in the kitchen, and the sounds of the house drifted out to him. It reminded him of growing up, of all the good memories he'd left in California. He'd come to Bellemont for a new start in a simple place, not somewhere busy like San Diego. And his mother had remembered a different man than he was. He couldn't go back and have her always asking if he was okay and when he'd start smiling more. She wasn't the type of woman to understand that Dominick couldn't change the man he'd become since the war.

He did miss San Diego though, especially this winter. The soft sand on Torrey Pines Beach, the sound of waves lapping outside his window. If he could have that here in Wyoming, his life could be complete. That and Vera, and both seemed impossible.

The door creaked and Dominick sat forward, out of the way of whoever was coming out. Maybe Vera to say good night. However, Mr. Larson stepped across the skinny beam of light coming from the porch light above the door.

"Mind if I join you?" he asked.

"No, sir." Dominick had to chuckle at the older man asking permission to sit next to Dominick on his own front porch.

With care, Mr. Larson lowered himself onto the step. Dominick held back from offering a steady hand. He didn't know Mr. Larson well enough to know if he'd appreciate that or if it would wound his pride. They sat in silence, both staring out into the darkness. It wasn't an uncomfortable silence. Not between two men as comfortable inside themselves as Dominick and Mr. Larson were.

Dominick could make out only dim shapes in the yard, thanks to the almost-black night and only the lights from the house to illuminate anything. He looked forward to the coming of summer and the light lasting well into the evening. Short winter days had never suited him.

"Interesting what the war took from all of us, isn't it?" Mr. Larson said, breaking the silence. He folded one arm over his chest and waved what was left of the other before tucking it into the crook of his elbow. "Thought when I came out of the first one all right, I'd lucked out for the long haul."

"I didn't know you'd seen action in the first World War." Dominick leaned back again, resting against the door behind him.

"I didn't. I got in on the tail end, and things were winding down by then. I was a kid out of school and didn't know much about what war was really like. Downright unlucky, I'd say, to get caught up in it again. Guess I could blame it on this farm. Kept me in too good a shape for the army to turn me down, even at almost forty-five." He gave a short, bitter laugh. "Funny how the war made sure I'm not much use to the farm now."

Dominick couldn't comfort him. He agreed with Mr. Larson about the war taking away too much. Dominick had seen far too much of that. "How did you lose your arm, sir?"

"Bullets. Shattered too many bones and shredded too much skin to make it worth much of anything. Took one to the chest too. Can't say I've felt the same since."

"I know that feeling." It surprised Dominick that his own chest tightened. He hadn't felt the same since the day he'd found out about Ondine and Laurent—everything had changed then. His life had turned upside down, and he couldn't remember how to be happy anymore. How to believe in anything.

"I'm lucky—well, Katie hates it when I don't say blessed. I'm blessed that it got me home to her that much sooner. Lucky—blessed, I mean—to have that woman. Hardy Wyoming girl. Shoulda sent the likes of her to Germany. She would've had Hitler treed long before we managed it." He chuckled to himself and then pinned Dominick with a stare. "And the times I've come closest to feeling normal have always been next to her." He turned to the blackness before them.

Mr. Larson was onto something. The closest Dominick had come to being happy again, to believing he could be happy again, had been since he met Vera. "You're probably right," he said.

The door nudged against his back, and Dominick hopped up then reached out for Mr. Larson's good arm to help him up without thinking this time of what it would do to the man's pride. To his surprise, Mr. Larson grasped his hand and stepped off the step next to him.

"Oh," Vera said, a half-smile on her face. "Am I interrupting?"

"No, no," Mr. Larson said, moving away from Dominick and back onto the steps. He climbed them slowly and shuffled carefully by Vera to go inside. "I was coming in. Getting cold out here, and your mother doesn't like me out without a coat." He nodded at Dominick. "Good night."

"Night, Mr. Larson." He lifted a hand to wave, still somewhat startled over the man accepting his help so easily. Could it be so simple? Could getting back on his proverbial feet, being the husband Vera deserved and the father he wanted to be—could that be as easy as taking Vera's hand and trusting she could hold him up? But how could she shoulder such a burden? How could he ask it of her?

She closed the door behind her father and stepped down to the bottom of the steps where Dominick still stood. "It is getting chilly. Will you come inside?"

Dominick rested his hands on her shoulders and kissed her gently. "Good night, Vee." Mr. Larson had left him with much to consider, and he needed to mull it over. A future with Vera—one that he wanted—and one with her children suddenly felt within his grasp. In fact, falling in love with her had included falling in love with her children, come to think of it; they were so much a part of her it seemed silly to try and separate them. It seemed too much to hope that someday he could measure up . . . with Vera's help. At least, Mr. Larson seemed to think he could.

"Dominick . . . ?" she pressed.

He kissed her on the forehead. "Good night."

"Good night, then." She rested her hands on his for a moment before he turned to his Ford, got in, and drove away.

☰ ★ ☰

It was just Fay's luck that Oliver would come to the social. She had kept an eye on him as he mingled among the guests so that he wouldn't catch her off guard. Although she suspected she had concocted that excuse so she could watch him, even if he'd ruined all her plans. Right now he was talking to old Mr. Cropper with his face all lit up and enthusiastic like he'd been the night he told her about how he would change farming, and darn it if his enthusiasm for his work didn't make her beam with pride anyway.

"Fay, would you like some more to drink?"

Fay whirled so quickly away from getting caught staring at Oliver that the remainder of her punch flew out and splattered Joey's crisp blue shirt.

"Oh, I'm so sorry," she cried, grabbing her handkerchief and dabbing at him. "You surprised me, is all."

Joey took her hand and stopped her, an easy smile on his face. "No harm done, Fay."

Now why couldn't tingles spread through her arm at the way he held on to it against his chest? She sighed in defeat. Because he was a farmer. Because he didn't have half the excitement for it as Oliver had for his job. And the dimple—he was missing that, too.

"Hello, Miss Larson. Mr. Gibson."

Though her heart jumped at the sound of Oliver's voice, Fay forced herself to react more calmly than she had a moment ago. "Hello, Mr. Burns," she said in a cool tone.

"May I have a word with you, Miss Larson?" he asked.

He had contrition written all over his face, but it wouldn't do Fay any good to let him talk his magic at her again. His idea of changing farming and her idea of changing farming were too far apart.

"I'm sorry. I'm here with Joey this evening, and it would be quite rude," she said. "I'm sure we can talk another time."

Oliver colored and nodded. "Of course. Good evening to you both." He nodded to a confused Joey and turned away, stopping to chat with another man who stood a few feet away.

Fay turned her gaze so Oliver wouldn't catch her watching him again. "I would like something more to drink."

Joey took her cup, his eyebrows furrowed. "If you need to speak with Mr. Burns about farm business, I understand."

Fay's insides tightened. In what world would a man assume a woman needed to spend time at a church social talking farm business? "No," she snapped, which only increased Joey's confusion. "Tonight is for fun," she added with a forced smile, and he relaxed.

She shouldn't blame Joey. For more than four years, everyone in Bellemont had known that Fay took care of business out on the farm. It would be hard to change people's opinions about that here. Moving to a new city, starting over . . . a lump formed in her throat, but she got the better of herself. She'd waited four long years for the boys to come home, hoping every spring when she planted that it would be the last she had to take care of by herself. She could wait one more.

⸗ CHAPTER TWENTY-THREE ⸗

"ELEANOR?" VERA PUSHED OPEN THE unlocked door of her friend's home and called, "Knock, knock. Eleanor?"

"Up here," came the voice from the top of the stairs.

Vera stepped inside, shutting the door behind her with her foot, and hurried through the living room to the bottom of the stairs. Eleanor stood at the top, looking down, her belly well rounded with seven months of pregnancy.

"What are you up to?" Vera asked, holding up a box she'd brought in. "I've brought some baby things I found in the attic."

"Bring them up." Eleanor grinned and waved at her friend, disappearing into the room opposite her and Alvin's. Vera obeyed, smiling herself when she came into the room. She had helped Eleanor a lot over the past several months to make up many of the things decorating the room—the bed things, especially a pile of blankets they'd worked on all winter, and a drawerful of handmade clothes and knitted stocking caps.

"Maybe you ought to keep some of those things." Eleanor took the box and set it on a wooden changing table that Alvin had made for her. It was really quite beautiful work. One of Eleanor's friends from the bank had seen it and asked for one just like it. Eleanor had been ecstatic over the extra money it would bring. "You might need these again someday," she said with a mischievous glance at Vera.

Vera shrugged. Dominick had been so pensive when he'd left her house a few nights earlier and after the discussion they'd had, she didn't know where their relationship might go from there. "Do you think I'll marry again before I'm too old to have more babies?" She tried to make the statement light. Eleanor was in such a lively mood, especially now that she was over the worst of the sickness and the new little one would be arriving soon, that Vera hated to weigh her down with her own troubles.

Eleanor frowned anyway and put down the bibs she'd been looking over. "Of course I do. Don't you?"

"It's awfully complicated. I love Dominick so much, but bless his heart, he can't bring himself to believe he deserves it. Sometimes I wonder if he'll ever believe it." She sank into a nearby rocking chair and sighed.

"Poor man." Eleanor chewed on her lip. "Is it so bad as that? I just thought for sure he'd come around. He's so different than he was even a few months ago."

"He is." To her surprise, Vera actually smiled at that thought. It was the truth, and she was proud for the part she'd been able to play in helping him move forward in his life. Now if only he'd let her continue to do so—forever. That's what she longed for. "Anyway, how are you feeling?" she asked, hopping up to join Eleanor in sorting out the things she'd brought.

"Very large." Eleanor patted her stomach and grinned. "And impatient. It seems I'll never meet this little fellow—or little miss," she added and then shrugged. Happiness blossomed in Vera for the joy this occasion was bringing to her friend. Eleanor had waited for too long for this blessing, and she would be such a lovely mother. And what a miracle the little boy—or girl—was!

"Don't worry, Eleanor. No one has ever been pregnant forever, I believe."

"I would be the first." She blew out a laugh and fanned herself. "Having a baby in the summertime was a very bad idea, don't you think?"

Vera chuckled. "Yes, very poor planning." They both laughed over the absurdity of that.

"Let's go down, and I'll make us some lemonade. This can always wait. I thought I'd be bored to death at home just waiting for the baby to arrive, but as it turns out, I've thought of a million things that need to be done." She led the way out of the room and to the narrow stairs. "I thought I ought to make a couple dresses—just in case. I feel quite sure it's a boy, but I would hate for the poor thing not to have a dress or two if I were wrong."

"Of course." Vera smiled and followed, thinking of the busy stages of her pregnancies when she had worked like a bee to make things ready for her new arrivals. Would she experience that again? She hadn't exactly had time to miss those things in the time since she'd had Audrey, and she wouldn't say she exactly longed for another baby, either—bearing four children was no small feat.

But when she thought of marrying Dominick and how he must want to have children of his own—she did. She could imagine the joy a baby would bring to him. She'd seen it light up Jack's eyes with each one.

"Where've you gone to?" Eleanor asked in a quiet voice.

Vera started, realizing she'd stopped in the doorway of the kitchen and stared off into space as Eleanor busied herself in the kitchen. "Oh, the usual places, I suppose." She kept telling herself that if Dominick chose to end their relationship, she would be able to move on, but every time she thought it, pain barreled through her chest like a stampede. She had to quit imagining all the beautiful things the future could bring, like babies. It would only make it worse if it came to them breaking things off. She'd just never really imagined they would until the other night. Even now she didn't think her heart really believed what her brain kept trying to warn her against.

Eleanor put down the lemon she'd been about to slice in half and came over to Vera, putting her arms around her friend. "Don't you worry. Have faith, all right? Just like you told me."

Vera clutched her friend's shoulders. "Thank you, dear. I will." And for better or worse, it was all she could do.

≡ ★ ≡

Oliver swirled his straw around in his malt and stared across Alice's diner at Fay Larson. She hadn't looked his way once since he walked past her group when he'd first entered the diner. The way she sat rigidly, not even daring a look in his direction gave him some hope that the failed start of their relationship pained her as well—but that seemed like a desperate hope to hold on to.

"Mr. Burns, is there something wrong with that malted shake?"

Surprised to hear Alice's voice, Oliver jumped and looked up at the middle-aged woman who ran the diner. "Er . . . no?"

"Are you sure about that?" Alice quirked an eyebrow and put one hand on her hip. "All you've done since I brought it to you is stir it around—it's fairly melted," she pointed out.

Oliver glanced down at his drink. Sure enough, a wonderful concoction of milkshake and malt had gone to waste while he mooned over Fay as though he were one of the schoolboys gathered around her now. Well, they weren't exactly schoolboys. Most had seen a little action before the war had ended.

"Got distracted, I guess," he mumbled. "Bring me a Coke?"

Alice followed his gaze to Fay's group and bit back a smile that Oliver pretended to ignore. Fay might be young—nineteen or twenty, he'd guess—but he wasn't in the grave yet at twenty-eight. She was sweet, even with her fiery temper and opinion, and determined to boot. Reminded him a bit of Miss Holman, though both women would give him a talking-to for making *that* comparison.

"Shall I leave out the ice?" Alice asked.

Oliver laughed dryly. "Might be safer." Chuckling to herself, the waitress walked away and brought the Coke back a few minutes later. As she left, the music playing from a radio behind the counter switched to "Let's Call the Whole Thing Off", one of the many songs he'd danced to with Fay. The band down at The Twilight Café liked movie songs, and they'd played a lot of them the night he'd taken Fay there.

He took a long drink of his Coke. Better not to waste two drinks in one night. The carbonation burned his throat and he coughed. Fay whirled toward him, involuntarily it seemed. She went pink and turned back to her conversation with a girl he saw her around town with now and then.

So she at least remembered he was here. He took another sip of his Coke and slapped some money on his table for his unfinished drinks. He was going down to his office and figuring out some way to help that blasted Larson farm if he had to spend all night. He would do anything for another night of holding Fay in his arms, so he'd have to settle this right away.

⚏ CHAPTER TWENTY-FOUR ⚏

SAM PATTED THE SIDE OF the golden Jersey cow and leaned back on his stool, pushing up his hat to wipe his forehead before he bent to move the milking can away from the cow's hooves. He patted Sally one more time before getting up to lead her lazily to her stall. It'd been another long day, and though it was only seven P.M., he looked forward to sleeping. Well, sleeping as well as he could on the pullout couch in the living room, with everyone coming and going. At least Vera was already in for the night.

Sam had pictured his life within six months of coming home from the war so different from how it had turned out. His thoughts went to an idea he'd had: it wouldn't take much to build a little one-room house. He had some money saved up. Money he'd intended to use to take Emily on a honeymoon and get them started out. Buy her all new furniture for the old farmhand house that Andrew and Josette were living in—then later for someplace for them to live.

He led the cow into her stall. "None of that matters now, does it, Sally?"

"Knock, knock."

Sam turned to see the very woman who had been dancing through his thoughts standing at the door of the barn. Seemed like a big coincidence, but then again, Emily dominated his thoughts an awful lot, more so in the last few days since seeing her at the Soil Conservation Service office. He turned away at first, not trusting himself yet to speak or for what he might end up saying. He pitched some hay into the stall for Sally.

"Kathryn said you were out here," Emily said. From the sound of her voice, she hadn't moved from the doorway.

"Just finishing," he said evenly. He took his time with the hay. He could only hope that Emily would give up whatever she'd come here to say if he made her wait too long. He'd have to pass her to get into the house anyway—of course, he could sleep out here in the barn. Might get more rest than on the pullout couch.

"I came to say . . ." Emily paused and raised her voice. "I came to say that you ought to listen to some of Mr. Burns's ideas. He really does care about the people here."

He turned to face her, his ire rising quickly. "I suppose you've gotten to know him pretty well since we stopped seeing each other. Must have both of those men wrapped around your finger by now." Sam shouldn't have said it, but why did Emily have to come out here and push her way back into his life?

She colored. "That was rude."

He didn't apologize. "I have an early morning, Emily. I know you've studied all about farming, and I'm sure both gentlemen in the office have schooled you well in how a good farm is run, so I'm sure you realize that I'll be up at daybreak. Do you have something more to say before I go to bed?" He walked back across the barn toward the milk can. Darn it if he didn't ache to kiss that stubborn face anyway. She had nerve, and he had always admired every bit of it. It said something that she could work hard enough to become a soil technician after starting out as a secretary there. It said something that she cared enough to come here and try and talk him into using a dumb government check to help his farm.

"No, I suppose I don't have anything more to say," she snapped. She pressed her lips together, probably so he wouldn't see them tremble. Sam had to squeeze his fists together to keep from opening his arms to her. She wouldn't accept his comfort anyway.

"Good night," she said.

He nodded. "Good night." They stood there, both of them stubborn fools, waiting for the other to give in. Sam was on the edge of it himself, but she turned and disappeared into the darkness, and a moment later an engine roared to life and drove away.

He made his way slowly into the house, heading for the kitchen to wash up. His mom looked up as he passed her in the living room, where she sat mending a pair of pants. "You saw Emily?" she asked, pushing down her glasses.

He paused. No Larson man would dare disrespect his mother by walking away when she'd started a conversation.

"Yes." He let loose a heavy sigh.

"Sam, dear, if not being with her makes you so blue, maybe you ought to do something about that." She set aside the pants.

"I'm all right, Mom. It'll pass."

She clutched her hands in her lap. "I hate seeing you like this, son."

His lips quirked. Kathryn Larson hated seeing anyone in a rough spot. He couldn't count the times Fay had written him in a tiff over Mom giving away half the food they'd worked so hard to put on the table—though she'd always admitted that more often than not Mom had traded it for some help they needed themselves, and everyone came out well in the end.

"I've been through worse."

Kathryn stood and walked to him, laying her hands on his arms. "You've been through more than enough, and you shouldn't have to see another day more of sadness like you're carrying now."

"Mom, that's not how life works."

She patted him and sighed before going back to the couch. "I know, but you know better than to borrow trouble." She gathered up the mending she'd been working on. "I'll take this into the kitchen to finish if you're thinking of going to bed."

"That's all right," Sam said, but his mother had already hurried by him.

He followed her silently to the kitchen and washed up before returning to the living room to ready his bed. He heard the murmur of voices as he passed the downstairs bedroom, and he paused in the hallway a moment to watch Vera reading to her children. Tom and Audrey sat together in her lap and the older boys flanked either side of her, leaning in to study the pictures of the book. Was that something Emily would do? He shook the idea out of his head. It didn't matter—not to him anymore.

He tossed and turned that night, and not because of the uncomfortable bed. He kept wondering how *not* to borrow trouble, as his mother had suggested. Emily had come up with so many solutions when she'd told him she wanted to keep her job. How she could hire a housekeeper if the work came to be too much. How they could buy milk and butter and things from his parents. He had to admit she had applied that same attitude that got her a promotion at work in making Sam see that she could be his wife and keep her job. That keeping one didn't have to mean ending another.

He had been stubborn, insisting on having a wife like his mother and sister—women much different than the one he had loved—still loved too deeply to forget anytime soon. A woman whose tenacity he had cheered for in every letter and then crushed when it didn't match with his own plans.

And the truth of the matter was, sleeping on a lumpy old mattress in the living room of a crowded, noisy farmhouse didn't make him feel any smarter for it.

≡ ★ ≡

When Oliver came upon Fay doing hard farmwork—cleaning ditches in one of the fields—he should have known to turn around and head back to his car.

But fool that he was, he walked right on up to her, determined to straighten things out between them so he could take her out again sometime in the near future.

The scowl on her face when she turned and leaned against her shovel to study him made him sure today was not that day. "Good morning, Miss Larson." He'd like to call her Fay, and he wished she'd smile her greeting instead of narrowing her eyes.

"Morning, Mr. Burns."

"I hope you're not too busy to continue the conversation we started in my office. I have some ideas that you might be interested—"

"You ought to talk to Sam." She stuck the shovel into the ditch and dragged it along for a minute before pulling it out, full of mud, rocks, and weeds. She dumped that on the side of the ditch before looking at him again. "He runs the farm," she finished in a tight voice.

"Yes, I understand." He took a deep breath and held out the notebook he'd brought with him. "I brought a ledger." It sounded so insufficient for what he wanted this peace offering to mean. Perhaps he *should* have brought flowers or something sweet from the bakery downtown, but that had felt presumptuous. "It's one of the things we've been helping farmers with to help keep track of their spending and earning . . ."

The way Fay wrinkled her nose in disgust made him trail off. "Mr. Burns, the more you talk, the more I wonder if you know an actual thing about farming besides what they taught you in that big, fancy college you went to." She jabbed the shovel into the ground and took a step toward him. She might be pointing a menacing finger at him, and her eyes blazed like a forest fire, but he liked it nonetheless. "My mother has kept a ledger for as long as I can remember. How else do you think we managed not to get into debt and go under when every other farm in the county was doing just that? Gosh darn it, Oliver Burns, the Larsons have been farming this land since 1887 and we've figured out a thing or two about it by now. We already know every penny we've spent and every extra penny we have and how much it'll take to buy next year's seeds." She huffed at the end, and she didn't have to say *or to hire a farmhand* for him to hear that deeply held desire in her impassioned speech.

He stared at the ground, cursing his stupidity. "Of course, yes . . . well." He managed to look up again. "There are also subsidies available—"

"You know how we feel about government charity."

He held out his hands imploringly. "Miss Larson, you have to understand, I want to make things right between us. I've talked with some other farmers and ranchers in the area, and there is another option to manage your farm business in a way—"

"Mr. Burns, I was wrong when I encouraged you to think I believed like you did. Farming may be a business, but for us Larsons, it is a way of life, and it will be long after I'm gone." She turned her back on him, grabbing her shovel and sticking it back into the ditch. He hated every ounce of heartbreak in those words—words that took away a future of fancy party dresses, upscale dinner parties, going to college—a future she had dreamed about. A future that didn't include her cleaning out ditches. If only she'd let him explain his latest idea. He opened his mouth to begin, but she glanced at him over her shoulder. "Sam's down at the barn if you'd like to talk with him about our business." She spat the last word out and stalked away, farther along the ditch before she started up her dirty job all over again.

Oliver sighed and turned and headed for his car. After Miss Holman's interference, Sam Larson was unlikely to listen to anything Oliver said with objectivity either. Maybe Mrs. Larson could tell him where to find Andrew.

☰ CHAPTER TWENTY-FIVE ☰

DOMINICK HAD SCHEDULED WITH VERA to pick her up at seven for their date, so when she knocked on his door at 6:45, he knew she had something different planned for them than eating dinner at the diner.

"We need to talk, Dominick," she said, planting a kiss on his cheek as she strode into his tiny front room and let him help her with her coat. She removed her hat and turned to hand it to him, a determined expression set in her features.

He blew out a breath. Since their walk out at the Larson farm the weekend before, he'd dreaded this moment—Vera's insistence that he tell her about the past or that they go their separate ways. Spending the rest of his life with Vera stood at the top of his list—raising her kids, maybe having more, helping the Larsons on the farm, everything that involved living every day at her side. He loved Vera, and for her he wanted to be the kind of man it took to raise those four kids. He wanted to make the changes it would take, to ease some of the load she carried, and to spend his life caring for her with every bit of his soul. Sometimes, when they talked together for hours at a time, he would let go, for a moment, of the man he'd become in the war—the one who had let Ondine and Laurent die. He could talk himself into them simply being casualties of a war that had taken so many.

But it would come crashing back to him, how they weren't simply casualties, how he was responsible for their deaths. How he didn't deserve Vera at all.

She waited for several moments while he hung up her coat and hat on a leaning wooden coatrack near his door. When he'd turned around from the task, she walked forward and reached for his hands, squeezing them inside her small, soft ones and staring him right in the eye.

"Dominick," she said softly. "I understand if you can't tell me or if you're not ready to." He relaxed, like a man granted a reprieve. A few more weeks with his sweet Vee. Then she went on. "But I can't risk my heart anymore. Every day

I fall more in love with you. Every day I want more and more to heal everything broken inside of you. Every day more is another part of my heart that breaks, and too many more days of this without the promise of a future with you will be too much."

Dominick clung to her hands, gathering courage from them. Her words a few nights earlier about the war doing something to all men told him that Jack had confessed things to her—that she wasn't entirely unspoiled. A woman like her, though, didn't need any more of a burden. He hated the thought of doing that to her.

But the quiet strength that radiated out of her bled into him, enough that he could open his mouth. Enough to know that though his blissful time with her had come to a close, he would let her go knowing she didn't need to regret his loss. He loved this woman enough to hope she got the best life could offer her. But if she was willing to hold out her hand for him . . . he would take it for this moment and see where it led.

He took her to the couch, sitting down to face her. His stomach tightened and the nerves spread into his chest, freezing the words there and refusing to let them out. Unable to face her as he revealed the truth, he stood and paced in front of the couch. She waited, watching him as he went back and forth in front of it twice before speaking—and still glancing at her fleetingly at every turn he made to pace the other way.

"I worked in France for the OSS and the SOE, mostly recruiting operatives and training them. I had to get my hands dirty—sometimes it felt like it was the only way to even out the fight." Even now anger still burned hard as the images passed through his mind. Slain women and children, disgusting buildings in French holding areas where Jews waited to get shipped off to worse places like Auschwitz and Buchenwald. All of it ugly. Those details would muck up Vera more than necessary, so he kept his words careful.

"But I was good at getting those operatives out before . . ." He hesitated in his pacing, unable to finish that thought, but Vera nodded her understanding anyway. "The war had turned, and the Germans were panicking. Things could get ugly fast with them. I'd trained two green recruits out of Paris, Ondine and Laurent. Both of them barely out of their teens—kids really, like too many over there—and ready to take on the world. We'd done some real good. Stuff I figured I could be proud of. We'd worked together a long time. I thought of them as family."

This part of his story always weighed on Dominick. He moved to the couch and sat. He threaded his fingers through Vera's, needing any strength he could gain to get the rest of the story out. He relived this decision too often in his nightmares, but he so rarely repeated aloud what had happened.

His voice dropped low as he tried to capture the emotion and push it down, down, down. "We received word of a suspected SS infiltration in our network. Before I could act on it, one of my men was captured in Amiens on his way back from Belgium. I took the risk of ignoring the infiltration in order to retrieve him for his intelligence."

Dominick pulled his hands away and stood again, backing toward the window where he turned away from Vera and put his hands on the sill. It was cold from the slight chill in the evening air and the window being open, a stark contrast to Vera's warm, comforting grip. But guilt kept him from going back to her.

"By the time I got back to Paris, Ondine and Laurent had been captured, tortured, and killed. And the SS was after the rest of the network." He hung his head, breathing heavily to keep from breaking down. Ondine, Laurent, and too many others recruited by him—dead, thanks to his arrogance and selfishness—putting Hampton's intelligence over the lives of two kids without enough experience to get themselves out of a bad situation.

"Dominick," Vera called for his attention softly. He could tell by the sound of her voice that she'd stood and taken a few steps closer to him. "Why did you go to Amiens?"

He ground his teeth together. He had expected at first, before the truth of what he had done sank in, that she would try to exonerate him, to find excuses for what he did. He didn't answer. He didn't deserve exoneration, and the sweet, wonderful woman he loved would do all she could to find the good in him. She always had.

"Were you ordered there?" she asked.

"No," he said. "In fact, my commander considered the threat to my team of greater importance." She had to see the truth of it. That he had made a stupid, selfish decision, choosing information over people's lives.

"Was the man you rescued—was he important? Was his information important?"

Slowly he turned to face her. "Yes," he replied. She opened her mouth again, surely to argue the case that his choice was justified. He held up a hand to stop her. Many had already tried those justifications. "I'm not a hero like Jack. I'm not the kind of man fit to be your husband, and especially not the kind of man to teach Jack Junior and Peter how to be good men."

She stared at him, her lips pressed together and her jaw tense. He wondered what arguments worked inside her brain, so it surprised him when she nodded.

"If you really believe that, then nothing I say will change your mind. I've been trying to tell you for months now." She sighed and crossed the room for her coat and hat, brushing his shoulder on her way by. "I'm sorry."

Then she left, shutting the door softly behind her.

≡ ★ ≡

After the hard way Sam Larson had treated her on Friday evening, the last thing Emily expected was for him to show up on her doorstep less than a week later. She stiffened and pondered the benefits of slamming the door in his face—again. Perhaps this time it would catch one of his fingers or, better, his nose.

"What can I do for you?" she snapped, glaring at him.

Sam stepped forward and reached for one of her hands. "Forgive me, please?" Slowly, and observing her with what she thought was hope and caution, he raised it to his lips and kissed her hand. "Please," he said again.

"What has gotten into you?" She scowled, but perhaps angrier at herself for the heat rushing through her at his tender manner and the contrition emanating off him. He'd been so cold the other night. She had been firm with herself about putting him behind her once and for all. She might have still loved him, but she would not give up every single one of her dreams, as much as it killed her to give him up. She had to be strong. Capitulating for love now would bring her heartache later. He would spend their life together stomping out her dreams if she let him. It had seemed they had no chance of happiness together.

"It's what has gotten out of me—namely a bit of stubbornness," he said. "I don't care what kind of wife you want to be. I'll hire a housekeeper and a nanny and a chauffeur with my last penny. Whatever you want, Emily Holman. Whatever." He held her hand against his chest, and she could only stare at him, stunned. Stunned by the genuine desperation in his expression. How his voice had caught when he said her name with so much gentleness she could've melted on the spot. He raised her hand to his lips again, kissing her knuckles, and reason started slipping away from her.

But what did she need reason for anymore? Hadn't he promised her whatever she wanted? "Do you mean it?" she asked, and she cursed herself for sounding like some schoolgirl with a crush and not the steady, determined woman she meant to be.

He took her other hand and kissed those knuckles again before he took a deep breath. "I've been mean and immovable. I'd like you to come home to every night. That's all I need."

"And what if I never want to be a housewife? Even when we have children?" She had to say it, though with him still staring at her all contrite and humbled, it took a lot of effort to speak at all or to think about the reality of their future together. His soft kisses may upend her, but she must know if he would truly respect her goals.

"We'll face that when we get there. Together. And without me acting like a bullheaded imbecile—cross my heart." He slid his hands to her elbows, drawing her closer.

She gripped his biceps, stalling the inevitable a moment longer. "This is absurd. It's been months, and you've hardly looked at me civilly."

His hands made their way to her waist so that they stood a breath apart. "Does it count if I've thought of you almost every moment? And more than civilly, I promise you that."

She blushed. "Sam!"

"Sweetheart . . ." He pressed his lips against her forehead and then along her hairline, and Emily closed her eyes and reveled in how this man turned her insides to jelly in a way John Mason never could. Two dates had been enough to tell her that. "Sweetheart," he began again. "I've spent the last week, almost, lying in bed thinking about all the rotten things I've done. At first I blamed you—I did. But I didn't give an inch for you, and that was awful of me. I'm a new man. I promise you."

She tilted her head back, watching him closely. "You'd get a house-keeper . . . *and* a nanny?"

"It might be more efficient to hire one person for both jobs—" He cut off when she raised an eyebrow. "In any case, yes." He nodded firmly at her, and a smile crept onto his lips. "I'm thinking of hiring Fay. She says she'd do anything to get off the farm."

"Oh! Sam!" Emily drew back farther. His comment reminded her how Mr. Burns had lamented not being able to get anyone in the Larson family to listen to him. "Mr. Burns found a rancher to lease your land. You can grow grass on it, and Mr. Adams will pay you ten dollars an acre to let his cattle graze it. You can't get that from hay or beans or anything, and it's not government charity. At least not the way you're thinking of it." She bounced in Sam's arms with the excitement of it.

"Ten dollars an acre?" Sam lifted her into the air. "That's more than enough for next year's seed and a part-time hand. Why didn't Oliver say anything?"

Emily unwound her hands from around Sam's neck to put them on her waist. "Neither you nor your little sister would give that man a moment to say anything."

Sam grabbed her hand. "Let's go tell Fay. This'll put her over the moon." He dragged Emily a few steps before he stopped and gathered her into his arms. "Wait, there's something we have to clear up before we do that. Will you marry me as soon as possible?"

Emily broke into laughter. "After everything you've promised? I'd be a fool not to. But you'd better put it down in writing, Sam Larson, because you're keeping every word of it."

He pressed his lips to hers in an earth-moving kiss that Emily had no inclination to stop for several minutes—or perhaps hours. "Every word," he murmured. "How soon can you put together a wedding?"

It was a good thing that Sam still held her around the waist because Emily could not hold herself up on her own after such an eventful half hour. "Sam, these things take time."

"You have one week."

She arched her eyebrows. At least he sounded like his normal self again—his *better* normal self. He kissed her, probably to drown out any arguments she might have against such a hasty affair. She didn't mention that she already had the dress—or more correctly, still had it.

"I can't risk losing you again, Em," he said in a soft, and quite desperate, voice. He reached to take her face in his hands, this time kissing her lightly and tenderly before resting his face against hers. "Shall we go find Fay?" he asked.

Emily sighed with pleasure and laid her head against his chest. "I'm sure it can wait a few more minutes."

⹀ CHAPTER TWENTY-SIX ⹀

THE NEXT MORNING, FAY MADE only one stop before heading straight to the Soil Conservation Service office—and that was to buy a pair of new lace gloves. As she stood outside the office door, her mind racing over again and again what Emily and Sam had told her the evening before, her heart soared and she grinned. Soon her calluses would disappear. She might go to college. Her smile widened as she stared at Oliver's name on the door. Or she might stick around Bellemont for a while longer. Her victory was thanks to him. He'd gone out and found a solution even when she'd given him every reason to give up on her and the farm.

She yanked open the door, and since Emily wasn't at her desk, Fay marched right on through to Oliver's office. She hesitated, wringing her fingers together for a moment. After the way she'd treated him and for no good reason, he had every right not to want to see her. She straightened her shoulders. At the least, he deserved an apology from her.

"May I help you?"

Fay turned to see Mr. Mason leaning against the frame of his door, his eyes sparkling, his smile flirtatious. She almost wrinkled her nose in disgust. No, thank you, she didn't need his charm mucking up her day. It had been Emily's choice to go out with him a time or two, but Fay had no respect for the man.

"I'm here to see Mr. Burns," she said and turned her back on Mr. Mason, tapping on the office door.

Oliver's voice, distracted and deep in a way that made her shiver inside from her head to her toes, called, "Come in."

She pushed open the door and watched him from the doorway, waiting for him to look up. "Yes, Emily?" he asked, without glancing away from the papers he bent over.

"If she hadn't come to and decided to marry that obstinate brother of mine, I might be insulted by that." Fay put a hand on her hip and regarded him with a good-natured eyebrow quirk.

His head snapped up, and he hopped out of his chair so quickly, Fay wondered if someone had set a fire under him. "Fay—Miss Larson! I heard the heels on the floor and assumed . . ."

The red staining his cheeks goaded Fay on further. "Oliver Burns, why didn't you tell me that you went all over the country trying to find someone to lease our highly erodible fields?" She added her other hand to her hip.

Oliver folded his arms over his chest. "You hardly gave me the chance."

She dropped her posture and shrugged at him. "That is true." She took a step closer to the desk, watching the curiosity settle in his expression. "Do you go to such lengths for all your clients . . . or just the silly ones?"

A smile worked its way onto his lips. "No. Just the pretty ones I'm trying to impress."

It was Fay's turn to blush. She couldn't remember the last time a man in Bellemont had called her pretty. "It was very nice of you, Mr. Burns, to make my dreams come true."

He stepped around the desk to take her hand. "Seeing as how I seem to know you well enough to do that, you should call me Oliver. May I call you Fay?"

Oh, how she liked the pressure of his hand around hers, the warmth through the lace, and everything. Didn't that make a girl feel downright, well, girly? "Oh, I wish you wouldn't," she said with a soft sigh. "I really like the way you say Miss Larson, all sweet like you do."

He chuckled. "Well, *Miss Larson.*" He made an exaggerated bow over her hand and then kissed it before rising again. A delighted laugh burst from her. "Would you please go to dinner with me?"

"Only if you promise to tell me more about revolutionizing farming," she teased.

He took her other hand and shook his head at her. "Oh no. No more talk of farming for us. I know better than that."

Fay leaned toward him, resting their joined hands against his chest. "Now that you've saved me from a life of calluses, you can talk about whatever you want. I'll like it all the same."

"And kissing?" he asked, bending his head toward hers. "What are your feelings on that?"

"Oh," she breathed, already all starry-eyed inside his loving gaze. "I've been positively dying to talk all about that."

"Talk?" he asked.

"Mmmm," she murmured as their lips touched. "Later, perhaps."

Oliver released her hands to pull her to him. "Miss Larson, I believe that may be much, much later," he said against her lips.

And goodness, was it ever a kiss. "Tell me," she asked, breathlessly gazing up at him when they had drawn away. "Did you learn about revolutionizing kissing at college too?"

"No, *Miss Larson*." He dropped another light kiss on her lips, but it sizzled there all the same. "I learned all about that when I met you."

☰ ★ ☰

Vera carefully rolled her last bit of hair into place and then secured it with a hairpin. Leaning forward, she scrutinized her makeup. A girl could never go wrong with good hair and makeup when she meant to challenge a man like Dominick Whitaker. She figured she could use every tiny bit in her favor. He could be tough—especially when it came to himself.

"Practicing for tomorrow?" Sam leaned against the door of the bathroom, arms folded across his chest and eyebrows raised.

"Nope." She dabbed at her lipstick with a tissue and turned away from the mirror. "I have some business in town."

"Wouldn't it be better to let sleeping dogs lie, Vee?"

Vera gave him her best eye roll—one Jack Junior would be proud of—and sighed in annoyance. "It's a wonder Emily still wants anything to do with somebody as stuck in his ways as you, Sam Larson. I don't need any more of your rumors and stories. Dominick has told me the whole story, and I have gathered some information on my own. Through Andrew, of course." She straightened up her shoulders and stuck him with a good, stern glare. "He isn't guilty of anything you aren't."

If possible, Sam's eyebrows arched farther. "Oh?"

"Did you kill men, Sam?" she shot at him. When he flinched, the tiniest bit of guilt pinged in her stomach. But none of the men she loved deserved to have their pasts thrown at them, and it would do Sam a lot of good to remember that. "Dominick had the misfortune to lose people close to him, and he blames himself enough despite them being casualties of a horrible war. He doesn't need you or anyone else blaming him more. And if I hear another word against him from you, so help me . . ."

The tip of Sam's lip edged upward. "So help you what?" he asked.

She pointed a stern finger in his face. "Oh, you'll regret it. I may not be able to give you the swat on the backside that you deserve, but there are other ways to punish disobedient children."

He sighed. "Vera, you're still my little sister, and I'm always going to try to protect you." Vera opened her mouth to continue giving Sam a piece of her mind, but he shook his head and continued on, stopping her. "I know a lot of men who will never be the same—they're broken, thanks to things they've seen and had to do. All your love may never make him whole."

Tilting her head at him, she took his hands in hers. "I understand where you're coming from. You forget that I know a little about broken men too, like the one in this house who came home early and the one I was married to who never showed his pain. Dominick is broken, and he might never be like he was before the war, but I love that man all the same, and I'd be privileged to spend my life fixing him, even if it takes all that time."

She squeezed his hands, and to her surprise, his tough, farm- and war-hardened eyes shone. "All right, all right. I suppose I know when I'm beat," he said. He leaned over and kissed her on the cheek.

His emotion choked her up too. She swallowed and good-naturedly batted him away. "Good," she said, clearing her throat. "Then get out of my way." She pushed Sam aside and strode down the hallway, more determined than ever to get Dominick back.

Halfway down the stairs, Kathryn came to the bottom. "Oh, good, you're ready. There's someone here to see you."

Vera quickened her step. "Who?"

"Go on in and find out." Kathryn shooed her toward the living room.

When she stepped through the archway that separated the living room from the kitchen, she found Dominick standing with his hands in his pockets. He'd donned his crispest white shirt and a plaid blue-and-yellow tie she figured was new since she'd never seen it before.

"What are you doing here?" she asked, surprised. Her heart fluttered so rapidly she had to press her fingers against her chest in an effort to still it. She figured she would have to drag Dominick into seeing things her way, yet here he stood in her living room. Dare she hope he'd come to win her back?

He cleared his throat. "I hear congratulations are in order."

"Is that why you came?" she asked. The rapid pace of her heart didn't slow, despite his answer. He shook his head, and she hurried the rest of the way across the room to stand in front of him. "Why did you come?" she asked. She couldn't stay a moment longer apart from him, and every ounce of her prayed he'd come back to her.

He swallowed and studied her for a long time. Fear danced all over his expression, and she reached up to brush his cheek, to soothe him and assure him that no matter what he'd said the last time they'd seen each other, she was still here with him.

"Can you really love me?" His voice came out low and cracked, the product of desperation.

"Oh, Dominick." She pressed her cheek to his and wrapped her arms around as much of his shoulders as she could, gripping his freshly pressed shirt in her fingers. "You might not have been able to stop it, even if you'd stayed in Paris. It wasn't your fault, and the past is the past. I can—I will always love you."

"You're too good," he whispered.

She pulled back to stare him down, using the same stern expression she had on her brother a few minutes before. "Now, that's quite enough. I had Andrew make some calls—now don't you try and keep me from saying this," she said when he opened his mouth to protest. She placed two hands firmly on either side of his face to keep him from looking away from her. "It seems that information you rescued was a lot more vital than you let on. As in it saved thousands of people and helped the Allied invasion."

Dominick's lips had pressed into a firm line of disagreement, so she carried on, eager to prove to Dominick her high opinion of him and the sacrifices he'd made. He would never change that, no matter how many stories he told.

"You made a difficult choice, one that had consequences that will haunt you the rest of your life. You loved those people, and no one can deny that or the hurt you've carried over it. But you made the right choice, Dominick. You will never convince me—and many high-ranking men, so I've heard— otherwise. Allow Ondine and Laurent the honor of being part of the sacrifice that made it possible."

It took several moments of him studying her, his expression relaxing inch by inch before he let out a sigh and pulled her back to him, Vera melting into their embrace. She thought he might have let go of at least a piece of the guilt he'd dragged around for two years.

"You are the safest I've felt since coming home," he said against her cheek, his breath shifting the hair above her ear and sending tingles all along her neck and arms.

The beauty of that pronouncement settled deep into Vera's soul. "Remember that," she whispered.

"I will." He pulled away enough to kiss her soundly, sealing his promise.

⹀ CHAPTER TWENTY-SEVEN ⹀

KATHRYN LARSON LEANED AGAINST HER husband and sighed with contentment. For only having a few days to work at it, the decorations had come together nicely. They had invited a handful of people to the wedding in her front yard, and most of them already filled the assortment of chairs they'd gathered for the occasion.

They couldn't have asked for a better spring day either. The sun beamed brilliantly down on them, the way only the sun in Wyoming could—like it was asking how anyone could doubt that it would return. The breeze blew the exact right direction, bringing with it the smell of lilacs blooming instead of the smell of the cows and the barn.

Her gaze wandered over her family, already all gathered around where she sat in the middle of the front row. Andrew sat beside her, Audrey in his lap and Tom between him and Josette. Vera sat behind them, Jack Junior and Peter separating her and Dominick, but they both had their arms atop the chairs, fingers tangled together. The lightness in Dominick's expression brought more joy to Kathryn than she could describe. He carried much less of the weight he had since first coming to Bellemont. She'd watched a good deal of it slip away with every day he spent with Vera. Kathryn had already taken him in for one of her own, and his happiness filled her with hope the way it would any mother.

Fay stood near the front, Emily's only bridesmaid, but she wasn't looking around for the bride. She stared near the back, where Kathryn caught Oliver Burns sitting and shifting around like he might feel out of place, but Kathryn couldn't mistake the pleased smile on his face. Fay had told Vera during the wedding preparations that morning that she and Mr. Burns had another date planned for this evening, after all the festivities and when Sam and Emily had departed for their quick honeymoon in Jackson.

"If I'm not mistaken, we might have the house all to ourselves here soon," her husband said from her other side.

"Too soon," Kathryn said with a wistful laugh. "Vera came home just in time. Not because of the farm, but because that house of ours was getting too quiet."

Samuel Larson Senior glanced at the row behind them and lowered his voice. "I'm sure she'd be happy to let us keep a few of the kids. They won't all fit into that tiny house of Dominick's." He chuckled.

Kathryn nudged her husband playfully and laughed. "Oh, Samuel. Dominick hasn't said anything to her about that."

"He will soon enough. He's a smart boy."

"He is." Kathryn leaned her head on Samuel's shoulder, only to pop it up again as Mrs. Starry began playing the wedding march. Kathryn stood with everyone else and turned to witness Emily coming out of the house in her full white gown, with its princess waistline and the lace overlay almost sparkling in the sunshine. She met her father at the bottom of the steps, and when she began her trip up the short aisle, Kathryn couldn't help following Emily's gaze to Sam.

Kathryn had to swallow at the sight of her son in his dress uniform. Oh, he looked sharp. When he, Samuel, and Andrew had come downstairs in them earlier that day, it had nearly undone her. A wedding was a much happier way to see the dress uniforms, instead of for a funeral—which was the only time she'd seen Russell in his.

She lifted her lace handkerchief to her eyes and dabbed at them. Fay and Vera had spent too long on her makeup for her to ruin it before the kids said their vows. And for a woman who only put rouge on a few times a year, she had better take care that it didn't smudge too soon.

A hand slipped into her right hand, and she looked down to see Andrew holding it. She smiled at her youngest boy and pictured what his wedding must have been like. Had he worn his dress uniform? What kind of dress had Josette worn? Had it been a proper wedding gown?

Of course, little Audrey had to add her own hand into the mix, and it brought a gentle laugh from Kathryn's chest. She clutched Andrew's arm in hers, letting the simple vows that Sam and Emily spoke drift around her, reminding her of her own wedding in this yard as well. That summer had been almost a lifetime ago of course, coming up on thirty-two years.

Now Sam and Andrew were already married. And her husband was right. Vera and Dominick would marry soon as well. From the looks still passing between Fay and Oliver—neither paying a bit of attention to the wedding—

she'd venture a guess they'd follow before the end of the year. Kathryn glanced at Josette. And perhaps if they were lucky—or blessed—a new grandbaby would come as well.

Life had always been good on the old Larson farm. Even the war years, with all their scrimping and saving and working and worrying. Kathryn wouldn't take back any of that and lose the blessings it had brought.

And life would continue to flow and get better. Kathryn smiled and watched Sam dip his new bride and kiss her amidst the clapping of the guests.

Better and better.